The Great
CHRISTMAS
Knit-Off

Library withdrawn

Also by Alexandra Brown

Cupcakes at Carrington's
Christmas at Carrington's
Ice Creams at Carrington's

E-Novella
Me and Mr. Carrington

Alexandra Brown

The Great CHRISTMAS Knit-Off

WILLIAM MORROW
An Imprint of HarperCollins*Publishers*

HarperCollins books may be purchased for educational, business, or sales promotional use. For information please e-mail the Special Markets Department at SPsales@harpercollins.com.

FIRST EDITION

Library of Congress Cataloging-in-Publication Data has been applied for.

ISBN 978-0-06-238980-0

15 16 17 18 19   OV/RRD   10 9 8 7 6 5 4 3 2 1

For my Nanny Edie
Who always loved a good knit and natter session xxx

ACKNOWLEDGMENTS

Dear Reader

This is the first book in my new Tindledale series and I really hope you enjoy it. I have wanted to write a book about knitting for a very long time, since childhood in fact, when I loved rummaging through the tassel-trimmed Dralon knitting box that took pride of place in my Nanny Edie's front room, then sitting on the footstool beside her with my hands held up for her to wind the wool around them. The whole process fascinated me and my fondest memories are of knitting with her—of the comforting click-clack of the needles as we nattered away—and I truly hope to have captured the essence of these memories forever in this book. So my first thanks goes to my Nanny Edie, for sharing her love of knitting with me.

Next, I'd like to thank all of you, my darling friends, who chat with me on Facebook and Twitter, or who send me emails: you are all magnificent and your kindness and cheerleading spurs me on through it all—writing books can get lonely sometimes, but having all of you is like a family and that is something very special indeed. I really couldn't do any of this without you. You mean the world to me and make it all worthwhile. Thank you so very much xxx

Special thanks and gratitude to my agent, Tim Bates, for always telling me what's normal and without whom I'd most likely be lying in a babbling, incoherent heap somewhere. Many thanks and appreciation, as always, to my wonderful editor and friend, Kate Bradley, for being so kind and funny and for coming to see me when I was writing like a maniac to meet my deadline. Of course, none of the other stuff would happen without my dream team at HarperCollins, especially Kimberley Young, Martha Ashby, Jaime Frost and Katie Moss with their wonderful enthusiasm, energy and expertise.

Ann Faithfull, aka @GrannieF, for sharing her knowledge of knitting—any anomalies are totally down to me. Louise Zass-Bangham for winning the "name a character" auction and introducing me to the wonderful world of Ravelry. Julie Richards at www.thelittleknitkitcompany .co.uk for designing Sybil's lovely little Christmas pudding knitting pattern at the end of this book.

Jadzia Kopiel, for helping me to keep on keeping on—you're the wisest woman I know. Niki Lawal for making me significantly smaller. Immense thanks always to my dear friends Caroline Smailes and Lisa Hilton—your friendship and being there is what also keeps me going xxx

My darling QT, for bursting into my office to present me with a tiara that she had made because "it will help you write the magic words." Thank you my brave, funny, bright little girl, I love you with all my heart and will always make sure your light shines xoxoxo. My husband, Paul, aka Cheeks, for holding the fort, for bringing me Curly Whirly cake and for standing by my side when I finally found the courage to set myself free. And my dad and Christine for being proud of me.

Now, pour yourself a Baileys, sit back and I really hope you enjoy *The Great Christmas Knit-Off*. And remember always to keep calm and carry yarn.

Luck and love to you all, and wishing you a very merry Christmas,

Alex xxx

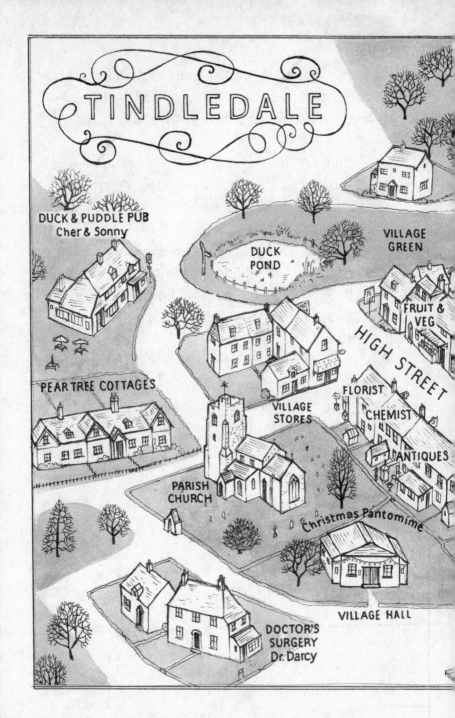

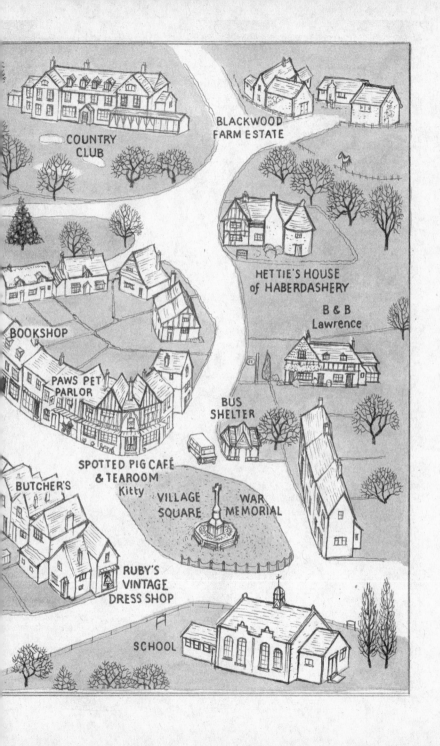

In the rhythm of the needles there is music for the soul.
—Anonymous

Prologue

Hettie Honey picked up a lovely lavender lace weight that a customer had abandoned by the till after pondering for what seemed like an eternity that, actually, it wasn't the right shade of lavender after all. She then walked across the shop floor of her House of Haberdashery to repatriate the ball into its rightful place—a wooden, floor-to-ceiling cabinet comprising twenty-four cubby-holes inset over three shelves crammed with every color, ply and type of yarn imaginable. Hettie smiled wryly, remembering the program she had listened to on the radio not so long ago. Knitting! It was all the rage nowadays and she hoped it would finally catch on in Tindledale, her beloved picture-postcard village and Hettie's home for the eighty-three years of her life to date. She ran the timber-framed, double-fronted shop adjacent to the wisteria-clad roundel of the oast house her father had built before she was even born.

Hettie lifted the tray on which sat the last remnants of

her afternoon tea; a cheese sandwich minus the crusts because her teeth weren't as strong as they used to be plus a pot of tea and a pink iced finger that had only cost ten pence on account of being past its best. Kitty, in the tearoom up on the High Street, had tried to give her the bun for free, but Hettie hated taking charity, especially when she felt there were other people in far more need. Hettie moved to the back of the shop, swept the curtain aside and went through to the little kitchenette area. Years ago this had been her mother's sewing room, and the wooden Singer machine with its rickety foot pedal still lived there, with a multitude of multicolored bobbins all piled up high on the shelf behind it.

After placing the tray on the draining board next to the age-veined Belfast sink and carefully wrapping the crusts in plastic to dunk into her warming homemade soup the following afternoon, Hettie picked up the picture frame on the mantelpiece above the fire and ran a finger over the faded black-and-white autographed photo. She allowed herself an enormous sigh. She wasn't usually one for self-pity or hand-wringing, but another one of the letters had come this morning, with FINAL DEMAND stamped across the top in ugly red type. Business had been so slow these past couple of years, and now, with her dwindling savings and pittance of a pension, she had come to realize that it was going to take a darn miracle this

Christmas for Hettie's House of Haberdashery to remain afloat come the new year.

There had been talk of retirement; of closing down the House of Haberdashery; of putting her feet up and going "into a home." Hettie's nephew, her brother Harold's son and last of the Honey family line, was all for it. On one of his rare visits, on the pretext of seeing how she was, he'd told Hettie he was concerned about her living on her own, that she needed the rest and that "it's not like you've got *that* many customers these days, is it?" He said he'd make sure she had her own bedroom or at the very least, a twin sharer. "And besides, it might be nice for her to have the company of people her own age." He'd put forward a strong case and had already contacted the council to inquire about a suitable place. But Hettie wasn't losing her marbles and she knew that what he was really after was to bulldoze her beloved home—the oast house surrounded by a meadow of pretty wild flowers, and the place where she grew up. There's her cozy bedroom suite, set upstairs in the roundel with its magnificent view of the valley, the lovely farmhouse kitchen with the walk-in pantry, the sunroom, the snug—it's got the lot, and that's on top of all her memories wrapped within its circular walls. Not to mention her beloved little shop, right next door, crammed full of all her favorite knitting and needle-craft goodies.

Then he'd be able to get his hands on the land for one of his building projects. He'd told her all about the one with ample parking and plastic windows that his company had created in the town where he lived, over fifty miles away. Seventeen months it had taken, he'd said, to fight all the objections from the local residents' association, and he had puffed on about it for the entire hour of that tedious visit. But Hettie isn't ready to be written off; to be carted away to an old people's home like a nag to a glue factory, not when there is plenty of life still left in her sprightly body. Besides, "going into a home" would mean leaving Tindledale behind, and Hettie knows more than anything that this is where her heart belongs. It always has, even when she'd had the chance of a different life, far, far away.

Three weeks until Christmas . . .

I stare at the radio mounted in the dashboard of my beat-up old Clio as I negotiate a particularly icy corner off Lewisham High Road. Jennifer Ford! Did the London FM newsreader guy just say Jennifer Ford had *absconded*? I wasn't really paying attention, but I know that name. F-O-R-D, the woman had even spelled it out for me, as in Harrison Ford, that's what Jennifer had said. It was about a month ago, and I had shuddered, which is hardly surprising given my monumentally embarrassing show-down at the altar of my own *Star Wars*–themed wedding just six months previously. I'm still cringing. May 4 it was, obviously. Luke, my ex—and for the record, a massive tool, I know that now, it's just a shame I didn't know it then—anyway, he thought it would be a brilliant idea to have "May the fourth be with you" in big swirly gold lettering on the wedding invites. He was literally leaping over the proverbial moon when we managed to secure the date with the church. So why then didn't he turn up?

Jilted at the altar! That's me. I'm the woman none of us ever wants to be. Stood there in a floaty neck-to-toe white hooded dress, complete with Princess Leia buns, having opted for the pin-on ones after my unruly red curls had refused to get involved, the realization dawning that he wasn't actually going to turn up. A *no-show*. And that's when I knew, really knew, what had been going on, because Sasha, my identical twin sister and far more glamorous than me—even her name is bursting with va-va-voom compared to my Sybil—wasn't there either. To be honest, I think I had known, deep down, in the weeks and months leading up to the wedding that something wasn't quite right. But I had chosen to ignore it—or perhaps that's the whole purpose of hindsight: its job is to protect you, to let you be obliviously happy for just a while longer before the reality swoops in to deal a cruel, mean blow.

I inhale sharply and let out a long breath, which forms a miniature Australia-shaped mist on the windshield. Sasha, golden and gregarious, the pony club princess to quirky and creative me, hadn't wanted to be a bridesmaid, citing a desire for not wanting to steal the limelight away from me on my big day. Ha! Instead she stole my husband-to-be. Turns out Luke had always had a bit of a twin fantasy thing going on in his head and had decided to make it a reality—they had been having a secret "thing" for ages. I don't know all the details, I really don't want to, and I haven't spoken to either of them since . . .

So, after wrenching the Princess Leia buns from my head, I had flung them into the crowd and run from the church, narrowly managing to avoid body-slamming into a late-arriving, over-furry Chewbacca as I burst out through the doors and into the sanctuary of the waiting tour bus. Yes, another one of Luke's brilliant ideas, a big bastard forty-eight-seater with STAR WARS: *May the fourth be with you, love Sybs and Luke* emblazoned down both sides for the whole world—well, the grayest part of London and beyond at least—to witness my humiliation. And I'll never forget the look on my parents' faces: disappointment mixed with embarrassment. I had let them down in front of all their friends. Even the flower girls were crying because the party was over before it had even started and I had promised them the DJ would do a special One Direction medley during the disco. I felt like an utter failure! And still do, a lot, to be honest.

I park the Clio and give the door an extra-hard slam with the full force of my left Converse trainer before picking my way through the dirt-stained leftovers from this morning's sleet storm and making my way down the path to my basement flat, deftly sidestepping the cracked paving slabs and trying really hard to ignore the mounting swirl of unease in my stomach. Maybe I'd misheard the newsreader. Let's hope so, because the Jennifer Ford I'd dealt with at work wouldn't take £42,000 in housing benefit wrongly credited to her bank account and blow it on a *crazeee* trolley dash around Westfield shopping center, and then be daft enough to post the pics of the shopping hauls across her multiple social media channels, would she? No! Of course she wouldn't. Don't be ridiculous, I tell myself, as I negotiate the crumbly old steps, push the key into the front door, retrieve the post from the mat and give Basil, my bonkers black Scottie dog, a stroke as he dashes to greet me with an expectant time-for-dinner look on his whiskery face.

It's Thursday evening and I've just finished work at the housing department of the local council office. I flick the switch to illuminate the miniature Christmas tree on my hall table and read the note from the dog sitter.

Basil had a lovely time today. Went for a run around the park followed by a long snoring snooze on my sofa lol. Sorry, I know you're trying to train him to keep off the furniture but he's just too cute, I couldn't resist a cuddle during Judge Judy. I'll try harder tomorrow.
Love, Pops xxx

Ah, Poppy is a godsend and I don't know what I'd do without her. After Luke left (he used to take Basil to work in his electrician's van) I very nearly had to rehome Basil, because I couldn't face leaving him on his own all day. Then Poppy moved in upstairs and she loves dogs but can't have one as she works nights as an administrator at one of the big law firms in the City, so she jumped at the chance to look after Basil when I'm at work.

I press the button on the landline phone's answer machine—I actually ventured out last night with a few friends, a bit of a rarity since the May 4 showdown, and then didn't have time to listen to my messages this morning. We'd gone to a Zumba class—so not my thing. My backside feels as if it's been pummeled by a trillion pygmy goat hoofs, and I really must get a new mobile, although it's been rather liberating being without one: no sneaking a peek at Luke's Facebook whenever the fancy takes me, or sending drunken texts only to agonize over them the following morning. I had hurled my old phone from the window of the *Star Wars* bus somewhere on the M4 on the way back to my parents' bungalow in Staines when Sasha had called to "apologize" with promises of "making it up to me" and explanations of it "just happened," all of the clichés rolled into one big ball of crushing heartbreak.

In keeping with tradition, I had stayed with Mum and Dad the night before the wedding and, after gathering up Basil and my special "going-away" clothes, I'd beaten a rapid retreat back here to my flat, called a locksmith and had the Yale lock changed. At least Luke had had the good grace to have already cleared his gear out before I got home, saving me the job of dumping it all in next door's trash bin. Although he did forget to cancel his *Star Wars* magazine subscription, so I store them under the kitchen sink to use when Basil sicks up grass, which I have to say is really rather satisfying. Especially the time the magazine came with a free Luke Skywalker plastic figurine: Basil and I played fetch with it until he'd had enough, bit Luke's head off, chewed up his body and spat it out in disgust. High-five, Basil!

After deleting all of Sasha's latest apology messages without listening to them—I can always tell them apart; there's a delay, then a bit of background noise, muffled voices (her and Luke, I presume), lots of shushing followed by the sound of her clearing her throat in preparation for yet another one of her convoluted "explanations"—there's a message from Mum.

"Sybil. How are you, darling? Just checking to see if you're still alive, only we haven't heard from you for a couple of days . . ." cue a short, nervous laugh, "and Dad was wondering if you'd like to join us for a pre-Christmas lunch soon. Help us all to really get into the festive spirit before we board the *Majestic* for the Christmas break. Are you sure you can't come too? I think they still have a few cabins left, inside lower-deck ones only, mind you." Her voice drops, just in case the neighbors are listening, I guess. Mum is very Hyacinth Bucket when it comes to keeping up appearances. "But still, leftovers are better than nothing, dear, and beggars can't be choosers, now can they?" I breathe in before exhaling a *looooong* calming breath, wondering when exactly it was that I became a "beggar." "Won't you be very lonely on your own?" "What about your turkey dinner with all the trimmings?" Cue a short silence before she changes tack. "We could invite Gloria from next door to lunch, the one with the handsome son who is a barrister with his own chamber! Fancy that." She pauses momentarily to draw breath. "And such a lovely fellow! Wouldn't it be marvelous if he—"

I press the button to skip to the next message. I know she means well, but I really don't want to spend Christmas on a cruise ship packed full of people twice my age and beyond, while Mum tries to fix me up with a "leftover" man or, worse still, Ian, the barrister, named after Ian Botham, the cricketer, but with a face like a moon landing, all craters and scars. We went to the same school and, a fellow horse lover, he dated Sasha for a while during sixth form and they rode together and showed off together in all the gymkhanas. After the end-of-year disco, he got hammered and then lunged at me for a snog, thinking I was Sasha. If that wasn't bad enough, he says things like "giddy up" in a ridiculously plummy voice instead of "hello" like everyone else, which is fine if you're astride a stallion and starring in a period drama or whatever, but he isn't, and therefore doesn't sound cool, just plain daft.

I unwind my most recently completed project from my neck, an extra-long, super-chunky knitted scarf with a tassel trim in Kermit green, and loop it over the banister before moving on to the next message.

"Sybs, babe, it's me, Cher. Listen, you have to see this new pub I've landed." Ah, she's there already. Last time we spoke Cher was still waiting to hear from the brewery about where they wanted to send her next. "It's called the Duck & Puddle and gorgeous is a massive under-statement. The village is just like something out of *The Darling Buds of May* and the locals—well, where have you ever heard of someone welcoming you with a whole hog to roast as a housewarming present? Tindledale, that's where! No joke. Cooper, he's the village butcher, came in yesterday with the pig flung over his shoulder, slapped it on the bar and said, 'There you go, love! I'll send the lad over later to set it up on the spit roaster for you.' So you'd better visit soon as I now have hog roast sandwiches coming out of my ears. Bring Basil too, I know he's partial to pork." She laughs warmly while I remember the time Basil stole a whole stuffed pork belly joint, and I had only turned my back for a few minutes to lay the table for our Sunday lunch. "Ooh, better go, babe, nearly last call." And the message fades to the sound of very jolly pub banter with Cher bellowing, "Time to drink up, ladies and gents" over the ding-a-ling of a ringing hand bell.

I smile. Cher, short for Cheryl, is my oldest and dearest friend. She and I first met at Brownies after her publican parents took over the local pub, "a step up," they had said, having come from a proper boozer in London's East End. By the end of Girl Guides, we were inseparable. Sasha was never keen on going, much preferring the Pony Club, but I loved it—all those craft badges to collect, just my kind of thing. Cher and I grew up together in the Home Counties town of Staines, until she moved away and her parents ran a number of pubs up North before retiring to the Lake District. Cher and I have always kept in touch and I've stayed with her and her husband, Clive, in many of the pubs she's managed over the years. The last one was in the pretty seaside town of Mulberry-On-Sea. The Hook, Line and Sinker it was called, and she did such a good job with it that the brewery asked her to go and rejuvenate this new one. Clive is a chef, so he spends most of his time in the kitchen or standing out the back by the industrial trash bins smoking a cigarette, putting the world to rights with whichever of the locals are his new best drinking buddies.

I take off my coat and saunter through to the kitchen. After dumping my bag on the counter, I flick on the kettle before reaching up to the top shelf of the cupboard to retrieve the biscuit tin, stashed up high in a vague attempt to curtail my sugar addiction, but it never seems to work. Well, it did for a bit, when I had a wedding to get ready for, but not now. I choose a Jammie Dodger and bite into its gooey sweet loveliness before firing up my laptop and typing *Jennifer Ford absconded* into Google.

The kettle boils so I swiftly make a mug of Wispa hot chocolate and it's just reaching the crackly, popping stage of the stirring process when an article posted just a few hours ago appears on the screen.

A young mum who went on a spending spree after a bungling council official accidentally deposited £42,000 in her bank account has disappeared. Police are trying to trace Jennifer Ford, who was last seen boarding a plane to Las Vegas dressed in designer gear including

£350 Gucci shades and seven-inch Louboutin stacked heels.

With sweaty palms, I swig the hot chocolate, scalding the roof of my mouth in the process. Ouch! I scroll down farther. And there she is. Jennifer Ford. My mouth drains of saliva. It's her. Definitely her. The woman whose claim I processed. Even with her new, superimposed, here's-what-she-might-look-like-now picture, complete with long, butter-blonde hair extensions, which the article then details were acquired from a "top salon in London's swanky West End, mainly frequented by celebrities." Oh goody, I shall rest easy armed with this important piece of trivia. Not. But part of me is thinking: good on you, Jennifer, I'm not sure I could resist such an enormous windfall, but then . . . what about the consequences? Surely there are laws about spending money that isn't yours, even if it has been paid into your very own bank account? I gulp, and try to ignore the hammering of my heart as I speed-read on.

A council spokesman has vowed to conduct a full investigation to ensure the bungling employee is identified and reprimanded for irresponsibly giving away such a huge sum of taxpayers' money.

And there, right in the middle of my laptop screen, is a picture of my boss, Mr. Banerjee, with his arms crossed and a furious look on his face. He's even wearing his serious black turban, and not his usual, colorful orange everyday one.

A wave of nausea crashes right through me and I actually think I might be sick. The kitchen sways slightly so I grip the edge of the counter to steady myself. What am I going to do? This has to be the cock-up to end all cock-ups, and I should know—I've had a few, and that's not including the wedding fiasco. Since May 4 I've been reprimanded several times at work by Gina, the team leader, mainly for trawling the Internet looking at knitting websites as a way to relieve the tedium of my boring job. The plan had been for me to marry Luke and then work from home—it was even his idea—because, he said, it made sense if we were to start a family. I'd be self-employed; I'd get to embrace my passion for knitting and needlecraft and see if I could make a proper go of it. I would take orders online at first and then, if it took off, I'd look for a shop, somewhere on-trend—like nappy valley, aka Clapham, where there are loads of people who love to create one-off masterpieces.

I had it all mapped out. But that dream has gone now, along with my heart, which shattered into a trillion tiny fragments on that day in the church. I swallow the last

16

of the hot chocolate in an attempt to shake off the pity party for one and delve into my bag to retrieve my knitting. I love making things—knitting, needlecraft, quilting, crocheting and patchwork—when dark thoughts threaten to overwhelm me. I'll just finish this tea cozy. Yes, it will calm me down while I come up with a plan of action to get myself out of this latest cock-up, because I have a horrible, sinking feeling that I'm the bungling employee. And if I am, then I could very well be facing the sack right before Christmas, because there are only so many warnings one can have before it just gets ridiculous. Not that I transfer the actual payments into the claimants' bank accounts; no, somebody else does that part of the process, for security apparently, which is a bit ironic. I process the claims, and calculate the payment amount due but with my mind not really being on the job recently, perhaps I did inadvertently add on a couple of extra zeros. It could happen. So easily!

I dart through the archway into my tiny lounge and slump down in the armchair. Knit one, purl one, knit one, purl one, knit one, purl one, KNIT ONE PURL ONE, KNIT ONE PURL ONE, KNITONEPURLONEKNITONEPURLONE! And on it goes, faster and faster and faster and faster until the prancing reindeer tea cozy is finished in record-breaking time, and my hands have fused themselves into the shape of an ancient Chinese woman's lotus feet.

I take Rudolph into the storeroom and place him on the bookshelf next to the others. Twenty-seven tea cozies in total. Not to mention all the other shelves housing the numerous beanies, cardigans, scarves, mittens and sweaters. My storeroom is jam-packed with knitted goods. But what can I say? I've had a lot of dark thoughts, and all of the sad feels, recently . . .

2

I try the key in the ignition one more time and say a little prayer, but it's no use—the Clio has definitely died. It's going nowhere. I rest my forehead on the steering wheel and let out a little whimper. Basil, sitting upright on the passenger seat beside me, tilts his head to one side in sympathy.

"So what now then?" I ask, giving him a sideways grimace before pulling the furry hood of my parka up over my crimson-and-white Fair Isle beanie. It's perishing cold out here, but I've made up my mind. I've come up with a plan and there's no backing out now.

Keep calm and carry yarn.

That's what I embroidered onto the front of my craft bag, so taking my own advice, in addition to a massive breath, I scoop Basil up under my arm, grab my suitcase from the backseat (you can't be too careful around here with all the street crime) and head back into the flat to call a taxi to take me to the station. We'll travel by train.

It'll be *fun*, and I'm sure it can't be *that* far to Tindledale. And I probably should call Cher to let her know that I'm on my way. I've already rung Mum to give her Cher's number and tell her that Basil and I are going on a mini-break for a few days; she'll only worry if she can't get hold of me, and she was delighted to hear that I'm venturing out and "dipping my toe back in" . . . Hmm. Mum also said to give Cher her love.

Of course, I didn't mention the cock-up to end all cock-ups at work and that I'm actually running away because right now I just can't deal with any more stress. Only for a long weekend, mind you, but enough time to give myself some space to figure out what to do and come up with a strategy. It's a chance to breathe, and I don't feel as if I've done that properly since the "wedding that never happened." Besides, Mum will only panic about everyone finding out that I'm the bungling employee. Plus, I don't want Sasha knowing. I feel so betrayed by her and the last thing I want is her knowing that I've messed up at work and could potentially lose my job too, in addition to the boyfriend that she stole from me. She's always wanted what I've had; as children she'd want the toy that I'd been given, even though it was exactly the same as hers, and she'd make me swap. As we've got older, I've often felt that she thinks she's better than me, more successful, just because she travels and has a full-on social life. It's well known within the family that she thinks my job and passion for knitting and needlecraft is dull—"provincial" is what she said on one of the rare occasions we were last all together—and I think she secretly feels the same way about our parents too, in their bungalow in the cul-de-sac in Staines—they and it are just not glamorous or exciting enough for Sasha.

Not that Mum and Dad are in constant communication with her; in fact, since May 4 they've been extremely diplomatic and have kept her very much at arm's length, which I guess is fairly easy given that Sasha spends most of her time gallivanting around, organizing spectacular events for her fabulously famous and wealthy clients in places like Dubai, and not forgetting her annual charity event here in the UK—the Christmas hunt ball—because she likes to "give a little back" as she says, to the horse community that helped launch her career. It's how she came to be such a successful event planner in the first place: she started out by organizing pony shows and polo parties for well-heeled people who recommended her to their even wealthier friends, who make up her glittering client portfolio. And now she's being fabulous all over the place with my ex-fiancé in tow, no doubt. Well, good riddance to them, I rally, mustering up a modicum of resilience. I wonder if Sasha has discovered Luke's penchant for farting under the duvet yet?

The Duck & Puddle number rings for what seems like an eternity before I hang up—I glance at the wall clock and see that it's just after 7 p.m.—Cher is obviously busy and I imagine the bar area is noisy so maybe nobody can hear the phone. I try her mobile, but it doesn't even ring, it goes straight through to the "person can't take your call . . ." message. Anyway, it'll be fine; Cher said to visit, so it'll be a nice surprise for her and I've already called work—well, luckily Gina's mobile went straight to voice mail too, so I left a message to say that since I have a migraine coming on and quite possibly a temperature, but I haven't actually confirmed this as I don't have a thermometer (Gina can be very pedantic), it was looking highly unlikely that I'd make it into work tomorrow. Not strictly a lie, as I really do have a headache, an anxiety one, and I'm starting to sweat in this furry hood and beanie. In fact, I think it's fair to say that right now I'm one very hot mess!

*

An hour later, the train to Tindledale is just about to depart—the last direct one, luckily, which arrives at 10:39 p.m. After that, you have to go to Market Briar, the nearest big town, and get a taxi or a lift on a tractor apparently, "so don't be planning any big late nights out while you're there," is what the man in the ticket office chortled when I told him where we were heading.

Basil settles at my feet after giving up on trying to snuggle on the seat beside me. A guy in a black duffel coat and a gray beanie hat (definitely machine-knitted) is sitting by the window in the bank of seats adjacent to me, reading a newspaper; he looks up and gives me a courteous smile. I smile back and instantly notice his kind-looking emerald eyes behind black-framed glasses that accentuate the stubbly dark beard and curly hair peeping out from under the sides of his hat. This is only a recent thing, noticing men. After being in a relationship for five years with a man that I was certain I'd marry, it still feels weird looking at other guys in a *snog/marry/avoid* way, as Cher would say. I guess, it just isn't something I'm used to; I really loved Luke, so it didn't ever cross my mind to notice other men, and then, after everything that happened . . . well, let's just say that it's taking me time to reprogram my head to an "I'm single" status.

"*Basil!*" I yell as he darts across the train car and goes to swipe the guy's Costa cake from a napkin on the table. I dive-bomb Basil just in time. "I'm so sorry, anyone would think he was starving, which he certainly isn't," I say, grinning apologetically to the guy. I grab Basil's collar and swiftly pull him back. Luckily, the guy laughs and shrugs it off, before moving the cake to a safer spot and lifting his newspaper back up.

A few minutes later, an older lady, sixty-something perhaps, arrives through the door of the adjoining car and sits opposite me.

"Ah, he's a fine-looking lad. What's his name?" she asks in a country accent as she glances down at my feet. "And what a superb coat he has on."

"Thanks, he's called Basil." I smile, straightening Basil's festive red knitted body warmer before unzipping my parka. Basil lifts his head on hearing his name so I give him a quick stroke. He laps it up before resting his chin back on my right foot.

"Well I never, that was my late husband's name, God rest his soul, and I haven't heard it in a while, I must say! Is it significant to you too?"

"Um, yes, I'm called Sybs, well, Sybil really. My friend, Cher, she came up with his name on account of—"

"Oh yes, I know it! From the TV series, *Fawlty Towers*, it was so funny. Basiiiiiiiiiiil," she bellows, taking me by surprise. "That's what his wife, Sybil, used to holler—it was a standing joke with my Basil and I. He always laughed when I did it to him." Her eyes close momentarily as she reminisces.

"I'm so sorry for your loss," I say gently.

"Oh, thank you, love, but it was a very long time ago

and he certainly had a good run. I'm on my second husband now, met him a year ago on a bus tour to Portofino. Colin was the driver," she chuckles, "and fourteen years younger than me. I'm Dolly, by the way."

"Nice to meet you, Dolly." I smile, loving her zest for life, and Dolly chuckles and winks before loosening her coat and removing her fur hat.

"You have the right idea, Sybs, it's mighty warm in this carriage, that heater is churning out the hot air." She frowns, pointing at the panel beside us.

"It sure is," I say, slipping off the parka.

"Cor! That's a beauty. Knit it yourself?" She nods at my Christmas sweater.

"Oh, um, yes I did. Thank you!" I beam and cast a glance down at the fleece-lined chunky red knit with Ho Ho Ho emblazoned across the front in sparkly yarn, and each Ho a different color. The heater in the Clio is so temperamental that I wasn't taking any chances on freezing to death during the long drive to Tindledale and this is the warmest sweater I've ever made, but then, when the taxi turned up right away, I didn't have time to get changed into something more suitable for a steamed-up train journey.

"You have a real gift. I could never get on with knitting." Dolly shakes her head and I smile politely, unable to imagine a life without knitting. Knitting has never let

25

me down: it soothes me, comforts me, excites me, calms me—it's multifaceted and it means so many things to me. It may sound silly, but all of my knitting projects have memories attached too: I can swing a silver pashmina around my shoulders, knitted on holiday in Ibiza, and it instantly puts me right there on the sandy beach under a parasol with Cher nodding her head along to the tunes on her iPod, us laughing together, sipping sangria and feeling carefree and happy. This was long before I met Luke, or Sasha betrayed me. "So where are you off to?" Dolly asks.

"I'm going to surprise a friend who's just moved to a village called Tindledale. Do you know it?"

"I most certainly do. My Basil was postman there for a while and his father before him. Colin and I live in Stoneley, four stops before yours."

"Ooh, you might be able to help me with something then, please?" I ask, eagerly.

"Always happy to help if I can, dear. What is it?" Dolly smiles kindly.

"I left home in a bit of hurry and haven't brought a housewarming gift for my friend, I don't suppose you can recommend a shop where I can buy something nice for her? I was thinking a candle or some Belgian truffles perhaps." Cher isn't really one for knitted garments, otherwise I'd have brought her a cardigan, or a tea cozy or two. I managed to grab a bottle of red wine from my fridge, and it's almost full, but it's hardly the same as a proper present, especially when Cher already has a pub full of alcohol. Dolly laughs.

"Well, it's been a long time since I've actually been in Tindledale, but I'm pretty sure there isn't anywhere that sells candles, certainly not the fancy fragranced ones that you'd be after. You might get some white Price's household ones in the village store—they always used to keep a few boxes in stock for the power outages," she says knowingly. "And as for chocolates, they won't be Belgian, but I'm sure you'd get a nice bar of Fry's Peppermint Cream in there too. They have quite a range in their small super-market section—through the archway next to the post office counter."

"Lovely. I'll head there right away," I say, not wanting to be rude, but I can't exactly turn up with a bar of Fry's chocolate. Cher will think I've really lost it.

"Oh, it won't be open this time of night, dear. The village store closes at four in the winter. You could try the pub though; they have a little shop that has sweets, crisps, cigarettes, milk, magazines, eggs, bread, fire-lighters, logs, lighter fuel . . . that kind of thing. There's an honesty box so take what you like and leave the money in the bowl." I smile again—I can just see Cher's face if I buy her a bag of crisps as a present from her own shop.

And who ever heard of a pub with an honesty box? At the fried chicken place on the corner of my street they have a metal grill that you have to pay through at the time of order, and they don't take notes over a fiver in case they're forgeries.

*

The train pulls into Stoneley and I can barely keep my eyes open after chatting to Dolly for most of the journey. I stifle a yawn and will myself to keep awake.

"Oh dear! You need a good night's sleep." *Hmm, this is true—I haven't slept properly in months.* "But not far now," Dolly says warmly, buttoning up her coat and giving Basil a parting tickle under his chin.

"It was lovely to meet you," I say, doing a little wave.

"You too, love. Enjoy your stay in Tindledale. And do look me up if you're ever in Stoneley. We have the import/export company on the old Market Briar road—can't miss our barn, which doubles as a warehouse. Cheerio."

"Thank you." I smile and wave again as she steps off the train and walks past the window and into the arms of her husband, who is waiting to greet her at the end of the platform with a big grin on his face and an enormous bouquet of festive winter blooms—rich reds, oranges and greens, and there's even one of those little dried pumpkins on a stick nestling next to a silver-sprayed sprig of mistletoe that he plucks from the bunch and holds high above her head before leaning in for a Christmas kiss. Laughing, she bats his chest before pulling him in close. They clearly adore each other and it's so nice to see. Maybe there's hope for me yet . . .

Leaning back against the seat, I close my eyes and realize that I really am exhausted. A few minutes later I become conscious that Basil's beside me, so I open one eye and do a quick scan of the car. The guy by the window is still engrossed in his newspaper and there's nobody else here, so I put my hand around Basil and stroke his silky soft ear. He takes the cue and snuggles into the side of my thigh, curling into a ball and making himself as small as possible, instinctively knowing that he needs to be on his best behavior or he'll be back on the hard train floor.

*

The train stops moving and I jolt awake.

"Er, excuse me . . . are we here?" I ask the ticket taker, as I wipe away the condensation that's gathered on the window, but he's already heading back off down the carriage, and the guy with the newspaper has gone too. I must have nodded off.

I peer out through the gap on the glass.

And gasp.

We're on the set of *Frozen*! Or so it seems. Outside there's a magical winter wonderland where Olaf could appear at any given moment—I'm convinced of it. The platform is covered in a beautiful layer of crisp, clean white snow, untouched and definitely not mottled with dirt like the sludgy gray sleet at home. It's perfect. Just like one of Mum's special festive placemats with the perfect Christmassy scene on them that she keeps for best, or for when Gloria from next door pops in for her annual New Year drinks soirée.

Feeling very excited, I quickly pull on my parka, loop my hand through Basil's lead and gather up my stuff before heading for the door. I can't wait to grab a taxi to the Duck & Puddle pub; with a bit of luck, Basil and I will make it there just in time to surprise Cher and Clive before last call.

B ut where's the taxi stand?

Basil and I are standing underneath an old-fashioned Dickensian-looking streetlight! And I don't believe it—we're in the middle of nowhere surrounded by snow-dappled trees and standing on a postage-stamp-size patch of tarmac that I'm assuming must count as a car park around here. And it's deserted, apart from what looks like half of a dilapidated two-berth caravan. It's hard to tell as the top has been cut off and the rest "left to nature"; brambles, ten feet high with an intricate crocheted maze of snow-dusted spider-webs weaving between the leaves, are sprouting from it at jaunty angles. Basil and I are the only ones here and the tiny ticket office, a prefab, is all locked up; we had to exit the platform via a rickety wooden side gate. So now what? There isn't even a bus stop or a phone box that I can see, and the snow is falling thicker and faster.

We start walking.

Well, I'm walking, trudging like a Sherpa really, dragging my wheelie suitcase behind me, whereas Basil is bouncing along up front, biting the snow as if it's a real thing and generally having a good time.

We've been walking for at least ten minutes when we come to a fork in the road. There's one of those traditional white wooden country signposts, so I stop walking and, after catching my breath, I reach up and wipe the snow away to see if we're even going in the right direction.

Tindledale 2¼

Two and a quarter miles! Sweet Jesus, when was the last time I walked that far? From what I can see, it's uphill all the way and my backside still aches from the Zumba class. Maybe coming here wasn't such a good idea after all. On the numerous occasions when the Clio has conked out, I've just taken the tube or jumped on a bus. Getting around is easy in London, but not here it seems. I scan the narrow, twisting country lane, hopeful for a bus stop, but there's nothing, just trees and hedges and darkness and silence. I never knew the countryside could be this quiet. No car alarms. No shouting. No TV. No belting Dubstep from next door at 3 a.m. on a school night. No nothing. Just nature at nighttime, I suppose. It's peaceful. And I never noticed it before when camping with the Brownies as a child, but then there were ten giggling girls in sleeping bags right beside me.

There aren't even any streetlights now. Only a pretty pearlescent hue from the full moon high up in the inky, twinkly starry night sky. Oh well. It could be fun, in a Dorothy-following-the-yellow-brick-road kind of way; only my road is glistening snow-white to light the way. I click the heels of my (fittingly) red Converse trainers together and try to ignore the fact that they're already soaked through. Right on cue, Basil, thinking it's some kind of new game, leaps up at me. Catching him with my gloved hands, I laugh and pull him in close, letting him nuzzle into my face, his whiskery nose tickling my cheeks and making me smile. He can be my Toto.

"Come on. We better get on with it then," I say, placing him back on the snowy ground, and making a mental note to buy a new mobile first thing in the morning.

Figuring it will be easier to push the suitcase up the hill, I lengthen the strap on my handbag and swing it over my head, cross-body style, before pulling the beanie and hood down over my forehead to act as a kind of snow shield, then I maneuver the suitcase into position like a mini snowplow, and start trudging. And trudge some more. And more again. Past a quaint, brick-built school with a tiny playground and an impressive clock tower at one end of the roof, a row of the cutest chocolate-box cottages I've ever seen, with wrought-iron gates leading into long front gardens surrounded by mature hedges and dotted with wooden bird feeders and wind chimes. One of the cottages has a pile of wellies and muddy boots stacked up in the porch by the front door and I can't help thinking how lovely it is, that they can leave stuff like that outside without the fear of somebody nicking it. That would never happen in London—I put an herb planter on my windowsill once and it lasted exactly a day before it disappeared. I keep trudging until, eventually, I spot a hazy glow in the distance. A flicker.

As we get closer, I see a single white column candle in a glass-covered storm lamp at the foot of a stone war memorial set in the middle of a very tiny village square. There's a festive holly wreath lying next to the candle, its crimson red berries a vivid contrast in the white of the snow, and for some reason it takes my breath away. It's poignant and magical and I stand mesmerized for a few minutes at the significance of the sight before me. Even Basil stops bounding and stands completely still, instinctively sensing the reverence of the moment.

The snow stops and I notice a bus shelter to my left

with a wooden bench inside. Hurrah! I stagger in and sit down, grateful for the breather. Two and a quarter miles, uphill, in deep snow, is very hard work.

"Evening!" a man's voice says in the dark, and I almost jump right off the bench. I didn't see him there, huddled up in the corner. "Sorry to startle you. Just waiting for the good lady wife," he explains, before rubbing his gloved hands together and stamping his welly-clad feet in an attempt to keep warm. "Nippy one tonight. Where are you heading? There won't be a bus along until tomorrow, you know. First one is at eight so you'll have a bit of a wait."

"Oh, um, hello," I start, awkwardly. I'm not used to complete strangers making eye contact in public, let alone talking to me. It isn't the done thing in London. *What if they have a knife?* But he looks harmless in the candlelight, wizened but friendly, jovial even, and Basil likes him; he has his front paws up on the man's knees and his tail is wagging from side to side. "Basil! Stop that. Sorry, he's still learning," I say, grabbing Basil's collar in an attempt to pull him away from the man.

"Ah, he's OK. Can probably smell my dogs. Got six of them at home. Not Scotties, mind. Working Collies—for the sheep." The man treats Basil to a vigorous rub behind his ears.

"That's nice. Are you a shepherd?" I say, and then

35

instantly wish I could push the words back into my mouth. I sound ridiculous—from what I've already seen of Tindledale, it's obviously a bit behind the times but hardly biblical. Then the man surprises me.

"Yes, I guess so. Ah, those were the days!" He chuckles. Wow! I've just met my first shepherd. "It's all changed now, but I've still got sheep, hundreds of the bleaters. So where have you come from?"

"Um, London" I reply, a little taken aback by his directness. "I've just walked from the station," I add, to clarify.

"Well, that's certainly a trek." He lets out a long whistle. "Oh, here she is." The man stands up as a mud-splattered old tank of a Land Rover judders to a halt in front of us, its diesel engine still chugging as the window is cranked down a few inches, gets stuck and a woolly-mittened (definitely homemade) hand appears over the top to force it down the rest of the way.

"Been bothering you, has he?" A blowsy woman in a floral silk headscarf pops her head out.

"Oh, no, not at all." I shake my head vehemently and smile to assure her.

"Well, that makes a change—fancies himself as a ladies' man when he's got his drinking goggles on, don't you, dear?" She chuckles as he plants a big kiss on her plump cheek before heading round to the passenger seat. "Do you need a lift?"

"I don't actually know," I say, feeling ever so slightly displaced, a bit parallel universe, even. It's surreal. I'm standing in Narnia with the shepherd and his wife chatting like they've known me my whole life.

"Where are you heading to?"

"The Duck & Puddle pub, do you know it?"

The woman roars with laughter like I've just cracked the funniest joke ever.

"Indeed, I do! Very well, in fact. It's my husband's second home. End of the High Street, over the village green—watch out for the duck pond—and Bob's your uncle." She points into the dark over my left shoulder.

"Is it far?" I ask, looking in the direction of her index finger.

"Minutes. But here, you'll need this." And after leaning down and rummaging around in the footwell for a while, her head bobs back up and she hands me a flashlight. It even has its own plastic carrying handle. "Switch that on and you'll be able to see as far as Market Briar," she instructs. "I would give you a lift, but you can be there in the time it'll take us to load you, the dog and the suitcase into the car." She roars again.

"Thank you," I say, flicking the flashlight on and thinking how generous she is. I could run off with this for all she knows.

"There's a girl!" She nods cheerily. "It's not usually this

pitch-black in the village. Blasted snow puts the power off, you see. The power lines don't like it." And she points again, this time above the bus stop to an overhead cable that's laden with snow. So, Dolly was on the ball. "Good night."

"But what about the flashlight?" I say, waving it in the air.

"Just leave it with the others in the crate by the bar." And with that, she pulls the window back up and chugs away.

With the powerful beam from the flashlight guiding the way, Basil and I step onto the cobbly street that's flanked either side with rows of small black timber-framed, white wattle-walled shops that I presume is the village center—a far cry from London with all its multi-story concrete tower blocks and big flashing neon signs. I shine the light toward the end of the little street and sure enough, there's the pub, the Duck & Puddle, cloaked in darkness, just past the village green. I take it we've missed last call, then.

Pushing the suitcase, Basil and I make our way toward the pub, but I can't resist having a nose through the mullioned windows of the shops. There's what looks like a clothes boutique on my left across the road, vintage maybe, because there's a swishy pink polka-dot fifties prom dress on a headless dressmaker's bust in

38

the window. Opposite is a place called the Spotted Pig—a double-fronted café, by the looks of it; there's a menu in a glass case on the wall in the little alcove by the front door. I take a closer look and see that the Christmas special is panettone bread pudding with creamy rum custard. Cor, I love the sound of this; maybe I can bring Cher to the Spotted Pig for afternoon tea tomorrow. Aw, a pet parlor is next door. I can see the sign, PAWS, in elegant mint green and cream letters above the door.

"One for you, Basil." But he's too busy biting the snow. There's a bookshop now, a proper musty, old-looking one. Using the sleeve of my parka, I wipe a space on the window and press my nose up to the glass. Wow! There must be a billion books filling every shelf, table top and nook and cranny; old books too, ones that you might have to wear special white gloves for before being allowed to thumb through them. A fruit and veg shop is next door with a stack of empty fruit boxes piled up neatly in the doorway.

We cross over and next to the one with the prom dress in the window is a butcher's, a traditional one with a ceramic-tiled counter and a row of silver meat hooks dangling in the window. Next, there's an antiques shop, then a chemist, a florist and a bakery. And here's the village store that Dolly mentioned, and, last of all, there are a couple of empty shops at the end nearest the green. I'm impressed: a butcher and a baker; all they need is a candlestick maker—which, given the apparent frequency of the power failures around here, might very well be a good thing. A real money maker.

We reach the green. Ah, this is nice. There's a very plump Christmas tree set right in the middle, and it must be at least twenty feet tall. It has glittery baubles hanging from the ferny fingers, glistening in the glow from the flashlight. My heart lifts. It's truly magical—so quiet and peaceful and in such utter contrast to the noisy hustle and bustle of what I've left behind. I think I'm going to really enjoy my weekend here. And then I realize that I haven't thought about May 4, or indeed, Jennifer Ford, since I stepped on the train in London, which right now feels like a million miles away—and that's a good thing, surely? These past few months, I have honestly been rapidly reaching the point where I feel as if my head might actually explode. A mini-break in the beautiful, cozy, bubble of Tindledale is just what I need.

4

It's like that film, *Deliverance*, when I push open the door of the Duck & Puddle—all that's missing is a man in dungarees chewing tobacco and strumming a banjo.

Ten or so pairs of eyes turn to stare at me as I stamp the bulk of the snow from my legs and feet, push down the hood of my parka and pull off my beanie. It's like a furnace in here. And I haven't missed last call at all; in fact, from the number of full pints lined up on the bar, I'd say "drinking up time" has only just begun. The windows all have heavy velvet blackout curtains blocking the light from the numerous candles dotted around the tables, which explains why the pub looked closed from the other side of the village green, and the source of the heat is an enormous real log fire with crimson, blue-tinged flames crackling and wheezing in the ceiling-height inglenook fireplace to my right.

I smile tentatively and scan behind the bar, but Cher isn't here.

"Well, don't just sit there. Give the girl a hand," a chunky woman wearing a woolly poncho (hand-knitted) bellows to the extremely tall, robust-looking man sitting beside her, before elbowing him sharply in the ribs.

"Will you turn it in, woman?" he pretends to chastise her as he shoos her hand away. "I was just getting my bearings." There's a collective good-natured laugh from the crowd as the man downs his pint in one gulp and then steadies himself on the table before hauling himself into an upright position.

"That suitcase looks heavy enough to house a body," the woman continues. *Oh God, don't say that!* They're already eyeing me suspiciously—probably thinking I'm some kind of *crazeee* woman on the loose, come to their village to strangle them all in their beds as they sleep.

The man strides toward me and hauls the suitcase up over his shoulder in one swift movement. He extends his free hand.

"I'm Cooper." He nods firmly, as if to punctuate the point. *Ah, yes, I remember, the butcher with the hog roast.*

"Pleased to meet you." I quickly pull a woolly mitten off with my teeth and shake his hand. "I'm Sybs," I finish quietly, but he's already dropped my hand and turned his back to go in search of a suitable spot in which to deposit the suitcase.

"Now, where do you want this?" he yells back over his shoulder.

"Oh, well, I've come to visit Cher, so behind the bar perhaps, for now?" I suggest, quickly going after him, scanning again and thinking *where is she?* This is really awkward. They are all still staring at me—and the only sound comes from the pop and whizz of the log fire. I spot the crate next to the bar, stacked high with an assortment of torches and flashlights, and deposit my borrowed one on top of the pile.

"SONNNNYYYYY!" Jesus, that was right in my ear. Cooper sure has a big, booming voice. And Basil has obviously heard him from outside as he's now barking like a mad dog—woofing over and over and over. Another guy jumps up.

"That'll be the cocker from the country club," he says to nobody in particular. "Perishing thing is always getting free and roaming around the village like it's lord of the manor. I'll herd it up and take it back." He heads toward the door with a determined look on his ruddy weather-beaten farmer's face.

"Oh, well actually, that could be my Scottie, Basil. He's tied up securely though," I say, shrinking a little inside as they clearly don't approve of dogs barking late at night. I wouldn't usually risk leaving Basil on his own outside, certainly not in London, where he could get kidnapped in the twinkling of an eye, but I'd figured he was probably safe until I found Cher and could get him upstairs out of the way. Besides, I thought the villagers would all be in bed asleep—I mean, don't they all have to be up at the crack of dawn to milk cows or something? Obviously not, they're all in the Duck & Puddle—the shepherd's second home, theirs too by the looks of it! I glance at the wall clock and see that it's after eleven. The farmer guy stares at me like I've just sprouted another head.

"Why would you do that?"

"Pardon?" I blink, wondering what he's going on about.

"Leave your dog outside?" he says, frowning and giving me an up-and-down look.

"But, I thought—"

"Get him in quick before he wakes up Mark." *Who's Mark?* "And put him by the fire—he must be freezing half to death, the poor thing." Oh God, now they think I'm cruel to animals. He points to a dog bowl brimming with water next to a tartan blanket by a log basket at the corner of the tiled hearth.

"Oh, that would be lovely. Thank you." There's a little

ricochet of chuckles as I dash back outside. How was I supposed to know that dogs were actually allowed inside the pub? And with special provisions too—blanket, refreshments, cozy log fire to bask beside—Basil is going to be in his element.

"Did someone bellow?" Clive has appeared behind the bar when I return with Basil. "Sybs! Hello darling. What a nice surprise," he beams on spotting me. "And Cher will be made up to see you." He lifts the hatch and motions for me to come through. I smile with relief at seeing a familiar face, and then, as if by magic, everyone starts chatting and laughing among themselves, doing normal pub banter—just like a scene from *Emmerdale* in the Woolpack Inn when the director has just yelled "action." How strange . . . I feel as if I've passed some kind of initiation ritual and that they've all relaxed and gone back to whatever it was they were doing before I burst through the door of their local pub, a stranger in their midst, but it's all OK—*now Clive has verified me, that is.*

I take off Basil's snowy wet coat and settle him in the designated spot by the fire (he instantly looks right at home, sprawled out on the blanket and he's practically comatose already as he relishes the intense heat) before I head toward Clive. Cooper follows behind, dumping my suitcase in the hall next to a mountain of boxes containing cheese and onion crisps.

"Thanks, Cooper," says Clive.

"No problem, Sonny." And he strides off through to the other side of the bar.

Clive gives me a hug and then steers me through to a cozy private lounge out the back. Once the door is closed and I'm satisfied that the locals can't overhear us, I give Clive a quizzical look.

"Er, why is he calling you Sonny?" I ask in a hushed voice, creasing my forehead. Clive smiles and shakes his head in amusement.

"Because I'm Cher's boyfriend." Clive shrugs as if it's the most obvious reason ever, and then he explains. "On our first day here, one of the regulars said it for a laugh, you know, as in, so if our new landlady is called Cher and you're her fella, then you must be Sonny and it's stuck. Now everyone in Tindledale calls me Sonny, as in Sonny and Cher." And he belts out a line from their iconic song, "I Got You Babe."

"Ha ha, of course they do," I laugh and give him another hug. "And my second question—who is Mark?" I shake my head.

"Oh! He's the local bobby—lives in the police house next door to Dr. Darcy, who's the village GP. Mark gets upset if he's woken up in the middle of the night, hence Pete wanting to get Basil inside quickly," Clive explains in a matter-of-fact way.

"But Mark is OK about you serving after hours?" I ask, lifting my eyebrows. I'm surprised; it's not something Cher usually goes for.

"*Weeeeell* . . ." He gives me a shifty look and shoves his hands into his jeans pockets. "Cher isn't actually here. She's on a course at Brewery HQ. A last-minute space came up after one of the others dropped out so she jumped at the chance of staying in a hotel for a few nights."

"Oh no!" My heart sinks.

"But she'll be back by Sunday afternoon," he adds quickly, seeing my face drop. "And Mark's fine about a bit of banter after hours as long he doesn't know about it, if you know what I mean. Discretion, that's the key." Clive winks and grins before tapping the side of his nose with an index finger. "Now, how about I get you a drink before we find you somewhere to stay." He rubs his hands together.

"Er, I thought it was OK to stay here. Cher said . . ." My voice trails off and for some ridiculous reason I can feel tears threatening. I push my top teeth down hard on my tongue to focus my mind and stop the tears from tumbling out. I've cocked up again. I should never have just showed up here. What was I *thinking*? I can't imagine there's a Travelodge anywhere in Tindledale so I'm going to have to go back home—which is where I probably should have stayed to face the music in the morning with Mr. Banerjee.

"Hey, of course it is," Clive says kindly. "Cher has been going on and on about you coming. Like I said, she'll be made up that you're here. And it'll sweeten the blow when she returns."

"What do you mean?"

"Come and see." And Clive pulls open a little timber-slatted door in the corner that I hadn't even noticed, and after ducking his head under the low frame, he motions for me to follow him up the narrowest, twistiest, higgledy-piggledy stairs I think I've ever seen. I feel like Alice in Wonderland as I crouch down and place the palms of my hands on the steps in front of me just to get low enough to climb up to the next floor.

"Oh dear! I see what you mean." We've emerged into a tiny, exposed-beamed bedroom with a mattress on the floor, one side of which is propped up on a row of wooden blocks next to a window so low and bowed it's practically a continuation of the carpet. "What are they for?" I point to the blocks.

"So we don't tumble away when we're fast asleep in the middle of the night and end up going through the window." He manages a wry smile, but he also has a very good point, because the floorboards slope so severely that there's every chance this really could happen. "We can't get any of our furniture up those doll's house stairs. The pub was built in 1706 as a coaching inn originally—even the old stable buildings are still intact. And currently storing all of our furniture, I hasten to add. People were clearly pocket-size in those days." He shrugs and pulls a face. "We're lucky to even have the mattress; if it wasn't for Pete lashing it up tight like a bale of hay, we would have never squeezed it up the stairs. No, we need a new bed, one that can be assembled in situ, as it were." He pauses and shrugs. "But until then, this is it, I'm afraid. So unless you and Basil fancy bunking down with me on the mattress . . ." He laughs, slings a friendly arm around my shoulders, and jiggles me up and down in a big bear hug.

I like Clive, always have. When Cher first met him, he was washing dishes in her parents' pub in Doncaster to pay his way through catering college, and they've been together ever since. He's so solid and uncomplicated. When I ran out of the church, Cher and Clive arrived at Mum and Dad's house within moments of me getting there. I learned later that Clive had grabbed Cher's hand, run her from the church (she was bridesmaid, of course) and driven at breakneck speed to find me. No fuss, just a "well, she's your mate and he's a wanker," and he was all for hunting Luke down and giving him a "good slap," but Cher talked him out of it. Yes, Clive is a what-you-see-is-what-you-get kind of guy, and there's a lot to be said for that. Not like Luke, who clearly has very hidden depths. You know, Luke even tried telling me once that he mistook Sasha for me and that's how the "mix-up" had all started in the first place. He snogged her by accident and it "sort of went from there." I didn't buy it of course—because for starters, our faces may be the same but that's where the identical twin bit ends these days. And Sasha wears completely different clothes from me—expensive body-con dresses and designer stacked heels to my hand-sewn Renfrew tops or chunky sweaters in winter with jeans and flats. Anyway, Sasha could easily have pushed him away, or laughed it off at the very least.

"Um, think I'll pass if you don't mind. Cher has told me all about your super-loud snoring," I play-punch his chest, trying to make light of the situation and wondering if perhaps Basil and I could sleep on one of the sofas in the bar. If the villagers ever decide to head back to their chocolate-box cottages, that is.

5

Leaning back against the plum-colored velvet head-board with Basil snuggled up on a blanket beside me, his front left paw on my thigh as he snores softly, I snuggle into the enormous squishy bed in my ditsy floral-themed bedroom.

After Clive and I had made it back down the tiny stairs and into the saloon bar area earlier, the woman in the poncho, who it turns out is called Molly and has a pet ferret she walks around the village on a leash—it was under the pub table apparently, and I didn't even notice—anyway, she's Cooper's wife, and she kindly rang the only B&B for miles around. It's located in the valley on the far side of the village and doubles as a hair salon too, apparently. As luck would have it, there was one room left, and dogs are very welcome, so Pete, who I later found out farms cattle—"three fields over near Cherry Tree Orchard, which supplies apples to all the major super-markets"—loaded me, Basil and my suitcase into the cab of his tractor, I kid you not, and then trundled us all the way down the hill in the snow and right up to the front door that doubles up as the B&B and hair salon reception.

So now I'm wrapped in a fluffy white bathrobe trying not to think about the contents of my suitcase. All of my clean clothes, pajamas, underwear—the whole lot's soaked in red wine. *Ruined*. Even my almost-finished knitting project, a lovely little Christmas pudding, is now stained a vivid claret color and stinks like a barrel of rotten grapes. The top on the bottle wasn't screwed on properly so had come off and seeped wine into everything. And as if that wasn't bad enough, in my rush to escape London and the wrath of Mr. Banerjee, I left my makeup bag and hairbrush behind on the hall table, so I will now have to spend the whole weekend wearing my super-warm, fleece-lined Ho Ho Ho sweater and snow-sodden jeans.

I say good night to Basil and switch off the lamp—the electricity in the village flicked back on, just like magic, as Pete and I left the Duck & Puddle. I was climbing into the tractor when the festive fairy-tale scene literally took my breath away. The pretty red, gold and green Christmas lights twinkling all over the tree on the village green before cascading the length of the High Street, with a grand finale—the cross at the top of the tall church steeple illuminated in silver as if bathing the whole village in a ray of tranquility and spiritual peace.

I lie in the silent night of the countryside, except for the intermittent ter-wit-ter-woo of an owl, and try to let everything wash over me: Jennifer Ford, Mr. Banerjee, Mum and her "make do with whatever's left over" implications, Luke the tool, *Star Wars*, Princess Leia buns, Chewbacca and, worst of all, the betrayal by my very own twin sister. I'm not sure I'll ever forgive her; men come and go, I know that, but *my own sister*? How does one deal with that? It's not as if I can just cut her out of my life! What would that do to Mum and Dad? And it would certainly make things very awkward at family events. But then again, Sasha did this, not me. And I can't help wondering if she has difficulty sleeping at night too!

I breathe in and out, desperately trying to slow my racing thoughts, in the hope of actually getting to sleep and making it through to the morning without waking up for once. It's been ages since I managed to get a proper night's sleep. Soon after the wedding-that-wasn't, my GP prescribed sleeping tablets, saying they would help with the "overwhelming feelings of sadness too" and they do, a bit, I guess. Which reminds me. I sit bolt upright and switch the lamp back on. Basil stirs before settling again at the end of the bed. I reach over to my handbag and

53

check the inside pocket, but I already know the answer; the packet of tablets are on my nightstand at home. I've forgotten them too.

Sighing, I lie back down and focus on breathing in and out, desperately trying to evoke a sense of calm. Basil moves up the bed and snuggles his chin onto my shoulder as if willing me to relax too, but it's no use. I fidget and plump the pillow over and over, dramatically, like they always do in the films, and resign myself to yet another restless night.

*

Satisfied that I won't scare the other guests with my appearance—I've managed to tease my curls into some kind of normal-ish state, which given that I had to use the flimsy little plastic comb from the complimentary vanity pouch in the bathroom, was never going to be easy—I scoop Basil up under my arm, grab the *Tindledale Herald* (I must have gathered the newspaper someone had left in the train in among my stuff when I got off the train last night), pull the bedroom door closed behind me and head off in search of breakfast. I've decided to keep the bathrobe on after flicking through the B&B's brochure (at about four o'clock this morning when I gave up on trying to actually sleep) and saw a picture of a couple wearing theirs in what appeared to be the dining room. Let's hope it's OK, otherwise I'm going to look like a right fool, yet again. An image of me in the Princess Leia dress and buns flashes into my head like a still from a Hammer horror film. I shudder and instantly shove the sorry sight away. Years ago, Cher told me that she read in one of those psychology magazines that a Buddhist monk said it can take a whole year to get over a breakup. Hmm. So by that reckoning I have another five months of these dark thoughts. Oh joy.

"Welcome to Tindledale." A very tall, fifty-something, debonair man with a shaved head, clad in a gorgeous soft gray cashmere cardigan (hand-knitted) over a checked shirt and chinos, walks over to where I'm standing by the breakfast cereal table. Underneath his stylish black-framed retro glasses, he's wearing diamanté-tipped lash extensions. "I'm Lawrence Rosenberg," he says, sounding very polite and stately in an old-school gentlemanly way, with the faintest hint of an American accent. He holds out his hand, the nails of which are painted a glorious pearly plum color.

"Oh, um, hi, I'm Sybil," I say, trying not to stare. It's not every day you meet a man wearing lashes and nail polish, and it's certainly not something I expected to find in this sleepy little village from a bygone era. "Lovely to meet you."

"Do excuse the . . ." He circles an index finger around his face. "I'm an actor. I run the Tindledale Players." I must look bemused as he quickly adds, "Amateur dramatics, musical theater, that kind of thing. It's my passion, and we had a dress rehearsal last night for the Tindledale Christmas pantomime—I'm the fairy godmother. In addition to being the scriptwriter and chief gofer." He smiles, rolling his eyes and shaking his head.

"Well, I think you look fabulous," I say, instantly warming to him. He smells of toasted almonds mingled with cigar smoke, and has sparkly blue eyes. "How did the rehearsal go?"

"Thank you." He does a gentlemanly bow. "Very well, considering we had no electricity in the village hall, so it was very much *'he's behind you'* and *'oh no he isn't!'* and all the other pantomime catchphrases that we love, albeit by candlelight."

"Sounds fun," I say, remembering the Brownie pantomimes—Cher and I had loads of laughs one Christmas playing Happy (me) and Dopey (Cher) in *Snow White and the Seven Dwarfs*.

"It is. You should come to a show, it's *Puss in Boots and His Merry Band of Santa's Elves* this year and I wrote it myself. Tickets include a mince pie and a mug of mulled wine. First proper performance is a week before Christmas

Eve, so not long to go, but we have another dress rehearsal tonight so you're more than welcome to pop along," he says brightly.

"Oh, I might just do that. If I can bring Basil too," I venture, wondering if the same dogs-allowed-in-the-village-pub rule applies to the village hall as well.

"Sure you can." Excellent. "And what's your name, little one?" Lawrence strokes Basil under the chin.

"Meet Basil, and thanks for letting him stay too," I say.

"It's our pleasure to look after you both." Ah, how nice.

"Thank you. And it is OK to wear . . .?" I lift the collar of the robe.

"Of course, anything goes round here, hadn't you noticed?" Lawrence says, raising one eyebrow, which makes me smile.

"And I don't suppose there's somewhere I might take him to . . ."

"Follow me." Lawrence leads the way to a utility room by the back door. "You can just pop in here and let him out here whenever he needs to go. Did you bring his food?"

"Yes!" At least I remembered Basil's pouches. I pull one from the pocket of my robe and waggle it in the air as proof.

"Well done. You'd be surprised at the number of our guests who forget. That's why I keep an emergency supply in the cupboard; I can't see the dogs going hungry." Lawrence shakes his head and selects two dog bowls from a shelf next to the sink. He fills one with water and places it on the floor before taking the pouch from me and squeezing it into the other. "I'll meet you back in the breakfast room."

"Thank you so much," I call after him, thinking how nice he is—nothing is too much trouble, it seems.

After Basil has finished eating and had a dash around the garden, we head back to where Lawrence is waiting.

"Now, why don't you go and sit down by the window and I'll fetch you a nice cooked breakfast," he says kindly. "All the trimmings?" I nod and grin before making my way over to the oval-shaped two-person table he's gesturing toward. It has an exquisite festive orange-and-clove pomander arrangement set in a crystal glass bowl, and underneath the table is a faux suede bed for Basil to lie on. Wow, this place is just like a dog hotel.

Fluffing a crisp white napkin over my knees, I gaze out through the big bay window to watch the snow. It's just started falling again, a light sprinkling like powdered sugar, swirling all around as if somebody has just shaken a giant snow globe. I feel a swell of excitement, a magical fairy-tale feeling that only a pristine duvet of crisp, clean, white snow invokes. Untouched, it stretches out before me like a virginal safety blanket across a rolling field and up to an interesting-looking building with a huge circular chimney that has smoke spiraling from it up into the white sky, like cotton candy in a breeze. And there's what looks like an adjoining double-fronted shop. It's really cute with a little white picket fence around the garden although it seems odd to have a shop in the middle of a field. I can't imagine they get much business being so far away from the center of the village.

"Marvelous view, isn't it?" Lawrence is standing next to me, gripping the edge of an enormous dinner plate with a blue-and-white striped tea towel. "That's Hettie's place you can see. The Honey family have been in Tindledale for centuries and her father used to own the hop farm before he passed away. It was sold off, but Hettie kept the oast and all the land around it. And her House of Haberdashery shop next door, of course."

"Oh, it sounds fascinating! I love knitting and needle-craft," I say, a surge of excitement rising within me.

"Then you should stop in, I'm sure she'd be pleased to see you. I don't think she gets many visitors—which reminds me, I must pop over and see if she needs any groceries. She does a weekly trip on the bus up to the village store, but it's not quite the same as having Ocado deliver," he laughs. "Plus, I've heard she buys barely enough to feed a sparrow. Please be careful, the plate's hot," he adds, sounding warm and mumsy as he places my breakfast in front of me, and for some bizarre reason that I can't fathom, tears burst onto my cheeks. "Well, this is a first—I know our breakfasts are good, award-winning, in fact, but I've not had one evoke this sort of emotion before! Sybs, what's the matter?" Lawrence dips down into the chair opposite, concern darting from one eye to the next and back again, both slender hands clasping the tea towel that's pressed to his chest. He's clearly not used to his guests crying for no apparent reason, talking of which, a group of ramblers arrive, clad in check shirts and corduroys tucked into chunky knee-length socks (hand-knitted, by the looks of them). They take one look in my direction and beetle off to a large table on the opposite side of the room before whipping up menus to hide behind. Oh God! And how does Lawrence even know that I like to be called Sybs? He checked me in very quickly last night, seeing as it was so late, saying I probably wanted to get off to bed right away, and as Cooper's wife, or "the funny woman with the ferret" is what Pete called her, had already vouched for me in any case . . . well, it was all very laid-back. He didn't even ask for a credit card to do the usual pre-authorization checks in case I stayed the night, nicked all the bathroom products and coffee packets and then ran off without paying. It's like another world here in Tindledale.

"Um, I don't know. I, um, er . . . just feeling a bit overwhelmed and . . ." My voice fades as I think of the plans, the dream I had to have my own haberdashery business just like Hettie. I rummage in my pocket in search of a tissue, getting flustered when I can't find one. "I'm so sorry."

"Don't be silly." Lawrence hands me the tea towel instead.

"Thank you." Dabbing at my face with the soft cloth that smells of bluebells, I press it to my nose and inhale. It reminds me of day trips to the forest in springtime, the ground carpeted in a layer of delicately scented flowers that stretched for miles, swinging between my grandparents, one on either side, gripping my chubby, little-girl hands as they whispered tales of fairies and angels hiding among the sun-dappled trees. Feeling happy, loved, and long before Luke and Sasha broke my heart. And Sasha hated those walking trips, preferring to stay at home and look at her pony annuals or what-ever. The moment vanishes and I take a deep breath, willing myself to get a grip.

"Maybe you'll feel better when you've had something to eat." Lawrence reaches a hand across the table to gently pat my arm. "I hope you're not coming down with something. If you don't mind me saying, you do look very tired." He smiles gently, the corners of his eyes tilting upward. I manage a half-smile.

"You're very kind," I say, in a wobbly voice, feeling embarrassed. "And I really am so sorry to cry on you like this. I don't know what came over me." I hand the tea towel back to Lawrence before picking up a knife and fork as a diversion tactic.

"Well, eat up and try not to be sad, you must look after yourself." He scrutinizes my whole face in one quick scan. "And just so you know, I'm here if you ever want to chat. I'm a very good listener."

Lawrence leaves, squeezing my shoulder reassuringly as he goes and I think about what he said as I prong a chubby sausage and cut it in two, before dipping one end into the filmy egg yolk. A complete stranger spotting how tired and fed-up I look. Well, it isn't good, but I have been feeling so down since everything happened with Luke. And then turning into a recluse and not going out very much, apart from to work and back, and then with all the cock-ups, culminating in the cock-up-to-end-all-cock-ups, well, Lawrence has a very good point. I am tired. Exhausted, in fact, from all the worrying. Which reminds me, I must check online and see if there have been any developments in the hunt for Jennifer Ford or, indeed, Mr. Banerjee's investigation into the "bungling employee."

After finishing the scrumptious breakfast, I put the napkin down, push the chair back and I'm just about to stand up when Lawrence appears again with something hidden behind his back.

"Now, we're not going to have any more tears, are we?" he asks hesitantly.

"Oh, I hope not." I paint a half-smile onto my face. "And I really am very sorry about earlier."

"Ah, it's fine. Please, there really is no need to apologize, these things happen. We all get emotional sometimes," he says, very graciously.

"Thank you," I smile. "Oh, I forgot to ask earlier . . ." Lawrence lifts his eyebrows inquiringly, "how do you know that I like to be called Sybs?"

"Well, I probably shouldn't have been so nosy, but I noticed it there on your newspaper." I stare blankly. "The message." And he taps the *Tindledale Herald* on the table next to the pomander. I pick the paper up. "See, right there."

And I do.

Sybs, give me a try x

There's even a phone number next to the message that's scrawled in black marker pen. A feeling flits through me. A feeling I haven't felt in a long time. A fluttery, flattering feeling. I glance up into Lawrence's diamanté-tipped eyes and then cast a glance around the room, half expecting someone with a smartphone to pop out from under one of the tables to Snapchat me and scream "gotcha" in my face. Things like this don't usually happen to me.

"Oh." I hesitate, unsure of what to say and much to my dismay, I see that my hands are trembling slightly. I really need some sleep.

"Sorry." Lawrence lifts his eyebrows in concern. "See, you've got me at it now. Have I embarrassed you? Only you look a little bit taken aback."

"No. Not at all. I—just—I—well, I didn't see the message before now." I shake my head.

"Not from someone you know then?"

"No, definitely not. No chance of that," I say wryly.

"Well, this is rather exciting. It's very flirty," Lawrence says.

"It sure is." I quickly rack my brains to work out how it came to be there and then it dawns on me—the guy sitting next to the window on the train. He had a newspaper. Yes, it has to be the guy in the duffel coat with the glasses and nice eyes and the curly hair peeping out from under his beanie hat who didn't seem to mind when Basil tried to snaffle his Costa cake. Because there wasn't anyone else in our car, which means that he must have left the message while I was sleeping. And he was quite cute. My head goes into overdrive trying to fathom it all out. But what does he mean "give me a try"? It's a bit forward, and with a kiss too. He didn't strike me as the type of guy to be like that, not at all; he was very unassuming with his polite smile. No, flirty swagger is much more Luke's style—he was very cocky—I used to think it was cheeky, in an appealing, banter-type way, but looking back now it really wasn't. Hmm, funny how things can seem so different at the time. Lawrence coughs discreetly.

"I have to say that it's very intriguing! Are you sure you don't know who the message is from?" Lawrence asks.

"*Weeeeell*, there was a guy on the train, but—"

"Then I urge you to call the number, Sybs! It's like a modern-day *Brief Encounter.* You must find out who your secret admirer is, but before you do, I thought one of these might cheer you up!" And he brings a four-tiered wire cake tree out from behind his back. And I gasp. I've never seen anything quite so spectacular. It's bulging with cake—slabs of lemon drizzle, chocolate brownies the size of doorstops, delicate pastel pink and white fondant fancies, sugar-dusted squares of stollen and loads of gorgeous festive red and green cupcakes with jaunty reindeers and snowmen piped over their bulging mounds. And the smell is heavenly; a cocoon of warmth and sweetness surrounds me instantly, lifting my mood another notch.

"Wow, they look amazing," I grin, helping myself to a wedge of stollen, my favorite festive treat, and even Basil stirs from under the table to see what's going on, his little nose twitching as he licks his lips in anticipation of a cake somehow rolling off the table and into his salivating mouth—ha ha, dream on, Basil! "Did you make them?" I ask, scooping a sliver of icing sugar off with my fingernail before popping it into my mouth.

"Sadly not. Kitty is the baker in Tindledale." He pauses before adding, "And some of the other villagers bake too—the WI ladies' Christmas cake sale in the village hall is legendary and always gets a good turnout, but Kitty owns the café called the Spotted Pig and she takes orders for special occasions and does all the village birthday, christening, and wedding celebration cakes."

"Ah, yes, I saw her café yesterday when I first got here. The menu looks amazing," I say, remembering the panettone bread pudding and rum custard Christmas special.

"Oh, you really must try her food while you're here, it is to *die* for." He stops talking abruptly, and glances away. "Oh God, I really shouldn't have said that."

"Is everyone OK?"

A flash of sorrow shoots into his eyes.

"Yes, yes, fine," Lawrence shakes his head, sounding

flustered. "It's just that, well, the whole village was devastated when it happened, and she's such a lovely, warm, kind person, and everyone knew him—his family has lived here in Tindledale for generations too, still do— that's why she moved here, to be closer to them as she doesn't have any family left of her own."

"What happened?"

"Her husband, Ed, he died, you see. Recently too, and he was only twenty-nine. It was insensitive of me . . ." His voice trails off.

"I'm so sorry," I say, immediately realizing what a close-knit community it is here. Back home in London I'm not sure I would even know if my next-door neighbor had died, unless it was Poppy, of course, and even then I might only realize that something was amiss because she hadn't been downstairs to fetch Basil. "Was he ill?"

"Oh no! No, nothing like that—he was a soldier in Afghanistan. A land mine. It was terrible, he was due home on the Sunday, a gloriously sunny day and the village square had even been decorated with banners and balloons for his homecoming—but then Kitty got the visit—she was pregnant too at the time, with little Teddie. Dreadful, dreadful business it was—she was in the café and the vicar heard her screaming all the way from the pulpit at the far end of the church. He was conducting a wedding rehearsal for Gabe and Vicky from Pear Tree Cottages and they all stopped and ran across the village to the café." I clasp my hands up under my chin. Lawrence looks down at the floor. Silence follows.

"I, um, I don't know what to say." And it's true. Poor Kitty, I don't even know her, yet I feel bereft on her behalf. To have the person you love snatched away without a second's warning . . . I only have an inkling of what that feels like because when I think of Luke I know it's absolutely no comparison: at least he's still alive, even if he doesn't want to be with me, but in that moment at the altar when I realized, it was as if he had died and taken all my dreams and hopes for the future with him. Disappeared in an instant—just like the flame of a candle snuffed out between a thumb and index finger. And then I remember the column candle burning brightly in the snow beside the memorial. A scratchy sensation forms in my throat as a cold shiver trickles down my back. I wonder if Kitty left the candle there for Ed. Oh God, that's so sad.

"Sometimes there just aren't any words," Lawrence sighs and another momentary silence follows. "Would you like to take the rest of the cake upstairs?" I nod solemnly. "I'll get you a plate and bring you up a nice mug of hot chocolate with whipped cream too."

*

Back in my room, having polished off the truly scrumptious cake and settled Basil on the complimentary dog bed, I lean back in the armchair next to the window and close my eyes for a few seconds, letting my mind wander. Crying earlier, what was that all about? I know I'm exhausted, so maybe that's why I'm feeling so emotional and then, with Cher not being here, well, it's another letdown, and on top of everything else that's happened, I've just had enough, I suppose. And I need to break out of this rut of sleepless nights—keeping going on practically no sleep doesn't help, it makes me extra emotional. I have to find a way to stop the dark thoughts and pity parties for one. I want to sleep all night long and feel invigorated and excited about life, and do my knitting and needlecraft for fun, just like I always used to before May the flaming fourth.

Opening my eyes and pushing the chiffon away from the window, I stand up and look out toward the puffy sky and watch the snowflakes sprinkling down like tiny diamonds against an almost Tiffany blue backdrop. The same sky that everyone around the world can see, and it makes me think of all the happy couples doing happy things, and I really want to be happy too—what's that old adage? *Love like you've never been hurt.* But it's hard, *really* hard. I think of Kitty again, and her husband, Ed, and how the whole thing with Luke just pales in comparison. And I make my decision. I'm going to call the number on the newspaper. Why not? What have I got to lose? Nobody will know, not even Lawrence if I don't tell him, especially if it turns out to be a big joke.

And then when I've done that, I'm going to venture over to Hettie's House of Haberdashery and see what treats she has in store. I'm going to buy loads of wool and some needles and knit something just for fun, like I always used to, and I might even get the material to start a new quilt. A lovely, cozy Christmassy one. Ha! I could even sell it online. Oh yes I could! I can still have my dream; I'll just go about in a different way, tweak it a bit and see what happens. And I can worry about Jennifer Ford and Mr. Banerjee on Monday morning, but until then I'm choosing happy!

I pick up the newspaper and wander over to the phone on the nightstand next to the bed, and take a deep breath. OK, I can do this. It's just a phone call. The number is ringing. One, two, three, four *bbrrrrring-bbrrrrrrings*. And then I get cold feet and quickly end the call. I sit on the bed. Basil is staring at me with his head tilted to one side as if to say, "You big wimp, get a grip, Sybs!" So I do, and lift the receiver back up. This time I'm going to speak—I'll just say "Hi, it's Sybs," in my best breezy voice, and the man with the kind-looking eyes will say, "Hi, I'm so pleased you called," and we'll have a laugh about Basil trying to pinch his Costa cake, and it'll be brilliant. Yep, of course it will.

The phone stops ringing.

There's a pause.

And then: "Tindledale Books, how may I help you?"

It's a woman's voice, which completely throws me, so I promptly slam the phone down.

Basil is right. I am a big wimp—but at least I now know where to find the mystery man from the train.

Invigorated by this key milestone in my as-predicted-by-a-monk year of heartache, I press an index finger down too hard on the brass bell, nearly causing it to shoot right off the reception counter. Luckily, I manage to grab it just in time and I'm carefully placing it back where it belongs, when Lawrence appears through an archway from behind a crimson velvet curtain.

"OK, OK, where's the fire?" he asks, making big eyes and pulling a face. It makes me giggle.

"Er, no fire, I just wanted to return this." I hand him a Clarice Cliff crocus pattern tea plate.

"Oh, you didn't need to bother with all that. You're a guest, just leave it outside the door next time."

"Thank you, but I didn't like to. It's such a pretty plate. Art Deco. I wouldn't want it to get damaged."

"Well, that's very kind of you. I just came off the phone with Sonny—he rang to say that if you want to call in later for your dinner, he's doing steak and ale pie with hand-cut chips followed by sticky toffee pudding for today's special." It takes me a moment to realize that he's talking about Cher's Clive at the Duck & Puddle.

"Ooh, sounds delicious."

"Does, doesn't it? Very hearty winter food and talking of which, how was the stollen cake?" He glances down at the crumbs left on the plate as he takes it from me to store under the counter.

"Mmm, delicious, thank you." I smile. "Lawrence, I was wondering if you might help me with something."

"Of course. Always happy to oblige if I can." He pats a stack of tourist information leaflets offering two-for-one tickets to Santa's grotto at a garden center in Stoneley into a tidy pile, before tilting his head to one side and smiling at me encouragingly.

"I was wondering where the nearest shops are to buy clothes—jeans, underwear, that kind of thing? And some suitable footwear for walking in snow—I wasn't expecting it and I can't believe how deep it gets here in the country-side." I make big eyes. "And I should probably get a mobile phone too; I don't want to get stranded again with no means of even calling a taxi. And maybe a hair-brush, toothbrush and some makeup because I forgot to bring mine and the stuff that I did remember to bring is ruined after wine spilt all over it and . . . well, I thought I might go for a wander around the village, maybe pop into the pub for today's special." I smile. *And Tindledale Books too!* I know I panicked when the woman answered but I'm still intrigued to know why the man on the train, who I'm guessing must have something to do with the bookshop, would leave a flirty message on a newspaper for me, but I can hardly venture out in soaking wet jeans that cling to my legs like a pair of needy toddlers, squelchy Converse trainers and hair that resembles a cuckoo's nest to find out.

Lawrence falls quiet for a moment, and then lets out a long whistle before looking me straight in the eye.

"OK, clothes I can help you with. Makeup too. But a mobile phone?" He shrugs and shakes his head. "Well, there's really no point." I frown, wondering why on earth not. "No signal for miles around," he quickly adds as if reading my mind. "Although I think someone said Dr. Darcy—he's the village GP—can occasionally get one bar, but only if he's in his loft conversion, hanging out of the skylight window with his arm waggling in the air."

"I see." Blimey, Tindledale really is a blast from the past and I wonder if this Dr. Darcy is anything like his famous namesake, Jane Austen's dastardly Darcy? Probably not: I'm imagining a kindly, traditional country doctor in a tweedy suit who looks as if he's just taking a break from an episode of *Heartbeat* so his matronly secretary can bring him Garibaldi biscuits with a nice cup of Darjeeling.

"Does that go for broadband too?" I ask, thinking there's no time like the present to peruse online to see what hand-stitched quilts are selling for.

"Oh no, we have our own village hub or whatever it's called, so we get superfast Internet, and there's a laptop for guests to use in the conservatory; just give me a shout when you want to log on and I'll set you up with the password and everything," he says, cheerily. "Although it does tend to slow down a bit when all the villagers jump on in the evening to download their Sky Box Sets, so you might want to avoid the teatime period."

"Brilliant," I grin.

"And as for a taxi?" Lawrence laughs, making his shoulders bob up and down. "You could try Tommy Prendergast in the village store, but he only takes bookings for after 4 p.m. when the shop is closed and then you'll have to put up with him complaining about one of his many ailments for the duration of the journey. There's a bus though, every hour on the hour, and you can go as far as Market Briar for just four pound." He gives me a helpful look.

"I see. And does the bus go from the stop in the village square?" I ask, wondering if it's walkable from the B&B. Last night, Pete drove the tractor in a loop round the top of the village, past the country club, before dipping down a long snowy tree-tunnel winding lane, so I've kind of lost my bearings a bit. Lawrence slowly places the map down on the desk and nods his head like he's deep in thought, before lifting the hatch up and walking around the counter until he's standing square in front of me with his hands resting on his slim hips, and a big kind smile spread across his face.

"That's right. Did you spot it on your way here?"

"Yes, last night, and I met a man—a shepherd, um, er, sheep farmer," I correct. "He was waiting in the shelter for his wife who gave me a flashlight when she turned up. So kind."

"Ah, that would be Lord Lucan," Lawrence says with a deadpan face. It takes me a moment to cotton on.

"Ha ha, you're winding me up. Come on, I know there's been speculation for years over the whereabouts of Lord Lucan—I saw the docudrama on TV not so long ago, but I think someone would have noticed if the actual Lord Lucan was hanging out in a bus stop in a snowy rural village late at night," I snigger.

"Don't laugh, Sybs, it's true. That's his name, Lord Lucan. Well, Lord Lucan Fuller-Hamilton to be exact. He and Lady Fuller-Hamilton live in Blackwood House—a breathtakingly beautiful Queen Anne mansion set in the grounds of the Blackwood Farm Estate."

"Wow, really?" Well, it just goes to show how first impressions really can be very deceiving.

"Yes, really. There's no grandstanding in Tindledale— doesn't matter who you are, or if you have an ancestral home here or not, we all rub along together. Did you call the number, by the way?"

"I sure did," I grin, feeling light and enjoying our chat; it's as if I'm somebody else, or another, more relaxed, version of me and not the tetchy, can't-be-arsed, worn-out Sybil that I am at work in London.

"And?" he asks, looking intrigued.

"A woman answered and said Tindledale Books, so I hung up."

"Why would you do that?" he frowns.

"I don't know—what if she was his wife? Or girlfriend? You never know . . . she sounded very stern, as if she was far too busy to be trifling with mere phone calls. In fact, I'd go as far as to say that she was quite snappy. I panicked, I guess."

"Ah, no need to panic, that'll just have been Mrs. Pocket, a retired headmistress—she ran the village school for years—and you're right, she is very stern, sits on the parish council, and between me and you, thinks she's the boss of us all, that someone put her single-handedly in charge of Tindledale." He smirks and shakes his head. "She volunteers in the bookshop on Fridays, cataloging

77

all those musty old books. Lots of them detail the history of the area, which she's very keen to preserve—she's a stickler for heritage and is into all that family tree stuff. Apparently, she's charted the whole village and can prove that most of the villagers are actually related in one way or another—going back centuries, of course," he quickly adds, "that would just be weird otherwise. But I can't imagine for a single second that she would leave a flirty message on a newspaper. Absolutely not." He tuts in a way that makes me stifle another snigger. "So that leaves Adam. It has to be him who left the message."

Lawrence rests an elbow on the counter. "Now he *is* a dark horse. I know hardly anything about him though, unfortunately, other than that he bought the bookshop just a few months ago when old Alf Preedy retired and moved into the addition in the garden of his daughter's house in Stoneley. Adam is very mysterious, keeps himself to himself, and is hardly ever there. One of the Tindledale Players said that he travels a lot searching for rare books—some of the tomes in his collection are worth a mint, apparently." He stands upright and folds his arms.

"Interesting," I say, liking the sound of Adam because, after all, there is just something about a man who loves books.

"So are you going to see him then?" Lawrence probes,

even slipping his glasses off and letting them dangle on the chain around his neck as if to scrutinize me further.

"Well, I thought I might pop in after I've been to Hettie's House of Haberdashery," I say, trying to sound casual and like I do this kind of thing every day—sashay up to secret admirers. Eek! "If it's not too far."

"Wonderful. You can walk to Hettie's from here—the snow has stopped, so perfect timing—and then right opposite Hettie's is a bus stop; time it right, on the hour every hour, remember, and you can hop on a bus that'll take you all the way up the hill. Jump off in the village square and you're right there. How exciting!" He puts his glasses back on and gives me a quick up-and-down look. There's a short silence before he adds, "Will Basil be OK on his own for a bit? Or you could always fetch him down if you like."

"Oh, I'm sure he'll be fine; he was asleep when I left my room, snoring away—it's his favorite pastime, apart from eating—why do you ask?" I say, casually.

"You'll see. Give me five minutes—I just need to make a quick phone call to Ruby, who has a clothes shop in the village and I'm sure she'll have something you can borrow to visit Adam in." And he disappears behind the curtain. I busy myself by thumbing through a copy of the *Tindledale Parish News*, a lovely pamphlet; it has a pencil line drawing of St. Mary's church on the front, and costs just fifty pence to buy with profits going toward "community projects." Ah, that's nice. It has a selection of adverts in the back—chiropodist, handyman, undertaker, Indian takeout in Stoneley, wedding-dress shop . . . hmm, on second thought . . . I place the pamphlet back in the rack.

Lawrence returns.

"Right. Now follow me." He grabs my hand and gives it a quick squeeze before gliding me up a small flight of stairs toward a door marked *Private Staff Only*.

Inside, I stand for a moment to take it all in. The scent from an enormous Yankee candle, called Christmas Cookie, floats over from a side table giving a glorious festive welcome to the room. There's an elegant mink-suede chaise longue running the length of one wall that's covered in framed photos, stills from Lawrence's stage performances by the looks of it, and a cozy log burner set in the center with a tiled hearth surround and a pavé chandelier hanging from an exposed-beamed ceiling, bathing the room in a glittery sheen. Wow, it's a pretty impressive hair salon—the Tindledale villagers are very lucky indeed. No need to get the bus, on the hour, every hour, to Market Briar when they can trundle down the lane for a cut and blow-dry with Lawrence. And reasonably priced too—there's a laminated list on the wall and it's only £35 for a full head of highlights!

The entire length of the opposite wall houses a clothes rack crammed full of costumes for the Tindledale Players,

I presume. Agatha Christie–style thirties silk dresses and fur stoles, Jersey Boy crooner suits and puffy prom dresses—they're all here. There's even a plastic watermelon hanging on the end of the rack in a big cellophane bag.

"*Dirty Dancing*! We did the musical in summer 2010." Lawrence informs me as I instinctively cup both hands around it.

"I carried a watermelon!" I say, and we both laugh.

But seriously, it's like having a Hollywood dressing room in your back bedroom. A large, open-shelved cupboard is stacked full of shoes, hats and all kinds of fluffy, puffy-looking accessories. In the corner is a sink, a proper hair salon one, the kind you can lie back in to have your hair washed before wafting over to sit in front of the enormous gilt-edged mirror framed in a circle of miniature lightbulbs. A shiny glass shelf on the wall to the side of the mirror houses a dozen polystyrene mannequin heads, each displaying a different, seriously big, bouffant-style wig. And the biggest collection of lash extensions I think I've ever seen: every conceivable color, design and sparkly type lash imaginable. Crazy Horse, Paris . . . eat your heart out; this is *serious* show girl territory. Moving toward the costumes, I let my fingers trace a line along the exquisite fabrics as I walk the length of the rack.

"This is amazing." My eyes widen and my pulse quickens.

"Why thank you." Lawrence laughs and waves a

dismissive hand in the air. "Now, settle yourself down and let's sort your hair out first. If you don't mind me saying so, it's looking a bit, hmm, well, snowswept."

"Is that next up on the scale after windswept?" I laugh, lifting a limp wedge of sausage curls away from my face.

"Yes, something like that. I can wash and style it for you if you like. I'm a trained stylist with years of experience—good job too as it was something to fall back on when the acting work dried up, and I used to own a hair salon, many moons ago. That was before I grew tired of having to do everything at breakneck speed and retired to Tindledale for some much-needed R&R."

"In that case I'd love you to, if you're absolutely sure?" I can't remember the last time I went to the hairdresser's, certainly not since the wedding showdown because I haven't really felt like it, but it's different now. "But what about your other guests? Don't they need you?"

"You need me more right now." Lawrence pats a red leather chair by the basin, and I don't need telling twice. I sit down and he shakes out a black nylon cape before securing it at the nape of my neck, scooping my hair back and turning the hand shower on. "How's the temperature?" He lets the warm water gently seep from my hairline and down over my scalp, protecting my face with his free hand.

"Perfect." I close my eyes, savoring the relaxing sensation.

"Hey, are you sure? You look a little anxious, clutching the armrests like that." He moves the water away from my head and I open my eyes.

"Yes, sorry, I'm fine, honestly. This is such a treat, I just didn't realize—being tense has kind of become second nature these last few months." I release my grip and place my hands in my lap instead.

"Ah, I see. Well, then try to relax. You're going to look great, I promise." He brushes his hand over my shoulder reassuringly.

Lawrence finishes and wraps my hair up in an enormous sunshine-yellow fluffy towel.

"Makeup time, and then I'll blow out your hair," he says, leading me over to a chair in front of the mirror. He opens a drawer as I sit down. "Now, shall I do the honors or would you prefer to do your own?" I open my mouth, and then quickly close it again. In the drawer are billions of pots, tubes and tubs of all kinds of lotions, potions and scrubs. I've never seen so many beauty products in one place before, except the beauty hall at Selfridges, but even then I reckon Lawrence's drawer could be a very serious contender on the huge-ness scale.

"Blimey, that's quite a collection." I smile. "I don't tend to wear very much makeup so I'll just borrow some blush and a touch of eye shadow, if that's OK?"

"Of course, help yourself and I'll get some tea. Posh or normal?" he says, his eyes dancing.

"Er, what's posh?" I ask, hesitantly.

"Well, we have peppermint, camomile, rooibos, Earl Gray and Lady Gray—now that's *really* posh." Lawrence cocks an expectant eyebrow.

"Camomile please."

"Good choice. Coming right up." He takes a bow, laughing as he leaves the room. I take the opportunity to look more closely at the pictures on the wall—they're mostly of Lawrence in a variety of Shakespearean-looking costumes; velvet and brocade jackets with big billowy sleeves and a serious look on his face, with famous actors such as Ian McKellen, Patrick Stewart and Helen Mirren. The last one is him hugging Dame Judi Dench and they're laughing like they're best pals. How lovely! Lawrence has obviously had a wonderful career.

Lawrence returns a few minutes later with a silver tray holding a teapot, covered in a lovely spotty pink and purple cozy (hand-knitted), and two fine bone china cups on saucers. "To Sybs, and her mysterious secret admirer," he says, pouring the tea and handing it to me before carefully chinking his own cup against the side of mine. I glance up at him. "Oh dear, what is it? You're not going to cry again are you?" he says, pulling a face to lighten the mood.

"No, no, of course not," I say, sipping at the grassy-smelling liquid before glancing away.

"What is it then?"

"Oh, I don't know," I lie. So much for my grandstanding and feeling of lightness earlier on; I'm never going to make it through to the end of my year of heartache at this rate. I'm all over the place, upbeat one minute, then miserable for the other twenty-three hours and fifty-nine minutes in the day. And hot, boiling hot; maybe that's the lack of sleep sending my hormones haywire. Or perhaps it's just because I'm exhausted. How on earth do parents with new babies function? If I were the Queen, I'd put them all on the honors list followed by a nice long rest in a super-king bed somewhere very, very quiet. Or maybe it's the menopause, come early, just to tick me off even more.

"Well, it must be something. Tears before breakfast and now you look like you're bracing yourself for the first day of an IKEA sale instead of Tindledale's hottest newcomer. Apart from your good lady self, of course." He winks and places his cup back on the tray before pulling up a chair alongside me.

"Ah, thank you Lawrence." I manage a smile. "You mentioned a doctor earlier?" I need some sleeping pills because there's no way I'm going to make it through the weekend without them. This must be how inmates in dodgy prisons feel after months of sleep deprivation torture, only much, much worse.

"Oh, I'm sorry, you're not ill are you?" he says, his face clouding with concern.

"Well, not exactly, not physically anyway." I'm not sure a broken heart counts as an actual illness. "I'm just finding it hard to sleep at the moment." I take another sip of tea before glancing away.

"And why is that, if you don't mind me asking?"

"Oh, I, um, I'm not really used to talking about it." And it's true, I'm not. Cher has tried to make me open up, but I didn't want to drag her down with my self-loathing and angst and perpetual analyzing of my disastrous relationship with Luke. I must have gone over and over our time together a trillion times in my head looking for clues, something I missed, or didn't do, or did do but did it wrong because if I did screw up, then how do I know the same thing isn't going to happen again? I'll go mad and be like Miss Havisham, cloistered away, wringing my hands over yet another ruined wedding breakfast! And let's face it, nobody likes a Debbie Downer, so I figured it was best just to bury all the dark thoughts into my knitting instead of burdening my best friend with the metaphorical wah-wah-wah of a muted trombone sounding out after everything that comes from my mouth.

"Sorry. I didn't mean to pry," Lawrence says gently.

"It's OK." I turn to look at him and take a deep breath. "It's just been this way for quite a long time now . . ." I hesitate.

"Go on."

"Um, ever since my boyfriend failed to turn up to his own wedding." I smile wryly. "To me, I hasten to add." I pull a face and take another sip of tea, willing my bottom lip to stop trembling—what am I? Five years old? Sweet lord of heartache, I really need to get a grip, I can't keep crying all over the place.

"Ouch. Hmm, I guess that would do it." Lawrence tuts. "Well, it's his loss!" He stands up defiantly. "You know, I believe in fate, destiny, whatever you want to call it, and him not turning up happened for a reason. And do you know what that reason is?" He has both hands on his hips now and a resolute look on his face.

"Er, because he wants to be with my twin sister instead of me?"

Lawrence does a double take, then opens and closes his mouth before swallowing hard and carrying on.

"Because there's someone far better out there for you! Now, let's get your makeup on so you can go and find him. Trust me, after you've clapped eyes on Adam you won't need a doctor. Oh no. Unless it's to resuscitate you after you've fainted from sheer lust." We both laugh. "You know, I met my late partner, Jason, on a blind date. Well, kind of, it was a balmy Sunday evening, standing in line for the *Saturday Night Fever* wrap party at Studio 54. It was 1978." He pauses to take a sip of his tea. "Yes, back in the day, this was. Anyway, I couldn't take my eyes off the vision standing right there in front of me, looking resplendent in peach cord flares and a chest-hugging top. He had that whole *Shaft* thing going on." I frown. "Oh, never mind, before your time, I guess. Well, I made a beeline for him on the dance floor. You should have seen it, Sybs. It was sublime—a strawberry-hued mural of the man in the moon, with his very own coke spoon twinkling and glistening under the disco lights. Dancing away making history we were." He closes his eyes for a second, looking like he's savoring the nostalgia. "I was very young and naive," he offers, by way of explanation as I try and picture the scene in my head. It's hard; I can't imagine Lawrence ever being naive, not when he seems so assured and worldly-wise. "So, after a few too many glasses of Midori, we had a snog and a bit of a fumble on one of the balconies, and then he ended up back at mine testing out my new magenta silk sheets. And the rest really is history. *Marvelous*." He drains the last of his tea before placing the cup back down on the tray. "Oh, don't look so scared—you'll not end up in Adam's bed, no, this is the sleepy, quaint little village of Tindledale, not NYC in the hedonistic seventies. Besides, you're a far nicer girl than I ever was." Lawrence winks, and I take another mouthful of tea.

"Ha!" I grin, feeling relaxed; it's great chatting with him and so nice to just hang out and drink tea—it's been awhile. All of my free time recently has been full of dark thoughts, with Basil and my knitting to keep me company. "It seems strange to be talking about dating, when not so long ago I assumed I'd be married by now and, well . . . that would be that. Sorted. I guess." I shrug.

"I bet it does. But lots of marriages don't turn out the way they were intended to. You know, Jason had a wife for a while. She lives in Australia now!" Lawrence says casually.

"Really? Wow!"

"Yes, Queensland, which is just so ironic when you think about it." He pauses to muse. "She went there when he eventually mustered up the courage to jump out of the closet, and confess all. Years ago this was, but she's happily partnered now to a used-car salesman and they have three gloriously tanned grown-up children together— she still sends me birthday cards every year, which is very lovely of her. We're the best of friends and she was such a comfort to me when Jason went to the big Studio 54 in the sky." Lawrence smiles contemplatively.

"Well . . . that's refreshing," I say, thinking how incredible Jason's wife must be and wondering how I might have felt if Luke had turned around and said that he much preferred men to me, after all. Although I actually think that may have hurt less than him jilting me at the altar for my twin sister. I'm convinced the feeling of hurt would have been lessened if he'd left me for a stranger, man or woman, and it still cuts me up inside that my own sister could do that to me. "And I'm sorry to hear about Jason. Do you miss him very much?"

"I do. Every day, but it was inevitable, I guess; he was quite a bit older than me and not in the best of health toward the end. It was very peaceful though and just as he wished, at home with me," Lawrence explains. "My sadness is for him really, that he didn't come out sooner and get to live as he truly wanted to for more of his life."

"But he had you and your life together. I'm sure that made him very happy," I say softly, and Lawrence leans forward to pat the top of my hand. A short silence follows as we both sit with our respective thoughts.

I finish my tea and start dabbing a smoky eye shadow into the crease of my eyelid.

"Now that's a perfect color on you. A touch of mascara, maybe, or how about some Cheryl lash extensions?" Lawrence asks.

"Cheryl?" They sound fascinating.

"Yes, here. That's the name of them." And he reaches into the box and pulls out a dainty pair of feathery lashes.

"The nation's sweetheart—you know, Cheryl Cole, or Fernandez-Versini or whatever her name is now. Exquisite, isn't she? And a phenomenal performer too—the young girls in the Tindledale Players are always trying to emulate her moves up on the stage of the village hall. But I'm not sure the villagers are quite ready for a pantomime with added grind just yet. And you're going to look just like her." He smiles.

"Ha! Hardly."

"You're not a million miles away. Such a cracking figure and pretty face you have."

"Yeah, right. Only she'd fit twice over into my body, possibly three times, and I'd need a whole factory full of hair serum to smooth out my bushy locks," I say, wondering again how Sasha, my so-called identical twin, always seems to manage to get her curls transformed into a poker-straight and glossy sheet falling down her back with never a hair out of place.

"Nonsense, don't put yourself down. Now, do you want to try the lashes? We can always trim them if you think they're too much."

"Er, I'm not sure, I don't want to look too . . ." I pause to choose my words carefully, not wanting to upset him, especially as he's batting his diamantés at me pleadingly, "spectacular," I settle on.

"Wonderful. I'll just pick out a few for the corners and

then you'll look totally natural. Trust me, you're going to love it; they'll be tossing rose petals wherever you walk when I'm finished with you," he says in a very grand actorly style voice. Then, chuckling and shaking his head, he busies himself with gathering the equipment together.

"OK then," I nod, with only a hint of apprehension after such a glowing guarantee. But I needn't have worried; because when I open my eyes and look into the mirror it's like a mini-miracle. My whole face looks open and bright—even my eye bags have practically disappeared. And it feels so good. "They're incredible. And subtle too," I tell him. I'm impressed. Grinning at myself in the mirror, I flutter my new lashes admiringly as I turn my head from side to side to get a better look from all angles. Then I reach up and give Lawrence a quick squeeze.

"Thank you, I love them."

"Told you. Now, hair time." And he darts around behind the chair, whips the towel from my head and starts combing through. "Big?" he asks, widening his eyes hopefully and holding a length of my hair out sideways, letting the comb hover in midair.

"OK. But not too big, I don't want to look like Beyoncé about to go onstage as I walk down Tindledale High Street."

"Point taken."

Using a big cylindrical brush, Lawrence funnels the hot

air from the hair dryer down and around sections of my hair before teasing the brush free and scooping up another section and repeating the process all over again, each time gathering speed.

"Voila! How's that for madam," he eventually declares, grabbing a round mirror and holding it behind my back. I twist my head to get a better look, loving how he's managed to get my bedraggled, snowswept curls cascading in a way I've never managed to before.

"Oh, Lawrence I love it." I stand up and give him a hug.

"It's nothing," he says modestly, "as our Chezza says, it's because you're worth it." He hugs me back and then takes both my hands in his and squeezes them gently. "And don't you ever forget it." He pulls a stern face, pretending to chastise me. I look into his eyes, thinking what a lovely, kind man he is. I'm so glad I came to Tindledale—I would never have met him otherwise. Maybe Cher not being here happened for a reason too—not that Lawrence is better than Cher, just different, and exactly what I needed today.

There's a knock on the door, breaking the moment, and a few seconds later the door swings inward and a woman appears with a nonchalant look on her face. Tall and slim, she's wearing a lemon-yellow padded ski jacket and denim Daisy Dukes over thick opaque tights with knee-high wedged boots. She has scarlet shoulder-length hair set in a Dita Von Teese style, her face is a flawless powdery white and she has cherry-red lips and smoky gray eyes. She's breathtakingly beautiful and so sexy looking. Luminescent. Oh God, I think I may have my first girl crush—I have to forcibly resist the overwhelming urge to stroke her hair.

"Hello, Lawrence," she says throatily, and even her voice sounds super sexy.

"Ruby, this is Sybs. Sybs, this is Ruby, she owns the vintage clothes shop on the High Street," Lawrence says by way of an introduction. *Ah, of course she does.* We smile and shake hands. "Did you bring the clothes?" he asks. I grin awkwardly, bobbing from one foot to the other as she casts a lazy look over my body.

"Of course. And in a range of sizes too." And she turns and sashays back out of the room, leaving me to wonder what her verdict is.

"Don't mind her, she's a poppet really. We're the best of friends and I knew she'd help you out with some clothes." Lawrence picks up a silver-embossed cigarette case, selects a cigarillo and lights one up before offering it to me. I shake my head. "Are you sure? I find them very restorative." He smiles.

"No, really, thank you," I grin, inhaling anyway. There's just something about the nostalgic waft of a cigar—it reminds me of my granddad, he was a big cigar fan too. Keeping the cigarillo for himself, Lawrence pushes open a window to puff the smoke out into the cold, snowy air. "You won't tell anyone will you? Only it's not *really* a public place this room," he says, draping himself across a padded window seat before flicking the ash outside. He winks at me before pulling his cigarillo hand back in to brush a smattering of snowflakes away. I shake my head and smile in agreement.

Ruby returns with a pile of clothes under her left arm and holds a pair of skinny jeans out toward me, dangling them by the belt loop on the end of a scarlet red polished fingertip. I peer at the jeans suspiciously, as they look very small.

"Try them. They're your size." She dips her head slightly to one side as reassurance. I hesitate. Lawrence and Ruby are both staring at me, so I slip my soggy Converse off. And oh my God, what is that stench? Oh no. To my shame I realize it's the trainers, still damp from the snow and sweaty like an old wheel of Brie: my feet officially reek like a thirteen-year-old boy's bedroom. Eewww! Lawrence thoughtfully sweeps the offending shoes across the floor and straight into the naughty corner.

"Here," Lawrence gestures to a curtained section of the room, "you can change behind there."

"Thank you," I say, shuffling away gratefully, hoping the whiff evaporates very quickly. A few minutes later and I have the jeans on and buttoned. They fit perfectly. I poke my head around the curtain and Ruby hands me a top—a gorgeous polka dot chiffon blouse with a forties pussycat bow. I slip my arms in and she does the tiny little buttons up for me before tying the bow just right.

"Oh, you're good, Rubes. The clothes look like they were made for Sybs," Lawrence says, closing the window and joining us by the mirror after I push the curtain back, feeling like a woman on one of those TV makeover shows.

"Well, it is my job to guess a woman's size," Ruby smiles, confidently.

"Thank you, Ruby, you're a lifesaver." I grin, feeling happy that I've made it into a size ten. But then it's hardly a wonder as I've had no appetite and have been surviving on mainly chocolate chip cookies, Haribo strawberry gummies and the occasional fried chicken leg from the place on the corner of my street.

"No problem, but you can't keep them. The jeans are from my designer line. Oh, I nearly forgot—you'll be needing these too." She hands me three pairs of gorgeous silk knickers. "You can have them on the house."

"Thanks so much," I say impulsively, but then quickly add, "Oh, no I can't just take them. Please, let me give you some money." They're proper expensive French lace, but she just lifts an elegant hand to brush my offer aside.

"Oh wow! Then thank you very much," I say, clasping the knickers to me. My big old cotton clangers won't know what's hit them when these appear beside them in my underwear drawer. "And of course I'll bring the blouse and jeans right back to you." I grin again. "Mine should be dried out soon, with a bit of luck. They got drenched and covered in muck with all that trudging in the snow so I rinsed them and now they're hanging up over the bath . . ." I stop talking, feeling feeble, and I'm sure she doesn't want to be bothered with the minutiae of my wardrobe malfunctions.

"Sybs, you didn't need to do that. You could have used the washing machine. Fetch them down later and you can run them through the tumble dryer," Lawrence says.

"Thank you. I didn't think to ask earlier, but that would be great," I smile.

"Wonderful," Ruby says, and I make a mental note to return the clothes as soon as possible—I can't wait to have a nose around her shop. "And Lawrence can return the favor by way of cake—I take it you do have a selection?" Ruby purrs as she hooks her right arm around Lawrence's neck and smacks a big lipsticky kiss on his cheek. I glance away, feeling self-conscious and a bit in awe of her charisma.

"OK, that's enough," Lawrence chides, as he leans into a mirror and wipes the smudge away with a tissue plucked from a silver box on the shelf.

"Oh, you love it really," Ruby teases, in Lawrence's

direction. "Now, slight problem with footwear . . . what size are you?" She turns back to face me with a quizzical look on her face.

"Er, a seven." I wish I had dainty little feet like hers.

"Mmm, well, I can't give you a new pair because I need to sell them and I shan't be able to if they've been worn; different story if I had some genuine vintage ones in stock but I'm all out of them at the moment. The blouse is fine to be resold and the jeans I can use in the Christmas window display when you've finished with them. I'm planning a traditional tobogganing scene—jeans, festive knitwear, Christmas sweaters, beanies and scarves, that kind of thing. Very kitsch, very *It's a Wonderful Life*," she says, having it all worked out.

"Ah, I love that film," I beam.

"Oh, me too," both Ruby and Lawrence say in unison.

"And I could help you with the window display," I suggest, feeling excited.

"How?" she says in a very direct, businesslike way.

"Um, I knit. It's my passion, and needlecraft, crochet and quilting . . . I love it all. And I have a pile of Christmas sweaters in my spare bedroom at home."

"Do you indeed? Well, I'd like to see them. When can you show me?"

"I'm here until Sunday so I could post a selection to you on Monday?"

"Good."

"Or you could knit one while you're here," Lawrence suggests. "You know, as a teaser until Tuesday when the rest arrive. Hettie will have everything you need."

"Er . . ." I open my mouth to explain but Ruby does it for me.

"Don't be daft, Lawrence, I'm sure Sybil can't knit a whole sweater in a matter of days." They both turn to me with expectant looks on their faces.

"It really depends on the size of the project—the yarn, knitting needles, complexity, that kind of thing."

"OK. Well, how about a super-chunky sweater with a fairly simple pattern on the front, like a Christmas pudding?" Ruby lifts a perfectly groomed eyebrow and I nod my head, keen to help her out after she's been so generous to me.

"That's certainly doable, if I make a start right away." Three days. It's tight, but I'm willing to give it a very good go. Ruby claps her hands together, seemingly pleased with the plan. I smile inwardly, remembering my decision from earlier about going after my dream in a different way, and now one of my creations is going to be in a real shop window. And who knows, somebody might actually want to buy it?

"And I can drop you at Hettie's on my way back to the High Street," Ruby says, "the lanes are almost clear now,

Pete was out with the tractor first thing. Good job the parish news people invested in that snowplow attachment last winter or we'd all be stranded by now. Lawrence, where are those cowboy boots? We need to hurry up now so Sybil can get knitting."

"Cowboy boots?" Lawrence asks.

"That's right, the ones from *9 to 5*, the Dolly Parton musical you staged last year," she says, sounding impatient now. "Get them for me, please." Ruby waves a "hurry up" hand in his direction, and my heart sinks. I can't waltz into a bookshop to check out a mystery man wearing Dolly Parton boots. Lawrence does as he's told and starts rummaging around in the cupboard.

"Oh, it's fine. I can wear my Converse. Really, it'll be all right," I say, not even daring to ask how much her boots cost after spotting the Ralph Lauren label inside the jeans. I quickly grab the Converse from the corner and push my left foot back into the still-soggy trainer while Ruby throws both her hands onto her hips, before glaring down at my feet. Lawrence even stops flinging a pair of Puss in Boots thigh slappers around the room to stare at me too. Silence follows as Ruby sizes me up. Lawrence pulls a face behind her back and then instantly busies himself back in the cupboard when she looks daggers in his direction. She's circling me now, head tilted, as she supports her chin with a thumb and index finger, pondering an alternative solution, I hope. But I can sense that she's not feeling the love for the stinky-feet grunge look that I have going on, oh no.

"Found them," shouts Lawrence, waving a pair of purple mock-croc cowboy boots in the air. They even have silver-tipped toes and little wheelie spurs around the side of the heels. Oh God.

"Perfect," Ruby says, grabbing the boots from Lawrence's hand. "Try them; they might be too big, in which case we'll go to plan B," she instructs, handing me the boots. I take them, and go to slip my foot into the right one, not daring to challenge her or inquire about plan B. For all I know it could be much, much worse. Sasha has a pair of red patent leather thigh-highs that spring to mind. Can you imagine me sauntering into the village bookshop in fuck-me boots? Hardly. Mrs. Pocket will probably call Mark, the policeman, over to arrest me and I'll be banished from Tindledale forever, my heinous crime having tarnished its heritage irreparably.

"NO," Ruby shrieks, with such force that I can't help wondering where the sudden emergency is. "Tuck the jeans in. It'll help keep them clean." My heart sinks as I do as I'm told, eager to please my new girl crush, but at the same time wishing the spurs wouldn't whizz around quite so furiously every time I move my feet.

"Oh, yes, they're definitely too big," I say, eyeing up a

cute denim shoe-boot that Lawrence still has shoved under his arm. He catches my eye and mouths "Sorry" in my direction.

"Nonsense, they fit fine." Ruby crouches down to press the end of the boot to see where my toes are, making me feel like a kid getting measured up for new school shoes. It's the same sinking feeling when you know you're getting the sturdy black bricklike monstrosities when you really want the glossy red dainty ones with the sweet little Mary Jane strap. My heart plummets even farther. I wish I'd put my foot down, literally, but I keep my mouth shut and go with the flow instead. "There, let me see you." Ruby stands back to scrutinize me. "Yes, perfect." She presses her palms together in approval and then fluffs my hair forward over my shoulders, making me feel pampered, like a model, sort of. "Yes, cowboy boots with your winsome smile . . . very kitsch in a postmodern Doris Day way," she says, as I try to keep up, hoping she doesn't mean all thigh-slapping and cowgirly, or that she's going to pull out a whip from Lawrence's dressing-up box just to complete the look. "I like it, and so much better than those stinking Converse! And in snow." Ruby looks outraged now. "All that schlepping along looking grungy? No, no, no . . . Sooo not a good look. You must saunter along, bursting with swagger, and don't be worrying about going arse over tit on the ice. If you do, just laugh it off

103

and get right back up." She makes a big Elvis-style circle with her arm to demonstrate the point. "So, who's the man?" she asks nonchalantly, smoothing a perfectly arched eyebrow with her ring finger.

"Oh, it's not like tha—"

"Honey, it's *always* like that!" she says knowingly, her voice sounding all Mae West after several hundred cigars. "Now get the dog and let's be off," she glances at her watch before pulling her ski jacket back on.

"Thanks for sorting me out, Ruby," I give her a quick hug.

"My pleasure." And she sashays from the room.

"Hurry, hurry, you don't want to miss Adam. He could leave at any moment in his search for rare books and then who knows when he might return?" Lawrence tosses the shoe-boot back into the cupboard and makes a shooing action at me with his hands.

"Thank you, Lawrence, for everything," I say, feeling a bit overwhelmed by the kindness of strangers. Well . . . that's what Lawrence and Ruby were, but not anymore: they're friends, new ones. And to be honest I really need to make more effort on the friendship front—sitting in night after night on my own, avoiding my old friends, despite their efforts to cheer me up after the nonwedding isn't good for the soul; I need to get out more and I don't just mean Zumba.

"Ah, you're very welcome," he mutters, leaning down and gently squeezing my shoulder. "Oh, before I forget . . . Wait here, I'll be back in a moment." And he shoots out of the room, returning a few seconds later with an enormous silver foil parcel. "Lunch for Hettie. Just a few rounds of sandwiches—will you give them to her please, with my compliments?"

"Sure," I say, taking the sandwiches, thinking what a lovely man he is.

"Thank you. I know she doesn't eat enough, and I worry . . . Now, be off with you. I enjoyed the pampering session too, and just hide those damn boots behind a bookcase or something and Adam will be none the wiser," he says, lowering his voice so Ruby doesn't overhear, and elbows me gently in the side. We both laugh as we glance down at the purple shockers. I click the silver-tipped toes together and Lawrence shakes his head.

"I'll do just that." And I turn to leave in my Dolly Parton boots, all ready to find the mysterious bookshop man called Adam. But wait, there's more. I'm getting to go into a bona fide haberdashery shop, which is such a treat, and I swear that today is turning out to be the very best day in a long, long time.

8

After glancing up at the tired, paint-peeling signage above the non-existent window display, I go to push open the door to Hettie's House of Haberdashery and one of those old-fashioned bells makes a gloriously halcyon jingly-jangly sound. I'm hesitating, wondering what to do with Basil, when a man, head bowed, hands shoved into his overcoat pockets, comes barging out of the shop, almost flattening me into the snow as he literally bumps into my right shoulder, making me stumble backward. I reach a hand down to the pavement to steady myself and he stomps off down the lane to a shiny black Range Rover parked beside an old wooden bus shelter.

"Well, excuse me," I harrumph after him, but he doesn't turn back. Instead, he jumps into his car and wheel-spins away, making the snow spray up into a giant, furious flurry.

"I'm so sorry, my dear." A small old lady wearing two

hand-knitted cardigans over a navy serge dress with thick tan tights, fur-lined felt booties, and long silvery-white hair pinned up into a big Aunt Bessie bun comes padding toward me. "My nephew forgets his manners sometimes. Are you all right?"

"Yes, I'm fine, thank you," I say, brushing the snow from the sleeve of my parka.

"Bring the dog in with you. He'll catch his death of cold left outside in the snow," she admonishes, frowning and shaking her head, then quickly adds, "I take it he is housetrained" before holding the door open wide.

"Oh, yes! He knows how to behave," I say, inwardly praying that Basil doesn't let me down and lift his leg on her gnarly, age-dappled wood floor. Or worse still, on the swirly patterned rug in the center of the shop that has admittedly seen better days—it's frayed at the corners and is almost threadbare in the middle, but it could be an heirloom antique Axminster for all we know.

"Good. Then hurry on in, dear, we're letting all the heat out."

Inside the double-fronted shop with mullioned windows it's like stepping into a time warp, an old-fashioned emporium of haberdashery delight. Low-beamed ceilings and a higgledy-piggledy collection of wooden tables are scattered around with open-topped storage jars crammed full of all sorts of knitting and needlecraft paraphernalia—a veritable rainbow of felt balls, plastic buttons, wooden buttons, silks, needles, threads, pins, bobbins, tape measures concertinaed up and held together in rubber bands besides bundles of dressmaker's chalk. Then there are lots of vintage green glass dishes containing remnants of lace, circles of cardboard with lengths of ribbon wound round, waxed cotton, crochet hooks, a china jug crammed full of wooden knitting needles in a whole selection of sizes. It's all here—there's even a rotating wire display rack bulging with Simplicity patterns that must date back to the twenties; one of them even has a picture of a lady's flapper dress on the front, complete with beaded headband.

I gingerly walk Basil around the rug, making a beeline for the yarn section—there must be at least a trillion balls crammed into the rickety old wooden display unit, but on closer inspection the labels look as though they're from the fifties through to the seventies and in mainly dated colors, drab pastels with a few lurid greens and garish oranges thrown in. My heart sinks; this isn't what I had in mind at all. I can't even see any nice vibrant reds with which to knit a Christmas sweater, hat or bobble scarf for Ruby's window display.

"The dog can wait in the kitchen by the fire while you browse. Follow me," the old lady commands.

"Oh, sure. Thank you." I quickly place a sun-faded

lavender lace weight back on the shelf and give Basil's leash a gentle tug as if to say "follow me and be on your very best behavior or else!"

The lady (easily an octogenarian), who I assume must be Hettie, leads us through to the back of the shop and behind a heavy brocade curtain that smells of mothballs mixed with coal dust and into a little kitchen-cum-sitting-room with one of those old square sinks in the corner and the orange-hued charcoal embers of a real open fire glowing in the hearth. Picking up a poker, Hettie gives the fire a good stoke before throwing on the last two lumps of coal. Her hands are clad in black fingerless gloves (hand-knitted, naturally), which she wipes on a raggedy old tea towel before hanging it neatly over the side of the sink. On the draining board is a tray, which, by the looks of it, holds the remnants of her lunch: a teapot with a knitted canary-yellow chicken tea cozy, a plate with crumbs on and some bread crusts wrapped up in plastic—for the birds, perhaps.

"Oh I'm so sorry, did I interrupt your lunch?" I say, instantly feeling bad.

"Lunch?" Hettie says, looking momentarily confused, but then quickly adds, "No dear, that's from yesterd—" She stops talking, tugs her cardigans in tighter around her slight frame, and glances at the floor. The atmosphere is awkward all of a sudden. Oh no, I've embarrassed her, but why? There's a short silence while I slip Basil's red coat off and admire the traditional wooden Singer sewing machine in the corner, complete with marble workbench and brass foot pedal underneath. And then it dawns on me—she's either ashamed at not having cleaned her tray away or, oh God, please tell me that isn't all she has eaten since yesterday? It's highly possible given the minuscule size of her and I can't help thinking that a sudden gust of wind could have serious consequences for her— quite possibly snap her clean in two, she's that brittle and fragile-looking. I reckon my hands could span her waist, no wonder she's wearing so many layers; there's not an ounce of fat on her tiny frame to actually keep her vital organs warm. And for some reason I have an overwhelming urge to wrap my arms around her and give her a big hug. She seems so vulnerable . . . But there's something else, something I can't quite put my finger on; a sadness, sorrow, or loneliness perhaps. I inhale sharply before exhaling hard, quickly covering it with a big smile so as not to embarrass her further; I don't want her seeing my concern and thinking that I'm pitying her, but if it is the case and she's scrimping on food, then it's heartbreaking, and I'll speak to Lawrence to see about getting her meals on wheels or something substantial organized, because he'd be right—she's not eating enough. Old people like her shouldn't have to go hungry. Remembering the sandwiches, I quickly pull the package from my bag.

"Lawrence asked me to give you thi—"

"What is it?" she interrupts.

"Sandwiches." I smile, going to hand them to her.

"Oh, you can keep them. I have plenty of food" she adds sharply, before turning her back. She heads away to the shop floor and beckons for me to follow, which I do, after leaving the silver foil package on the side by the sink. She stops near the counter that houses an antiquated old wooden till and turns to look me in the eye.

"Are you the girl down from London that turned up in the middle of the night?"

"Um, er, yes, I suppose I am," I say, withering slightly under her scrutiny while thinking that news sure does travel fast around here, "but how do you know?"

"Peter told me. He called in earlier with a fresh pail of milk, still warm from the herd. Such a thoughtful lad, just like his father, and his father before him, dairy farmers all of them. Would you like a glass?" she offers kindly.

"That's nice. But, no, thank you anyway," I shake my head and smile politely, wondering if I could actually stomach warm, unpasteurized milk; I can't say that it's ever really appealed to me.

"Are you sure? It's so good for the skin, dear, and if

you don't mind me saying so, your face is looking a little gray around the gills, as it were. That'll be all the pollution up there in London. Blocks the pores! Fine country air and Mother Nature's recipes are what you need, then you'll be dewy-skinned and bright-eyed in no time."

"Oh, er . . . right. Um, thank you for the tip," I mutter. *She's very outspoken.*

"So what is it I can help you with, dear?" she says eagerly, swiftly changing topic and fixing her Wedgwood-blue bright eyes on me.

"Um, well I was hoping to buy some yarn to knit a Christmas sweater and possibly a matching hat. Mittens too, if I have time for them, and perhaps a selection of nice materials to make a quilt. But that's not so urgent as I'm not in such a rush to make that," I say, eyeing up some rolls of fabric stacked up on a table in the corner. I move closer to inspect the roll on top—a pretty black-and-cream birdcage print, but it's all yellowing and stained at one end. Oh no, it's such a shame. And then I look around the shop again and see that everything is faded, and I feel mean thinking this, but the whole place is a mess. There's stuff piled everywhere—old magazines, blankets, sewing books, there's even a decrepit old Silver Cross pram in one corner that's crammed full of material remnants. I take a step closer, wondering if the jumbled assortment will do for a quilt as I can hardly walk out of here without buying anything at all. I don't have the heart to do that, not when Hettie looks so expectant and well, if I'm honest . . . very much in need.

"Do you need a pattern for the pullover?" she asks, going to bend down toward a box on the floor.

"Oh, please let me help you with that, it looks heavy," I say quickly, as she tries to grasp the sides to lift the box.

"Thank you, dear. I'm not as strong as I used to be. Lift it up onto the table there, will you please?" And she hurriedly clears a space by tossing a stack of hand-knitted, lemon lace-weight shawls with a beautiful beaded picot edging into an ancient old open suitcase. The box is seriously heavy and full to the brim with crumpled paper knitting patterns. "That's a girl." She elbows in next to me eagerly, licks a couple of fingertips and starts rummaging through the pile. "Now, let me see. I have just the thing for you here." I smile politely, taking in the Technicolor pictures on the patterns—ladies in old-fashioned twinsets and schoolboys in tank tops dating back to the fifties. Oh well, never mind, I can always use Lawrence's laptop to find a pattern online. "Ah-ha, here it is." And she pulls out an old Bestway pattern priced at 6d (blimey, it's pre-decimal so it must have been in this box for decades) with a picture of a couple wearing his-and-her Christmas sweaters: two skiers mid-slalom over a row of fern trees, with matching headgear, Fair Isle knitted ear muffs for him with a knitted link over the head to hold them in place, and a lacy knit hat for her complete with knitted little strap to go under the chin and button fasten up by the earlobe. Oh God, I know Ruby wants vintage but I'm sure she still envisages people wanting to actually buy the garments on display in her window and nobody is going to want to walk around looking like a prize plum. But then, who am I to talk? I glance down at my feet, cough, and quickly push the now snow-coated spurs under the table.

"I was thinking something a little, um, er, simpler," I say delicately.

"Well, what about this one?" Ah, now this is more like it, a classic chunky-knit with a Christmas pudding on the front. "Too plain?" she adds, going to put it back into the pile in the box.

"Not at all, I'm tight for time on this project and the pattern looks pretty straightforward so I think it'll be perfect," I grin, taking the paper pattern from her to get a proper look and hoping she has some suitably colored yarn stashed away somewhere.

"If you're sure . . . How long do you have?" She stops thumbing through the pile of patterns.

"Three days—and that includes today. It's for Ruby's vintage shop window, up in the High Street."

"Hmm, well three days isn't very long at all," she muses.

"It sure isn't, but Ruby has been very kind to me—and Lawrence." I grin.

"Ah, yes, the B&B, that's where you're staying," Hettie states, matter-of-factly.

"That's right." I smile inwardly, guessing Pete must have told her this as well.

"Ah, Lawrence is a lovely man. An American too; I like Americans. Have you ever been to America?" she asks directly, her eyes lighting up.

"Um, no, I haven't, but I'd really love to," I say, remembering ages ago chatting to Luke about me going to Chicago for a big knitting convention—it never happened though as he had said it was a waste of money, what with the wedding to pay for—the bulk of which I had already saved up for myself, because he needed his money to cover the cost of his football season ticket. Hmm. I really was a bit of a wimp back then. Maybe that's why Sasha appeals to Luke: she'd never let a man tell her she can't do something. Anyway, live and learn, and there's knitting conventions every year; New York is next and there's nothing to stop me from going now, I can spend my own money on whatever I like! The thought lingers, lifting my heart until I realize that I could very well be out of a job quite soon. I instantly push the thought away, but not before thinking that maybe knitting conventions in America will have to wait . . .

"Oh yes. I lived in America for a while," Hettie says brightly, "many years ago and I had such a wonderful time." She pauses and a misty, faraway look comes into her eyes, followed by a soft smile as if she's reminiscing about another, more golden, age. "So, about this pullover," she adds, her face clouding over and her voice changing suddenly, and the moment vanishes.

"Yes, I'd really like to have it done before I leave on Sunday, to repay the favor if I can. Besides, I love knitting, and it feels a bit weird not having a project on the go." I had tried salvaging the lovely little Christmas pudding that I brought with me but even after soaking it in the bath in my en suite overnight, it's still a ruined mess.

"Well, this I can understand. Knitting is like oxygen, a necessity, isn't it?" Hettie's smile is back in place and I nod fervently, not having ever really talked to anyone about the emotional complexities of knitting before. "And some people have a cup of tea when they need cheering up, but I find there's nothing better than the comforting, repetitive click-clack of the needles and the feel of the wool looping over my index finger to make everything feel all right. It's been a wonderful tonic for me over the years." And the faraway look returns in her eyes.

"Ah, yes, me too," I say, wondering if I'll be like Hettie

when I'm in my eighties. I always had it in mind that I'd be surrounded by grandchildren. Luke and I would have a big rowdy family of our own; that was the plan, well, just my plan, as it now turns out. Not Luke's plan at all—with Sasha maybe, but I can't see it myself as she's not the settling-down-with-babies type at all. I put a smile on my face. Monday! That's what I promised myself; I have until then to ignore the reality of my life and enjoy being here in Tindledale, living in blissful ignorance. I must try harder to stop picking over the carcass that is my dismal, failed life. I take a deep breath as if to clear my head.

"I could help if you like?" Hettie offers. "We could knit the pullover together, the hat and gloves too; we might even squeeze in a scarf if we get a move on and if I knit the back and a sleeve while you do the front and the other sleeve. Or I can do the front with the pudding pattern on if you prefer? But you might be quicker as my eyesight tends to fade in the evening, which can make reading patterns problematic." Her eyes are dancing with delight now. "I'm a very fast knitter though, comes from years of practice," she adds proudly. "If we pull together, I reckon we can easily get it all knitted in time. Can you knit fast?"

"I think so," I say honestly, as I've never actually timed myself or done a comparison.

"Good. Then what do you say to a good knit and natter?" she eyes me eagerly.

"Well, when you put it like that, how can I refuse?" My smile broadens. "Yes please, that would be wonderful. If you're really sure and if you have the time—I wouldn't want to put you to any trouble," I say, surreptitiously taking another look at her cardigans which I'm guessing she made herself. They may be old and worn, but they're knitted beautifully so I'm sure her half of the sweater will be superb.

"That settles it then," Hettie says, grinning like a much, much younger person. A teenage girl, almost. It's incredible. And it lifts my spirit to see the transformation, to see her looking so happy. It makes me feel happy too.

"Now let's choose some wool and needles, or do you have your own?" Hettie says, her voice all bubbly with excitement. "I like to keep to the same ones," she adds enthusiastically, before practically skipping over to the other side of the shop and flinging open a wooden cantilever sewing box. All of a sudden, it's as if she has a new lease on life, a purpose. And so have I. It'll be fun to have a knitting buddy, and it's not like I have very much else to do over the weekend, with Cher being away on her course. I can come back here early tomorrow morning and Hettie and I can knit the Christmas sweater together, and on Sunday too—two clear days should be plenty—and I'll get the last train to give us as much time as possible, but with us both knitting, we're bound to have it done in record time and certainly before I have to leave.

My heart lifts at the prospect of a mini knit-off and I make a mental note to pop into the village store later on after swinging by Tindledale Bookshop to get a sneak peek at Adam, aka the mysterious man from the train, to see if I can get some nice biscuits and maybe some chocolate for us to munch on while we knit tomorrow; Hettie definitely strikes me as the kind of lady that might enjoy a chocolate chip cookie or two, or perhaps a bar of Fry's Peppermint Cream.

"Wow! Now that is some collection," I say, making big eyes as Hettie reaches into the sewing box. Inside are a trillion knitting needles, or so it seems, in every size imaginable.

"What size do we need for the Christmas pullover?" she asks and I quickly scan the pattern. It's pre-metric of course.

"Fours," I say, figuring she won't have the six-millimeter metric equivalent. Her collection looks ancient.

"Some of these belonged to my mother," she says, confirming my assumption as she lifts a bundle of cream-colored bone knitting needles high up into the air like a prize. If I'm not mistaken, they are probably worth a very tidy sum. I saw some just like these on eBay during one of my secret online sessions at work, after perusing the Ravelry knitting community website when I should probably have been updating a spreadsheet or something equally mind-numbing. Hettie leaves the bundle of needles on a table and checks the pattern. She rummages some more. "Here we are—my favorite size fours. Would you like a pair too?"

"Oh, yes please," I say, taking the needles from her. "I only have three and three-quarter ones with me," I say, and they still have part of a wine-stained Christmas pudding dangling from them. She creases her forehead, obviously trying to remember the conversion. "Sorry, size nines," I add. "And we need seven balls of chunky scarlet wool, and—"

"Follow me." And she hurries back out to the kitchen-cum-sitting-room, where Basil is snoring in an armchair. Loudly. Very loudly.

"Oh no, I'm so sorry, I'm trying to train him off furniture." I push the pattern under my arm and leap forward to remove Basil but she places her hand on my back.

"Let him sleep, dear," she whispers over my shoulder, as if he's an actual human baby and not an exceedingly cheeky hound. "I'm sure he's exhausted after that long walk from the station last night. Lord Lucan said you were puffing like a steam train when you staggered into the bus shelter," she chuckles and I shake my head, wondering what else she knows. So news really does travel fast in Tindledale; at this rate the whole village will know all of my business before the weekend is out. But to be honest, I'm not sure I mind; it's not something I've experienced before and back home in London it might

121

feel intrusive, but not here in Tindledale. No, it feels nice, in a warm, friendly, embracing way. It's like I belong—and isn't that what everyone wants?

"If you're sure it's OK . . ." I say, and to my surprise, Hettie grabs a child-size knitted granny patch blanket from a pile by the door and gently tucks it around Basil, who stirs for a second, does a massive yawn and has a good stretch before settling back down with his chin nestling over the edge of the blanket. And I swear he now has a big Cheshire-cat grin of satisfaction on his cheeky dog face.

"Right, now let's see what we have in here." Hettie pulls open a door to a cavernous cupboard under the stairs and I gasp. It's a treasure trove. New wool, yarn, whatever you want to call it, balls and balls and balls of it arranged on shelves in neat, jaunty piles ranging from one end of the rainbow prism to the other. And there must enough here to knit a trillion sweaters at least, or so it seems. But why is it hidden away in a cupboard when it should be out there on display in the shop? Nobody is going to buy the faded old stuff that's currently languishing on those rickety shelves. "Hold out your arms." I do as I'm told and Hettie selects seven balls of the richest scarlet yarn I've ever seen, before counting them out into my waiting arms.

"And a few extra for luck," she chuckles, plopping four

more balls on top of the pile. "If we make good progress, we'll be needing these to make a start on the gloves and scarf." She dives back into the cupboard.

"Good idea," I say, getting into the swing of things and enjoying her enthusiasm. "And please let me know how much this all comes to," I add.

"Thank you dear," Hettie says from inside the cupboard. "What's next?" she puffs after pulling herself back out and sweeping a stray tendril of hair away from her flushed face.

"Um . . ." I point with my chin to the pattern still under my arm. Hettie slips the pattern free and holds it out as far as she can before bringing it right up to her nose.

"It's no use. Blasted eyesight, I'll have to get my vari-focals," she tuts, seemingly cross with herself. "Now, I wonder where I left them . . ." She casts a glance around the room and so do I, but it's no use, I can't see her glasses anywhere and it could take ages to hunt for them among all the stuff in the shop.

"Not to worry, we'll work it out together. If you can hold the pattern out in front of me, I'll read out what we need and then you can load me up some more," I say. And she does. "Oops, can you lift it up a little bit higher, please," I laugh, and she goes up on tiptoe before moving from side to side so I can see over the wool mountain under my chin. Wow! I'm super impressed at just how sprightly she still is; I struggle to stand on tiptoe for any length of time and I'm less than half her age. "Perfect. OK, we need . . ." I pause to scan the pattern, "one ball of chocolate brown for the Christmas pudding, a ball of white for the pouring cream and a gorgeous emerald green for the sprig of holly that goes on top of the pudding."

"Thank you, dear. Coming right up." After rummaging in the cupboard some more, Hettie batches up the balls and then loads them into my arms before snapping the cupboard door tight shut. "That should do it," she says with a flourish before straightening up and turning to face me with her hands planted on her slim hips. "I can't wait to get started. You know, this reminds me of when I was a young girl with my mother—we often used to do knitting projects together. We did Jerseys for the whole Tindledale village cricket team one time and they looked truly dazzling out there on the village green. And I think they won the county cup that year. It was the summer of 1947—a gloriously hot one it was too—and we sat in the garden with jugs of cider and cartons of plump strawberries from the fields over at Cherry Tree Orchards. The farmer used to charge three and six and you could pick as much as you want."

"Ah, that sounds amazing," I say, happy to hear about

the olden days. "And Pete mentioned the orchard last night. So it's been around for a very long time then?" *I can't believe I just said that! She's going to think I'm so rude.* But much to my surprise, Hettie just throws her head back and laughs.

"I like you," she says very directly, after composing herself. "You remind me of myself when I was a girl, with your obvious passion for knitting. And that was a *very*, *veeeery* long time ago." She chuckles some more, shaking her head and prodding me gently in the ribs. I let out a little sigh of relief on realizing that she's teasing me and quickly decide that now might be the time to broach the subject of her tired-looking yarn section in the rickety old shelving unit, so I take a deep breath and hope for the best, really not wanting to offend her.

"Can I ask you a question, please?" I start tentatively.

"Of course, but let's walk and talk so we can get started on the knitting. We can sit upstairs—much more comfortable up there. Follow me." And she heads toward the stairs.

"OK. Um . . . Why do you have all that gorgeous new yarn hidden away?" I say really quickly as if to lessen the impact. She stops moving and turns around to face me.

"The wool? In there?" I nod as she points back into the kitchen-cum-sitting-room. "That's the stock cupboard,

125

dear. It's where I keep the good stuff so that when the old wool is all sold I can replenish the shelves. It's called stock rotation," she informs me earnestly.

"I see. But what if the old stuff doesn't sell? It seems such a pity not to show off the lovely new yarn," I half mumble, wondering if I'm pushing my luck, but to my surprise she doesn't miss a beat.

"Hmm, good point." She tilts her head to one side and cups her chin in her hand as if considering my point very prudently. "I've never really thought about it like that before. The shop was my mother's before it became mine and that's just the way it's always been. Where do you suggest I would put the old stuff if we were to display the new stock? You know, business has been so slow these last few years and I keep meaning to sort it all out but it just seems like such a big task . . ." Her voice trails off and the confusion from earlier, over the lunch tray, reappears. And then her face fills with alarm as she spots something on a nearby table. I follow her eye line and see that it's a pile of post. She grabs the papers and stuffs them underneath a cushion. Instinctively, and not wanting to add to her embarrassment, I pretend not to have noticed.

"Well, I could give you a hand if you like," I carry on, carefully, not wanting her to feel that I'm trying to take over. She stares me straight in the eye as if sizing me up. "I'd really enjoy the opportunity, I've always dreamt of having a haberdashery shop just like yours, so I'd love to help out if I can. Honestly, you'd be doing me a favor," I grin, pushing my chin out over the yarn to keep it from rolling away on to the floor. And it's true. Stepping inside here and envisioning just how glorious it could be is like seeing my dream come alive. She looks anxious, but then her face softens. "Only if that's OK, of course," I quickly add. Silence follows apart from the roar of Basil snoring.

"What do you have in mind?" she says eventually, still eyeing me shrewdly.

"Well, let's see it as a partnership: you're helping me with the sweater, so I'll help you to, um . . ." I pause to pick my words carefully. "Rotate the stock!" I finish, thinking: I can clear the old wool off the shelves, empty the cupboard of the new stuff and store the old balls in there. Easy. Ideally, they need binning but I reckon that might just be a step too far for her right now. Little acorns and all that, and then, when she's comfortable with me helping out, I can make a start on clearing the rest of the shop. I'm sure it won't take much to tidy the place up and make it look a whole lot fresher and brighter for her.

"But will you have time?" Her wrinkled forehead creases some more. "What with the knitting project to do by Sunday?"

"I'll make time. Besides, I have you to help me with the knitting now," I smile, letting the wool and needles drop from my arms into a nearby wire shopping basket before pulling my parka off and rolling up the sleeves of Ruby's blouse. "Come on, you'll see. It'll be fun." I move toward Basil. "But first, let's sort out some chairs to put in the shop—we don't want to be sitting upstairs and end up missing a customer. Plus, if we position them near the window we'll be like a living advertisement for knitting, which is bound to entice customers in to see your lovely new stock!" I add, already on a roll, feeling excited and exhilarated and optimistic—something I haven't felt in a very long time.

"Dear, can I tell you a secret?" she asks, keeping her eyes on the floor.

"What's that, then?" I prompt, making sure my smile stays in place. I'm so pleased that she's up for getting reorganized but there's clearly something serious bothering her, so whatever it is, I hope I can make it better for her.

"I don't really have many customers these days, apart from the odd rambler who bumbles in by chance, and to be honest with you, if things don't pick up soon then I'm afraid I may have to close the shop and move away. There's such a lot to keep up with, what with the house and the payments for the . . ." Her voice fades. She's wringing her hands and looking really distressed now, almost as if she's shared something she shouldn't have. I stop moving for a moment.

"And don't you want to do that?" I ask. "To close the shop, and move away?" I clarify, feeling so sad for her.

"No, I don't. I want to die here at home," she says adamantly. "But not for a while yet, I hope," she adds, "and when the time comes I don't want it to be in a strange place where my last moment of pleasure is sipping stewed tea from a sippy cup." She shakes her head stoically, but I spot the flash of fear in her eyes and I'm horrified that this is what she has to worry about. Oh God.

"Well, in that case we had better try to change all that," I nod firmly, figuring it best to keep up a jovial, positive attitude to spur us both on. Hettie does a half-smile and sags just a little in relief.

"I'm so pleased you popped in," she says softly.

After gently waking Basil, much to his disgust, I drag the faded old armchair from the kitchen-cum-sitting-room and out onto the shop floor. A few minutes and a bit of shifting around later, and I've got the chair in a perfect cozy-looking angle by the window. Hettie folds a pile of old blankets on the floor as a makeshift bed for Basil, who after licking her hand by way of thanks, hops on and is snoring again within seconds. I shake my head;

129

he really is the laziest dog in the whole of the canine kingdom.

"Here, we can use this chair too." Hettie, getting into the swing of things, lifts an enormous pile of old satin-quilted eiderdowns up to reveal an Art Deco design armchair in a beautiful buttery brown leather. "You'd better sit in it because if I do I'll never get up again. No, it's far too low for me," she laughs, her eyes dancing like a child's and for a second I get another glorious glimpse of the girl she once was, young and pretty and carefree— and quite possibly a little bit mischievous as she gives me a cheeky wink then sweeps a pile of old bobbins from a low table and into a bin before rubbing her hands together very vigorously. "I've been meaning to do that for such a long time. And will you look at the state of them? Most of these don't even have any thread left at all. Why on earth are they still here?" she says, tutting and pulling a face as she retrieves a bobbin, inspects it and then tosses it back into the bin. "Now, would you be a love and move this table into the gap between those two chairs for me? We'll be needing somewhere to put all our junk—tea, glasses for me, and I always like to have a hanky at hand and a packet of strong mints—they help me knit faster." She does a big belly laugh and it really touches my heart to see her looking so happy, and in such contrast to the bleakness emanating from her just a little while ago when I first stepped inside her lovely House of Haberdashery.

"I'd be delighted to. This is going to be amazing," I say, dashing toward the small table.

"But before you do, I'm going to ask you a question now," Hettie states, ominously and very directly.

"Um, sure . . ." I stop moving.

"Why are you so unhappy on the inside when you look so glamorous on the outside? Apart from the gray skin of course, but we can fix that!" She shrugs and tilts her head to one side. Silence follows while I reel again from her directness. I open my mouth to answer, and then close it again, realizing that I actually have no idea where to begin to explain it all to her, and to be honest, I'm not sure I even want to, because by doing so, it will be as if all the heartache over Luke and my very own twin sister hurting me, and then my feelings of inadequacy and letting everyone down on my wedding day added to messing up at work will just get in the way and tarnish the new life I have here, even if it is only for a weekend.

But it's a whole weekend to be anonymous with nobody nudging their mate and saying, "Ooh, yes, didn't you know? She's the one whose boyfriend dumped her *at the altar*," in a hushed voice, like they do at work. Yes, I've overheard them, but then I've never really fitted in there, never been a part of the clique. I've always felt as though I'm swimming upstream and that's probably because it isn't what I really want to be doing with my life. I dig my nails into the palm of my hand and try not to wobble into another embarrassing meltdown as I did over breakfast this morning. I really thought I was making some progress, being here in Tindledale and the whole change of scenery, especially after the pampering session with Lawrence earlier on, but maybe I got it wrong . . . It's Hettie who moves the moment on.

"Why don't I make us a nice fresh pot of tea, dear, and then you can tell me all about it—we can cast on and have a good old knit and natter?" She smiles kindly, momentarily resting her hand gently on my forearm, almost as a gesture of solidarity, and I can't stave them off any longer . . . tears well in the corners of my eyes. I instantly blink them away. Then, much to my surprise, I realize that I don't actually feel sad, not at all, not in the way I used to. Instead I feel calm and relaxed, free almost. I look into her eyes and smile.

"I'd love that so much."

"Me too, dear. Me too," Hettie says.

Later, and after many cups of tea and Lawrence's truly scrumptious roast beef, arugula, mustard and tomato sandwiches (I had to say that I was hungry and could really do with one, in order for Hettie to even entertain the idea and accept a round of sandwiches for her lunch) and having totally lost track of time, Hettie and I have made exceedingly good progress on the Christmas pudding sweater. We've each finished our sleeves, had a good natter while we knitted, and yes, I caved in and ended up telling her all about Luke and Sasha and what happened on that horrible day in the church. I tried asking her about herself and her own past, but she was very reluctant to talk, preferring to listen to me.

"So, Sybil" (Hettie told me that she can't call me Sybs because it's not "proper") "you must soldier on. No point in dwelling on the past. Believe me, it gets you nowhere," she says wistfully, carefully folding her sleeve and placing it neatly in her lap.

"But what about your time in America, Hettie? Surely that was exciting? And what took you there? Was it love?" I venture, finishing my tea and wondering if perhaps she'll open up a bit this time. Despite my own disastrous love life, I'm a sucker for a good romantic story. Plus, I'm keen to know if she has any family, someone to look after her when she can't look after herself any longer.

"I suppose you could say that . . ." A short silence follows and I will her to share the story. I'm fascinated, especially after spotting a black-and-white photo on the mantelpiece above the fire in the kitchen-cum-sitting-room out the back. It shows a beautiful, svelte woman wearing a jeweled turban and a leotard with black tights and high-heeled dancing shoes. She's sitting on a chair, leaning forward, with her legs crossed and her elbows resting on her knees, hands cupping her chin in a proper professionally staged pose. It's very glamorous. And it's signed too.

"Sounds intriguing," I prompt.

"Oh, it's not what you're thinking. Not a man! Although that did follow for a while." Hettie places her cup back on the table and looks me straight in the eye. "In addition to the knitting of course, my true love was dancing. Still is. It's what I went to America for . . . to Hollywood."

"Really?" I say, incredulously. "But that's amazing. I saw the picture on the—" I gesture to behind the brocade curtain.

"Yes, that was taken in 1953, I had just turned twenty-two," she muses.

"It's you?" I make big eyes.

"Yes, believe it or not," Hettie nods, smiling wryly. "I wasn't always this old." She glances down at herself with a look on her face as if she's seeing the wrinkled, bony body of an old lady for the very first time. "But that was before—" She stops abruptly and her face crumples slightly. I manage to resist the urge to leap from my armchair and scoop her up into an enormous cuddle.

"And the signature? Is that yours?" I say, trying to lighten the mood. She's clearly distressed again about something as she's now clasping and unclasping her hands and staring at the knitted sleeve in her lap.

"Oh no, Gene did that," she mutters, not looking up.

"Gene?"

"Yes, dear, Gene Kelly!" she says in a breezy voice before lifting herself from the armchair, placing the sleeve on the table and padding out to the back, leaving me to reunite my jaw with the rest of my face. I'm literally speechless. Wow! The actual *Gene Kelly*. But he's a legend. I know he's long gone, but honestly, he's up there with the icons— Elvis Presley and Frank Sinatra and the like, and everyone knows that these guys live on for all eternity. And it just goes to show; I would never have guessed that she was a dancer in Hollywood—the little old lady who lives in a tiny village in the English countryside. And didn't Lawrence say that her ancestors, the Honey family, had been here for centuries? If that's the case, then how did Hettie get to go to Hollywood and dance with Gene Kelly? But, more intriguingly—*why on earth did she come back?*

I'm contemplating following Hettie out to the kitchen, wondering if she might want to be alone for a bit, when the bell jangles and the shop door opens, bringing in a fine flurry of snow and a blast of chilly air. Basil galvanizes himself into action and does a lame bark before bouncing over to see who's at the door. The figure stamps welly-clad feet on the mat before pushing the hood of its tattered old brown waxy Driza-Bone Mackintosh down, and ah, I recognise her: it's the flashlight woman from last night.

Hettie reappears, darts a glance in my direction and I can instantly see that the moment has vanished; she has her stoic face in place and her guard well and truly back up.

"Marigold," Hettie says warmly, stepping forward to clasp the woman's hands in hers before dipping down into a little curtsey then standing tall again and giving her friend a hug. Marigold or should I say, Lady Fuller-Hamilton, squeezes Hettie's thin frame affectionately, and I'm sure I spot a glimmer of shock on her face as she rubs her hand up and down in between Hettie's shoulder blades but she keeps the smile firmly in place and, after letting Hettie go, she takes a step backward.

"Oh, Hettie, we'll never tire of that old joke will we?" Marigold laughs, shaking her head.

"I don't think so, but then it's your own fault for marrying the earl's younger son!"

"Hmm, much to the old earl's chagrin." Marigold frowns, shaking her head.

"And to think, you could have had your pick of the village lads." The two women chuckle some more at the seemingly in-joke. "So, what brings you in here?" Hettie says, the first to compose herself.

"Well, I drove past earlier on my way up to the village and saw you both through the window, knitting and nattering away you were, and I thought I'd pop in on my way back, and be exceedingly nosy." She flings her head back and does her trademark roar of a laugh—I realize it as such now, remembering the laugh from last night—which now seems like an eternity ago. I can't believe I've only been in Tindledale for less than a day—I feel as if I've been here forever, but what's that old adage? *Time flies when you're having fun.* "And hello again, dear," Marigold says, smiling in my direction. "Such a pity about Sonny and Cher's unfortunate sleeping arrangements, but I trust you are comfortable at the B&B? Lawrence will look after you, that's for sure. A true gentleman." And she does her roar again.

"Oh yes, he's the perfect host too," I reply politely, not

even going there on the "how does she even know that I'm staying at the B&B?" thing, because it's a given, of course she knows; everyone knows about everyone here in Tindledale. Apart from me, and I want to know all about Hettie and her amazing life as a dancer with Gene Kelly in the golden age of Hollywood. I make a mental note to see if Lawrence knows, or Ruby perhaps. And then it strikes me. Oh my God. What if Hettie was in that film, the famous one, the one Mum loves and always sets up the Sky+ to record when it's on over Christmas, to watch when she gets home after the cruise. *Singin' in the Rain*, that's the one. Oh, how exciting. I make another mental note to get on Google and type in Hettie Honey at the first opportunity. I wonder what Hettie is short for? Hmm, I'll ask Google that too.

"So come on then, what's going on? You two looked as if you were having a whale of a time together. And you know me, Hettie, never one to miss out on the fun. Are you sure you won't come along to my bridge club? We have such a marvelous time, I'm sure you'd enjoy it Hettie, and then there are the jollies; we're all off on a day trip next week to a Christmas market in Germany—perfect place to pick up some nice stocking fillers," Marigold says, and in my periphery vision I can see Hettie clasping her hands and looking anxious again, so I jump in.

"Knitting and natter! As you saw on your way past, exactly that. Hettie kindly offered to help me with a knitting project that I need to have finished in record time," I say brightly, and Hettie stops clasping.

"Knitting! Ooh, I'd love to see. I haven't knitted for years, but I always loved it as a girl. What are you making?" Marigold pulls her mackintosh off and wanders over to pick up the pattern from the low table between mine and Hettie's armchairs. "Ah, a splendid Christmas sweater. What a jolly idea. Lucan would love one, the grandchildren too. How much do you charge?" Marigold looks first to Hettie and then to me.

"Oh, we, er, well, we haven't really got that far." Hettie pats her bun and glances in my direction.

"Yes, we're still working out the prices for the bespoke knitwear but you're more than welcome to join our new knit-and-natter group if you wanted to knit a sweater of your own," I say, taking a chance on this being OK with Hettie—they are friends after all, and the more the merrier. Besides, it'll be nice for Hettie to have the company after I go home.

"I'd love to, but I'm not sure my knitting skills are up to a whole sweater," Marigold says.

"Then you can make yourself useful and knit the scarf to go with this set," Hettie says, in her usual brusque way, but Marigold doesn't seem fazed.

"Oh, what fun. When can I start?" She looks around the shop for somewhere to sit.

139

"No time like the present. Here," Hettie lifts a pile of old newspapers to reveal yet another armchair. Smiling, I jump up and push it over to the window next to the other chairs to form a cozy semicircle.

"In that case, I'll fetch in some mince pies from the car. I just picked up a batch from the Spotted Pig and can't wait to sample one. Kitty's cakes are always exceedingly good, as that Mr. Kipling would say. And I'm sure you two could do with a cake break." Marigold claps her hands together and does her roar, seemingly pleased with the plan, before turning toward the door.

"And I'll put the kettle on," Hettie beams, giving my shoulder a quick squeeze. Once Marigold has closed the shop door behind her, Hettie leans into me and whispers, "She's not much of a knitter you know. I used to babysit her when she was a child, and I tried my best to teach her. But you can hardly go wrong with a scarf now, can you?" I smile as confirmation. "You should have seen the flock of sheep she made for the church nativity scene one year, shocking they were." Hettie purses her lips and bats a bony hand in the air. "Only managed to knit two lambs and her sewing together was so atrocious, the seams unraveled within minutes. *Minutes*. Even the vicar was aghast." Hettie does a snort of disapproval and I have to stifle a giggle. "But she has a good heart; her father was a pig farmer and she married well," Hettie rushes to finish, barely drawing breath as Marigold comes back through the shop door with a cake box tucked under her arm and a bulging net of logs swinging in her left hand.

"Is the chimney open in here, Hettie?" Marigold yells out to the back, where Hettie has scarpered, before dumping the logs by the grate of the little fireplace set in the wall next to the old yarn section. Hettie pops her head around the curtain, her cheeks flushed.

"Yes, I think so, but I don't have any coal . . ." Hettie's voice trails off, not having seen the logs in her rush to scoot away after gossiping. I have to suppress another giggle. "I have firelighters and matches though," she adds quickly, before ducking back behind the curtain to retrieve them.

"Marvelous! It's perishing in here so let's get a fire going and then someone can cast me on; I'll be fine to knit away if you can help me with that—it's the bit I struggle with," Marigold roars, assembling the firelighters and logs around some scrunched up sheets of old newspaper she's taken from a pile. In no time at all, the logs are crackling and the shop starts to warm up nicely. Basil, seizing the opportunity, repositions himself on the tiled hearth to bask, yet again, in the heat. He's going to be ruined forever now when he has to make do with dull, inanimate radiators back home in the flat in London.

Hettie returns with the tea tray, which she sets down

141

on the table and then busies herself with sorting out wool and needles for Marigold. I stifle a yawn.

"Oh dear, keeping you up are we?" Hettie says, casting on for Marigold before handing her the needles and wool to continue. "Knit one purl one. Simple," she says to Marigold before looking back to me.

"Yes, sorry, I've not been sleeping well—"

"Then why don't you dart off up to the village?" Hettie says, giving me a knowing look. I'd told her about the message on the newspaper and she agrees with Lawrence. "Oh, how exciting. An illicit rendezvous," is what she said then. But now "Perhaps a nice *book* will help you to sleep," Hettie adds suggestively, making very big eyes, and Marigold cottons on—her knitting face (steely concentration, complete with poking-out tongue) freezes.

"What's going on?" She stops moving her needles and looks first at me and then to Hettie with a quizzical look on her face now. I inhale sharply.

"You can tell her," Hettie nods reassuringly. So I do.

"Then you absolutely must get up to the village. Oh my, this is so romantic!" Marigold practically squeals in delight. "Get into the bookshop before it closes. Oh, I'm so glad I popped in; this is the most fun I've had in ages. Just between us girls," she pauses to do illicit left-then-right eyes as if someone might be listening, while I smile at her calling us girls, "the bridge club can be *very* stuffy,

142

but Lucan likes me to be involved, says it's nice for us to show an interest in village life and the other members expect it now after all these years," she sighs, then takes a big bite of a mince pie, carefully cupping her hand underneath so as not to get crumbs on the scarf before pulling a hanky from her sleeve to wipe her fingers and mouth.

"And we've made good progress on the pullover so I'm sure we can spare you," Hettie says, reaching for her cup of tea. "If you go now, you can hop onto the next bus." We all glance at the wall clock and see that it's nearly four o'clock. On the hour, every hour.

"But Hettie, I can't just abandon you to knit on without me, not when you're doing me a favor in the first place," I say, feeling very cheeky.

"Nonsense. I'm here to help out now, and you'll be back tomorrow," Marigold insists. "I'll rope in some of the other girls too, for the mittens, and I'm sure Ruby won't mind a few extra items—hat and scarf sets make very nice stocking fillers." Cue her roar again. "My neighbor, two fields over, is a very keen knitter."

"Is that Louise?" Hettie asks.

"That's the one. Mrs. Zass-Bangham, do you know her?"

"She used to pop in for her wool, but not for a while now . . ." Hettie's voice trails off.

"I think she buys from online these days."

143

"Online? Where's that?" Hettie asks suspiciously, as if there's a mysterious competitor sprung up in Tindledale somewhere, which might account for her lack of customers in recent years.

"It's in the computer. Lucan does all the banking there too."

"It has a bank?"

"Well, not an actual bank like the HSBC next to the parish council office where Dolly's sister in Stoneley works," Marigold says earnestly, while I can't help thinking that this is just like watching a live episode of *Mrs. Brown's Boys*. Mind boggling.

"Dolly with the younger husband?" I chip in, hazarding a guess that there aren't two women called Dolly who live in Stoneley.

"Yes, that's the one. Lovely lady. And a very lucky one too with that devilishly handsome new husband of hers," Marigold roars. "Do you know her?"

"Well, not really, we just met on the train from London."

"Oh, *from London?*" they both chime at the same time, while exchanging inquisitive glances, their interest very obviously piqued.

"What was she doing up there?" It's Marigold who asks, but Hettie is leaning forward, eager to hear my answer too.

"I've no idea."

"Didn't you ask?" Hettie quizzes.

"Um, no." They both look deflated now, so I immediately add in a "sorry" for good measure, and they resume knitting with disappointed looks etched all over their furrowed faces. I try not to smile. Silence follows, bar the click-clack of Marigold's needles and a huffing noise from Hettie as she tries to read the pattern.

"You better get your coat on then," Hettie says a few minutes later, as if to dismiss me. She puts the pattern back down on the table and turns to Marigold. "So, tell me about the online shop."

"Well, it's all the rage. Hettie, if you opened one then you could have worldwide customers," Marigold tells her in a very impressed voice as I haul myself out of the armchair and lift up my parka.

"Do you know about it, Sybil?" Hettie asks with a baffled look on her face.

"Oh yes, I can organize it for you if you like," I say, figuring I can use Lawrence's laptop to set up a *Hettie's House of Haberdashery* account on Etsy where she can sell hand-knitted items and crochet and needlecraft stuff too. Those lemon lace-weight shawls are bound to sell well. And perhaps an eBay account for all the haberdashery paraphernalia she has piled up in here; most of it is vintage and will probably sell for a phenomenal amount. People love this stuff—in Clapham they would be beating a path to the door of Hettie's House of Haberdashery. "All you need to do is select some items to sell and then I can list them for you." I smile enthusiastically, remembering my thoughts from earlier about achieving my dream in a different way. It may not be my shop, but I reckon it'll be just as rewarding to set it all up for Hettie, especially if it means her House of Haberdashery doesn't have to close down and she gets to avoid having to drink tea from a child's sippy cup. "Those whalebone knitting needles are worth a lot of money, easily two to three hundred pounds." Hettie looks stunned. "So we can auction them with a decent reserve to maximize your return," I say and I wonder if Lawrence would be up for helping Hettie out with processing the orders once I've gone home? Even if it's just packaging and popping them up to the village store for mailing—Hettie might struggle to lug them all that way on the bus on her own (I make a mental note to ask him). Then Marigold, as if reading my mind, says,

"Oh, what fun. And I'll help you out Hettie; I can be your logistics girl—post the knitwear off to your worldwide customers to save you traipsing out to post them. And besides, you'll be busy knitting away to keep up with all the new commissions that will come, you wait and see." She makes big, impressive eyes. "You'll have to get some of those embroidered labels to stitch in too, they could say *Handmade by Hettie's House of Haberdashery.*"

"Fancy that." Hettie shakes her head, trying to take it all in. "Do you really think it might take off?"

"I'm certain of it. Sybil is such a clever girl, Hettie, and she knows how to set it all up for you." Marigold gives me a wink, and I really wish I could stay here and be a part of this exciting new adventure. But I'll be back, I quickly decide, as there's nothing now to stop me from coming to Tindledale every weekend, if that's what I want to do, and I can always keep an eye on the online store from my flat in London during the week. That's the beauty of the Internet.

"Do you really think the needles are worth that much? In the online shop?" Hettie turns to me, smiling eagerly, and it makes me feel happy as I seem to have been exonerated now from having failed to ask Dolly what it was *exactly* that she was doing up in London. "And to think, they're only cluttering up the place." Hettie shakes her head in disbelief.

"I truly do," I grin. "Do you have a camera?"

"No." Hettie's face drops.

"I do!" Marigold interjects excitedly. "On my mini iPad—never used it, mind you. Lucas got it for me last Christmas, heaven knows why, blasted thing keeps going upside down."

"Upside down?" Hettie creases her forehead, clearly confused.

"Yes, unless you keep it absolutely still, the picture on the screen moves around on its own. Causes havoc with my migraines," Marigold groans.

"Well I never." Hettie shakes her head in disbelief. "It's a marvel what they can do these days." There's a short silence while the two women ponder on this technological phenomena. "What is a mini iPad?" Hettie eventually pipes up.

"It's a miniature computer that you can keep in your pocket," Marigold tells her.

"Your pocket? But why would you want to do that?" Hettie frowns.

"An iPad would be perfect," I jump in, figuring their comedy double act could go on all day at this rate. "Would you be able to bring it with you tomorrow?"

"Consider it done," Marigold says firmly. "And it can roam!" she adds proudly, pausing her knitting needles for added impact.

"Roam? On its own?" Hettie's baffled look is back in place. "Is that why you have to keep it in your pocket?"

"Yes, I think so, but let's not worry about it now. I'll bring the iPad with me and then Sybil can sort it all out. She'll know what to do. We need to get on with the knitting while she goes off on her romantic adventure,"

Marigold takes charge. "You must tell us all about it tomorrow."

"Wonderful. I will do, I promise. And you're sure you don't mind me going?" I beam, feeling a tingle of excitement from the curiosity of seeing Adam. "I'll take some yarn with me and make a start on the matching mittens tonight; I won't need to take the pattern just for those."

"We insist," Hettie says. "There's plenty of time to get this sweater finished and it's a good idea to leave the pattern here as I've started the back already." Hettie lifts her knitting up as proof, and I'm impressed. She really is a *very* fast knitter. "Marigold will read the pattern for me, won't you, dear?"

Marigold nods.

"In that case I'll see you both later. Come on Basil," I say, pulling his knitted coat on over his head and legs before clipping his leash onto his collar.

"Shan't be a minute, Hettie, I'd better fetch my glasses from the car," Marigold says, putting her knitting on the table, then getting up and walking out with me. She grabs her mackintosh on the way and swings it around her shoulders as we close the door behind us.

"My dear, how did you do it?" Marigold says, in a low voice, leaning into me as soon as the shop door swings shut behind us.

"Do what?" I ask, pulling my hood up and slipping my

mittens on; it's freezing outside, but at least it's stopped snowing now.

"Transform our Hettie! She's like her old bubbly self, full of vigor," Marigold says, her voice rising a few octaves as she pulls her car door open and starts rummaging around in the glove box.

"Oh, um, I don't know really. I guess we just hit it off," I shrug, before pressing my hands up to my cheeks to keep them from going numb in the wintery wind.

"We've all been so worried about her." Marigold hauls herself back out of the car to stand squarely in front of me with her back to the shop, presumably so that Hettie can't lip-read what she's saying to me. "She clearly hasn't been coping, or eating by the looks of her. And she hardly ever ventures out these days, despite our encouragement, and it's such a shame as she used to be a leading lady in the Tindledale Players—what with her being a dancer and all, and she was a marvel with the youngsters, choreographing their dance routines, teaching them tap and how to do all that jazz dancing."

"Wow! That's amazing."

"Certainly is. But it all stopped awhile ago, and if that nephew of hers gets his way then she could be homeless very soon," Marigold tuts, shaking her head dramatically, and I'm instantly horrified.

"What do you mean?"

"I mean . . ." she pauses to sigh and shake her head ". . . that he's a mean piece of work and is after Hettie's land."

"Hmm, you know, he barged into me and knocked me to the ground in his hurry to leave the shop when I was going in."

"That sounds about right. He's an obnoxious shit," Marigold says fiercely.

"But she's an old lady. Where will she go?" I ask, dreading the answer. It's clear that Hettie's struggling to make ends meet and to keep on top of everything—she told me so herself—but even so, her own nephew!

"Exactly. She's not going anywhere," Marigold says sternly. "Not if we can help it, eh?" She gives me a conspiratorial wink and a big nudge with her elbow.

"Well, I'll do whatever I can to help." I make a mental note to get cracking on tidying up the shop first thing tomorrow, right after I've set up the Hettie's House of Haberdashery online shop and eBay account. I might even manage a simple WordPress website for her too, with a pretty snowcapped picture of the shop on it, some village scenes and a selection of her knitting projects. I can see it now, all traditional-looking but whimsical and appealing too. And I'll definitely put a picture of the Christmas pudding sweater on there. Everyone loves a wacky festive sweater.

"That's very kind of you, Sybil. You know, that nephew of hers talked Hettie into 'releasing equity' from the oast house years ago, with some cock-and-bull story about her becoming an investor in his building company and she's still struggling to pay back the loan without so much as a sniff of a dividend from him. And recently I heard on the village grapevine that he plans to get his hands on her land to tear down the oast and the shop and build a whole load of those monstrous shoe-box houses in their place." Marigold purses her lips. "*None* of us wants that to happen, least of all Hettie."

"That's terrible," I say, but it explains why she seems to be scrimping on the basics, like food and heating—I saw the look on her face when she thought Marigold was after some coal earlier—Hettie used the last of it when Basil and I arrived, which, while it's generous of her and a generational thing, I guess, to look after your guests ahead of yourself, I get that, it's shocking that a lady of her age is practically on the breadline. And what about that pile of post she didn't want me to see? We hear about the austerity measures all the time and I see it every day at work, people living in poverty, unable to even afford to keep a roof over their heads, but I never imagined it affecting people like Hettie . . . I bet that's why she got anxious, did her hand-wringing thing, when Marigold mentioned the trip to the German Christmas market. She can't afford a luxury like that when she can barely afford to eat. A lump forms in my throat so I inhale sharply and let out a long breath, hoping I never clap eyes on the nephew again, because right now there's a very real possibility that I could end up doing something to him that could have very serious consequences for my own long-term freedom. And spending any length of time in prison really isn't part of my life plan. Besides, where would Basil go? He'd never survive in a boarding kennel, or a rescue shelter, no; he's far too spoilt for all that. I shake my head as if to clear my vengeful thoughts.

"It certainly is terrible," Marigold puffs indignantly. "I could wring his neck." *Join the queue.* "Anyway, there's the bus coming now so you had better stick your arm out." I do, and the bus stops short of the rickety old wooden bus shelter so I don't have to trudge down the lane in the snow, which is nice of the driver. "I'm so glad you're here in Tindledale. At this rate, we won't ever want to let you go," she says and then Marigold does her trademark roar while giving my hand a hearty squeeze as I step onto the bus with Basil under my other arm, an enormous grin on my face and a fierce determination in my heart to help Hettie keep hold of her home and her glorious House of Haberdashery.

11

The bus eventually pulls up next to the snow-covered shelter in the village square. We had a slight delay after coming around a bend in a lane to be faced with a deer standing right in the middle of the road—all majestic it was, with enormous and very impressive antlers—and it took my breath away. The driver switched the engine off and we sat for a good few minutes while the deer eyeballed the bus before finally deigning to swagger off into the dense forest at the side of the road. I was beside myself with glee, whereas everyone else on the bus just carried on chatting or reading their newspapers like it's an everyday occurrence, which I suppose for them it is.

Basil and I jump off the bus, thank the driver who must be going on his break now as he's pouring a steamy cup of tea from a tartan-patterned flask and make our way along the High Street, past the Spotted Pig café, where we're treated to a burst of a truly scrumptious aroma that fills the air as a customer opens the door and steps out onto the pavement—it's cinnamon and nutmeg and it reminds me of a scented seasonal candle that Nana gave me one year on Christmas Eve. It was around the time they became an actual "thing" and Cher had got one for her twelfth birthday a few months earlier, so I had been thrilled to have one too. Past the Paws Pet Parlor where there's a magnificent Afghan hound standing on a metal table in the window having a blow-dry with a giant hair-dryer attached to the ceiling on a bendy hose. The dog's long, honey-hued hair is flowing and flaring out in the air as if it's starring in a shampoo advert.

On we go, smiling at passers-by, all of us trying not to skid on the hard-compacted icy snow, until we're standing right outside Tindledale Books, me with the fierce deter-mination from earlier still in place and Basil wagging his tail eagerly as if he can't wait to see what this next stop on our mini-break adventure has in store for him. I bet he's imagining another roaring fire and perhaps a lovely granny patch blanket to snuggle up to.

I pull my hood down and push open the door, reminding myself that Adam left the message for me, so I haven't really got anything to feel anxious about. But, still . . . and for some random reason, Mum's "dipping your toe back in" line comes into my head. Hardly, I'm just taking a look, that's all, nothing wrong in being curious, and if there's the slightest hint of him being another Luke, or even a *Star Wars* fan for that matter, then I'll be scarpering faster than anyone can say Han Solo!

"You can't bring dogs in here," a sturdy-looking woman barks before I've even pushed the door open wide enough to actually get a Dolly Parton boot-clad foot over the threshold. The woman folds her arms after tapping at a sign in the window that has a picture of a black dog with a big red cross right through the center.

"Oh, I'm sorry, I didn't see that there," I say, having obviously lulled myself into a far too relaxed state with Basil being allowed practically everywhere else in Tindledale—the village pub, the B&B and down at Hettie's. What on earth am I thinking? I take a deep breath, as this doesn't bode well for an exciting first encounter with a man that isn't Luke. And when you've been with the same man for five years, the prospect of chatting to a new one can be very scary indeed, so this is all I need. Not.

"He might damage the books, they're very precious," the woman quips. I assume she's the infamous Mrs. Pocket, aka gatekeeper to the mysterious Adam.

"I'm sure he won't, but . . ." And I'm just about to loop Basil's leash around a lamppost when he chooses this exact moment to cock his leg in the gutter and let me down. She shakes her head before tutting and crossing her arms underneath her ample bust but she still doesn't

156

move. She glares at Basil's offending stream of wee in the snow, as if expecting me to remove it at once. So, feeling awkward, I rummage in my bag for a bottle of water, flip the lid off and quickly sprinkle the liquid into the snow, hoping this will appease her.

"That's better. We like to look after our village," she smirks smugly with added emphasis on the "we" and the "our." I open my mouth to talk, wondering *what is her problem?* but quickly decide against antagonizing her further. She studies me for a moment, before carrying on, "Are you something to do with *that*?" and she releases one hand to point across the street.

"Um," I swivel around to look in the direction of her pointy index finger and see a big white van pulling into the village square behind the stationary bus. It has Mobile Library signage written down one side. "Oh, no I'm not. But how lovely! I might pop in there to take a look after I've been in here," I say, gesturing to the inside of the bookshop, like a clue for her of my intentions. *Why won't she let me in?*

"Hmm, so who are you then?"

"I'm Sybil, but everyone calls me Sybs." She pulls a face, making me wonder if, like Hettie, she doesn't approve of my shortened version of a classic, if dull, and quite frankly old-fashioned name, but it's the best I can do within the limitations. "I'm here to see Adam," I say, using my extra-conciliatory voice, usually reserved for the more "challenging" clients at work. She stares at me. A short silence follows while she sizes me up.

"Well, you still can't bring the dog in!" And with that she marches off inside.

I'm trying to secure Basil's lead around the lamppost when a young girl from the pet parlor next door pops her head outside.

"You can leave him in here if you like. I'll look after him." She smiles kindly, folding her arms against the chilly afternoon air.

"Oh, if you're sure. That would be great. Thanks so much," I say, walking Basil over to her, figuring it will be all right. Everything's so different here.

"Of course. He's so cute. And look at his gorge little coat," she laughs, reaching her very impressive Santa airbrush-manicured hands down to scoop him up. Basil, immediately sensing another opportunity to preen, just like he did on the train with Dolly, rests his chin on the girl's shoulder, making her go, "awwwww" before trying to nibble her shiny gold Christmas-present-shaped dangly earring. "You can't leave him outside in this freezing cold weather, no matter what that old cow from next door says." She rolls her eyes and I stifle a snigger as she then does a quick furtive glance to check that Mrs. Pocket can't actually hear her. "I saw her telling you off from the window, and I know how that feels 'cos I was always getting told off by her at school. She hated me—gave me detention once just for writing Robbie on the blackboard, you know, as in Robbie Williams." She shrugs and fiddles with one of the six loom bands on her left wrist.

"Oh dear," I say diplomatically.

"What's his name?" She gestures to Basil.

"Basil."

"Like Basil Brush, *boom boom!*" I smile, and a woman's voice shouts out from inside the pet parlor.

"Taylor, can you come here and give me a hand please, love?"

"Oops, better go, that's my mum, she'll be wanting me to sit on the reception desk and answer the phone while she finishes off Petula." I lift my eyebrows. "The Afghan," Taylor clarifies. "See you later."

"Yes, see you later. I won't be long. And thank you sooo much," I grin, giving Basil a little tickle under his chin. "Be good now," I say to him.

I walk up to the entrance of Tindledale Books and I'm just about to push open the door, when a hand appears on the other side of the small square of glass, swiftly flicking the *Open* sign over, so it now says *Closed*.

But hang on! So, after all that palaver, I now can't even go inside. Well, we'll see about that. Feeling bold, and a bit ticked off, I try the door anyway, and it opens so I

159

quickly step inside. Ha! I'm in now, and isn't the rule that once you're inside a shop, there's an obligatory bit of time left still to buy stuff before they close, or at least that's what they say over the Tannoy in the Tesco Metro just off Lewisham High Road. And I should know, I've run in there many a time to grab a bottle of pink wine on my way home from work to console myself with while knitting in front of the TV.

"What the hell do you think you're doing? We're closed. I'm locking up now," a gruff man's voice says from behind a red Neoprene balaclava. He's wearing a black leather biker jacket with tight, knee-padded leather jeans and has a shiny white crash helmet under his left arm.

"Hi, I'm Sybs," I say, grinning pleasantly and sticking my hand out, figuring it best to break the ice right away in case he thinks I'm here to rob his rare, but very valuable book collection. Hardly, but the way he's carrying on . . .

"Syb?" he repeats, with extra emphasis on the *b*, like my name is some kind of weird disease that he's never even heard of.

"Sybs, with an *s*," I press on. "From the train, remember?" I add brightly, reckoning his mind must have just gone blank, seeing as he's clearly in a massive hurry to leave.

"The train?" he huffs.

"Last night, you left a . . ." I pause, not wanting to say

160

"flirty" given his current mood, and desperately trying to ignore the swell of uncertainty that's building in the bottom of my stomach. Oh God, maybe it wasn't him after all. Maybe it was a prank, a silly joke. Gripping the strap of my bag tighter over my shoulder, I carry on, just wanting to get the conversation over with now. This is so awkward. "Um, that's right, you left a lovely message on a newspaper for me," I mutter very quickly, wishing I had brought the paper with me now to show him, to point out that the phone number given with the message saying "give me a try" is for his actual bookshop, so he doesn't think I'm some kind of fruit loop—that it's a perfectly sane conclusion to come to—that he was the one who wrote the message.

"A what?" he snorts, placing a gloved hand on the frame of the door, as if going to hustle me out of his shop. "What are you going on about? Is this some kind of a joke? Did Rachel send you here to wind me up? Because if she did then you can tell her from me that it's not funny." He's practically shouting now. "And you can also tell her from me that I will never give up fighting for proper access—she won't wear me down." His green eyes are flashing now, bearing no resemblance at all to the sparkly kind-looking ones that I saw on the train last night.

"I, um, I er . . ." I splutter, like an actual, proper idiot.

"You should be ashamed of yourself, coming here all

161

dolled up and trying it on with me. What are you? Some kind of a private eye? Or, oh I get it. Ha!" He nods his head slowly as if the penny has just dropped and he's worked it all out. "You're one of those honeytrappers and you reckon you can seduce me into a compromising position—I bet you've got an accomplice hiding somewhere with a long-lens camera to take pictures for Rachel to blackmail me with?" And he does an exaggerated, almost absurdly comedic (in any other circumstance), left-then-right swivel of his head to see up and down the street behind me. "Well, I've got news for you sweetheart; you're not my type." And I can see his Adam's apple bobbing up and down furiously as he attempts to choke down his anger. "Now clear off before I call my lawyer. You're a disgrace. And quite clearly desperate." And he actually grabs the hood of my parka as if to physically throw me out.

Saving him the bother, I immediately yank myself free, turn sharply and run as fast as I can.

And keep running.

I can't get away from his bookshop and Tindledale High Street quickly enough. My heart is pounding so hard it's making my chest ache and I can hear the sound of blood pumping in my ears as tears spill onto my cheeks.

I've just made it to the war memorial when the spur of the left Dolly boot catches on something and I'm

162

propelled forward. I end up face-planting in the snow. Thank God it's the middle of winter and it's already dark so nobody can see me—the stupid, ridiculous, and quite clearly desperate stranger from London who is obviously going to end up ancient and decrepit and all alone with just her knitting and a trembly old dog to keep her company. And it won't be Basil, my lovely, loyal companion, oh no, because he'll be long dead by then. Oh God. I squeeze my hands into fists and will myself to get a grip, but the feeling of disappointment, rejection and humiliation, all over again, just like that day in the church, is indescribable. Crushing is the best I can come up with. I just want to curl up and howl and then die right here in the snow, with my burning, pathetic, *desperate* cheeks mere centimeters away from Kitty's sad candle and holly wreath memorial.

But I can't. I have to get up. I have to walk. I have to carry on.

And what am I going to say to Lawrence? He's bound to ask how my trip to Tindledale Books went, to see the elusive, mysterious, and now, as is extremely evident, rude, dismissive, aggressive, belligerent, misogynistic—and I'd even go as far as adding in a wanker and a dickhead—newcomer, that is Adam!

I eventually make it back to the B&B after walking and half running and stumbling all the way from the High Street in the thick snow. I couldn't face taking the bus and risking everyone staring at the "girl from London with tears in her eyes and rivulets of mascara all down her face."

Thankfully the reception area is empty and Lawrence takes one look in my direction before flying out from behind the counter. He throws his arms around my shoulders and hugs me tight, almost winding me in the process. His kindness makes my chest heave and tears spill down my face all over again. I just cry. A full-on meltdown. Bawling until I'm exhausted and the heaving subsides into a whimpering tremble.

"Hush, it's OK." Lawrence rubs my back with the flat of his palm.

"I'm so sorry," I say in a quivery voice, pulling back and feeling stupid—it's not like it's the first time I've made a fool of myself after being rejected, but I haven't cried like this in years, not since Jingle my basset hound died—I didn't even cry like this after the "wedding that wasn't," but perhaps that's the whole problem: I've kept everything crammed inside me, tried to put a brave face on, just like I always do. Jingle was my first dog—Dad got her for me from the dog shelter and I had wanted a dog of my own for so long, but she got run over by a speeding 4x4 after Sasha left the front door open when she was in a hurry to be first in the queue for the ice-cream van. "Your cardigan, I've ruined it."

"What, this old rag? Meh!" Lawrence throws his hands up in the air dismissively. "A good dry clean is all it'll need," he adds, generously, especially as I can see a streak of smoky eye shadow daubed right across one shoulder. "Come on into the warm, you're shivering."

And then I realize.

"Basil! Oh my God, I've left Basil behind," I yell, and a fresh wave of panic flies through me. And another torrent of tears pours down my cheeks. I immediately turn to leave and run back up to the High Street.

"Hey, hang on!" Lawrence stops me by grabbing my hand. "OK. Now take a deep breath and calm down. Tell me where you left him." I do as I'm told. "Right. I'll call the pet parlor and sort it out. Don't worry; he'll be fine there. Trust me, Taylor adores dogs, she'll not let anything happen to him." He smiles kindly.

"But they'll probably be closed by now, and then what will they think of me?" I babble, remembering that *Closed* sign appearing in the bookshop window. I should have known better. I should have just left there and then, instead of hanging around like a spare part, just like I did as a bride at the altar! The feeling lingers.

Taking my hand, Lawrence walks me around behind the counter and through the velvet curtain to a drawing room. There's an enormous floor-to-ceiling Christmas tree in the bay window, covered in twinkling fairy lights and sparkly baubles, and there's a big squishy-looking sofa in front of an open log fire that smells all woody and comforting. He steers me toward the sofa and gently pushes me down before lifting up my left foot and easing the Dolly boot off. He repeats the process with the other leg and then after helping me out of my parka, slipping off my mittens and unraveling the Kermit green scarf from my neck, he smooths a soft cream cashmere blanket over my knees.

"Now, wait here. I'll be back in five minutes. Promise." And true to his word, Lawrence darts off to call the pet parlor, returning exactly five minutes later, according to the dark wood grandfather clock standing in the corner, the pendulum of which ticked off the seconds precisely.

"OK. It's fine," Lawrence says on his return. "Amber, she's Taylor's mum, wasn't fazed at all, said it happens all the time; people get distracted or delayed so their pooches spend a bit of time in the doggy-day-care section, in other words, their cozy cottage kitchen with the furnace-like Rayburn and the battered old sofa to curl up on. Apparently, that's where Basil is right now, next to Taylor; they're watching that Christmas film, *Elf*, together, on her laptop. Amber said you can collect him anytime, just press the bell when you get there, really hard, because it sticks sometimes and doesn't always ring. And she also said that she's sure Taylor would be delighted to have him snuggle on her bed if you wanted to leave it until tomorrow to pick him up." I manage a feeble half-smile.

"Thank you," I say, feeling slightly relieved. "But I shouldn't leave him there all night; I'll collect him later," I add, panicking now at the prospect of venturing back into the village. I dread to think how many people witnessed my embarrassing scene earlier by the war memorial.

"I can always collect Basil after tonight's rehearsal," Lawrence says, as if sensing my unease.

"Ah, thanks, but it's OK, you've done so much for me already. I'll go and fetch him." I grin bravely, figuring I'll just have to laugh it off if anyone mentions me lying in the snow in the middle of their village—they can think I'm the crazy woman from London who got overexcited, having probably never seen real snow before, just the dirty, dog-poop-streaked sludge usually found in suburban streets.

"Well, if you're sure." He pats my arm before throwing another log on the fire. "So, tell me what happened."

And I do.

When I pause to take a breather, having told him all about the hideous encounter with Adam, plus a bit more about my relationships with Sasha and Luke, May 4 and the whole *Star Wars* thing, right through to the situation at work with Jennifer Ford going AWOL after having frittered away £42,000 of taxpayers' money that I most likely just handed over to her, Lawrence hands me a tumbler.

"It's mulled wine, take a little sip." I hesitate and he gestures toward the glass adding, "It tastes delicious—sweet and sharp like a liquid blackberry crumble." Doing as I'm told, I let the flavor linger on my tongue and it tastes cinnamony too and feels warm in my throat, radiating down my arms and through into my stomach. I can feel my body starting to relax. Inhaling sharply and then exhaling long and hard, it's like the Nurek Dam has just burst inside me.

There's a long silence while Lawrence looks at me and

I'm sure I spot the glisten of a tear at the corner of his left eye. He pushes a finger in behind the lens of his glasses.

"Damn lashes. You know, I have to be very careful with them, but it's so much easier than keeping taking them off just to put them back on again for the next dress rehearsals. Top it off?" He jumps up and grabs a jug from the Art Deco–style sideboard and I must be mistaken; probably a speck of log dust from the fire has caught in his eye.

"Um, no thank you. This is enough," I say, taking another mouthful of the delicious mulled wine. I don't want to end up getting plastered and quite possibly making an even bigger fool of myself by going all maudlin and Miss Havisham on him. Lawrence places the jug back down, picks up a bottle of vodka and quickly mixes himself a martini. Using a cocktail stick, he plucks a stuffed olive from a jar and pops it into his glass before joining me back over on the sofa. "I'm so sorry. I shouldn't offload on you like this." I avert my eyes toward the fireplace.

"Listen Sybs, would you mind if I gave you some advice?" He swivels his body to face me square on.

"Er, sure, go on," I reply overbrightly but feeling uneasy inside. He takes hold of my hand and gives it a little squeeze.

"If there are things in your life that aren't working well for you—that are making you sad—well, then you must find a way to be brave and deal with them; action is always better than inaction, I find." He pauses, and an ominous silence follows while I wonder if I should call Gina at work, face my demons and find out what's going on, instead of just wallowing in self-pity and oblivion. It's not going to change the outcome, I know that now, and I feel like a coward, running away again, just like I did on that day in the church: that's not how grown-up, confident, thirty-something women carry on when faced with a challenging situation at work. Lawrence finishes his drink and bites the olive from the stick. I take another mouthful of the mulled wine, pondering some more on what he's just said.

"I wish it were that easy, Lawrence." I feel dim, as if there's a key to it all out there that everyone else knows about apart from me, but I can't just flick on a happy switch when most of the time my heart feels as if it's shattering all over again. And I've even started getting physical pains, like someone is piling up bricks on my chest, one on top of the other, to squeeze the air right out of my body. Every time it happens, it makes me feel panicky and I can't breathe.

"In that case it's just not bad enough," he says kindly, but firmly.

"What do you mean?"

"Oh, my dear, where do I start?" He pulls out a silver-embossed cigarillo case from his cardigan pocket and lights one up before walking over to a window and opening it an inch or so; the breeze of cold, crisp air is refreshing against my tear-stained, flushed cheeks. I finish my mulled wine and Lawrence takes a couple more puffs before carrying on. "OK, here's an example." He makes a circle in the air with his cigarillo. "Me, growing up in a New Jersey suburb, an effeminate little Jewish boy with a passion for 'prancing about on stage.'" He pauses to do sarcastic quote signs with his fingers. "And all this, living amongst a community of Mafia wannabes hollering to all and sundry to 'keep off their lawns. *Or else.*'" He rolls his eyes upward. "Think homemade prison tatts . . . *on their faces.* Teardrops. The works." He pulls a mock-scared face before puffing some more on his cigarillo. "Tough, yeah?" he adds, his American accent getting stronger as he gets fired up. I nod. "But I had good, resilient, Jewish parents who loved me and who had witnessed and experienced firsthand how prejudice can persecute humanity and scar one's soul. They were survivors, immigrants from Berlin, strong. So one afternoon when I got home after school with yet another bloody nose, trashed shirt and sneakers stolen at the hands of the playground bullies, my parents were there waiting for me. My mother stood in front of me in her apron, hands on hips and looked me straight in the eye. She asked me if it was bad. I nodded, and she asked me a second time, and I nodded, and then she said, "But is it bad enough, Lawrence, is it bad enough?" And you know what? I nodded and told her, "Yes, it's bad enough." And she said to me right there and then, "So you change it." The following day we left. Everything, not that we had very much, suitcases, boxes . . . all of it was loaded into a U-Haul trailer and we went and lived with Dad's sister, my aunt Hana, over in Manhattan. You know, Mom had been asking me that question every single day since I'd started at that hateful school a whole year earlier."

He takes a few more puffs of his cigarillo before throwing another log on the fire, his eyes flicking to me and away again.

"Oh, Lawrence, I'm so sorry!" I wish I'd managed to contain myself now. My self-pity feels pathetic compared to what his family must have endured all those years ago. I should have kept my mouth shut. Kept my battered, broken heart to myself.

"Don't be, I'm not telling you this to make you feel sorry for me, quite the opposite. You see, what happened had happened, and I learnt right there and then, standing in the kitchen in front of my mother, that we can't change the past—but we can choose not to let our past experiences define our future ones. When you get to the point of 'enough is enough' then you'll know—and that's when you'll let go of the past. And that's when the fun starts." A naughty smile dances on his lips. "A whole new future to be excited about. You'll see—you can live whatever life you want to live. Be and do whatever you want. Reach for the stars. Heal your heart and achieve your dreams—when you free yourself to feel the passion for life and look forward instead of backward." He laughs and nods firmly to emphasize his point.

Another silence follows, broken only by the crackle and wheeze of the logs in the fire. I look over at him, letting my eyes reach his, and I take a deep breath.

"Lawrence, I think I've reached that point," I say, my voice all wobbly and my heart clamoring so hard it feels as if it might burst right out of my chest to race across the room and set a new world 100-meter sprint record. And Luke, Sasha, Mum, the wedding that wasn't—it's all swirling around inside my head, but I'm the common denominator, I know that, so I'm the one who has to make the effort if I want to stop living in the past and move forward. I remember Nana telling me once that if you don't plan your own life then someone else will plan it for you, and that's what I've allowed to happen, in a way, by not taking control, by shying away and letting things happen instead of facing them head-on. I did it with Luke. I knew things weren't right before the wedding; in fact, long before the wedding things had changed between us, I should never have agreed to marry him, but I did. I compromised and went along with it, got swept up in the excitement of the proposal, the ring, the feeling of fitting in, being normal, of having achieved a significant life event like all of my friends, of being partnered up and happy. Or so it seemed. Or was it fear? Fear of reaching forty and being on my own, while everyone else was settled down with babies? It's ridiculous, the pressure, the expectations, and I got sucked into it all.

Well, no more. I'm going to take control of my life, I don't want Mum feeling sorry for me with her "beggars can't be choosers" lines, and then trying to fix me up with men like Ian. I want to feel happy, do what I want and be amazing just the way I am.

"Good, because you know what." Lawrence looks at me. "It was the best thing ever, us moving to Manhattan. My father staged his first play just off Broadway and it's where I first got to touch and feel my dream. Stand on a stage and perform," he says, proudly. "Now, Sybs, can you feel your passion? What is *your* dream?"

He winks at me as I push the blanket off my knees to join him over by the window. I know what my dreams are and they're full of knitting and needlecraft and quilting and being my own boss and moving on from the past. I've known for years the things I want to do and be, but somehow it all seems to have got muddled up and lost on that day in the church when Luke Skywalker went off on a very different kind of walk. And my sister betrayed me, broke my heart and stole something I had, that I thought was mine, yet again, and just like she always had, but toys, clothes, shoes, makeup are nothing in comparison to a fiancé, a husband-to-be, and she knew how much I believed I loved Luke. But I can't change any of that now. Lawrence is right—what's happened has happened, and it made me feel sad for a while and, truth be told, I'll probably always have a little pocket of sadness in my heart whenever I think of Luke and what might have been before he lost interest and we drifted apart. And me have no idea if things will ever be OK between Sasha and me again. Not that we've ever been particularly close, but there was always a link, the bond that comes from being sisters. I give Lawrence a hug and swallow hard before telling him my dream, saying the words out loud.

After flicking the last of his cigarillo into the fire, Lawrence squeezes my shoulders.

"Wonderful. So your new life begins right now!" he says, stretching a theatrical hand out high and wide, like he's back on Broadway and the curtain has just gone up. Fixing his eyes on mine, he raises an eyebrow and I think I might cry again. Just telling him, letting the words out and sharing them with someone else, those things that have been buried deep in my battered and bruised heart for months and months . . . well, the relief is overwhelming. "But first, I'm phoning the doctor's office to see if we can get you an emergency appointment with Dr. Darcy. You need to sleep, and he's the man to make that happen. You know, he does hypnotherapy, homeopathy and lots of other holistic therapies too, so I'm sure he's bound to have something that will help grace you with some much-needed sleep! You can't start a new life when you're running on empty." Lawrence shakes his head. "Why don't you go up to your room and have a little lie down? I'll slip a note under the door with your appointment time on, and that way I'll not disturb you if you do actually manage to get some sleep." He smiles reassuringly.

*

Back in my room, I sit in the armchair by the window and pull out my knitting, figuring I might as well make a start on the mittens, as it could well be a very, very long night. I have to give at least a week's notice to get anywhere near an appointment at my doctor's office, so I'm not holding out on getting to see Dr. Darcy anytime soon. Taking the crimson yarn, I cast on, quickly getting into the familiar rhythm of knit one purl one, knit one purl one, knit one purl one; soothing and calming, it sweeps all the awfulness of that encounter with Adam away. I keep knitting until a folded piece of white paper slides under the door. I put my knitting down and pad across the room to retrieve the message.

Sybs,
Your appointment is at 6:30 p.m. Dr. Darcy said no problem at all about fitting you in at the end of his office hours and if you don't mind hanging around for a bit, I can drop you off there on my way up to the village hall for tonight's rehearsal.
Meet you in reception around 6:15ish.
Lawrence x

Hmm, clearly I was wrong to be so cynical; seems you can actually see a village doctor at a moment's notice, how very modern, which is a complete contradiction given that Tindledale doesn't even have proper mobile phone coverage . . .

"He won't be long. Doctor is just finishing up with his last patient," a matronly-looking woman sitting behind the reception desk says, after I check in at the doctor's office. I push the pump underneath the bottle of antibacterial hand cleanser, mounted on the wall beside the touch-screen computerized appointment system. "Ooh, you're good! Most people don't bother doing that, and then complain when they catch a cold after coming in here with some totally unrelated ailment." The receptionist shakes her head and hands me a form and a black pen. "I've already filled in your name at the top, but if you can pop your details on as well, please— home address, phone number, that kind of thing, the B&B address as well—we have to know where you're staying, for the EU thingamajigs." She does a tinkly laugh before patting her perm and waving a hand in the air. "And your own GP's details and any medical conditions

178

the doctor will need to know about. Oh, and if you're taking any medication. Here, you might find it easier to lean on this." She hands me an old edition of *Country Life* magazine—it has a picture of a shiny black Labrador on the front and is dated June 2002. It throws me slightly, her being so helpful and kind, in complete contrast to the hostile hag who polices the office of my doctor in London. Last time I called to renew the prescription of my sleeping tablets, the receptionist was so indignant anyone would think that I had asked for a kilo of cocaine to be couriered round to my flat, immediately, free of charge, and by one of her very small children.

"Thank you," I smile, when she draws breath, and I start filling in the form. I've just finished, when a red light buzzes on the wall.

"Ah, there you go. Dr. Darcy will see you now. Down the corridor, turn left and look for the door that says Doctor B. Darcy." She smiles nicely and I so want to say, "I never would have guessed that for myself," but I don't, of course. Instead, I hand her the form and say,

"Thanks so much for your help."

"You're very welcome." She pauses to scan the top of my form, "Sybil! Oh, that was my mother's name; how lovely," she beams before picking up a mug with *Best Granny Ever* inscribed on the side.

179

I find the door and, after pausing for a second to whip my parka and scarf off to loop over my arm, I tap the door before pushing it open. Inside—and Dr. Darcy isn't here. There's a big mahogany desk by the window, with a computer screen shoved to the far corner, as if in disgrace—it's facing away from the chair, so he's obviously not a fan of technology, presumably preferring an old-school, traditional country doctor approach, because the rest of the desk space is a jumble of papers, pens, empty specimen pots, a stethoscope, one of those ear light things, a blood pressure kit and an open book with the pages facing down and BNF printed on the front cover. The floor is covered with files—cream-colored folders that, I assume, contain the medical details of every single Tindledale villager, the deceased ones too, because there are so many stacked up, practically covering every inch of floor space.

I sit down in a chair near the desk, guessing it's where patients are supposed to sit, but it's hard to tell, as there are several chairs dotted around the room. I'm just about to move to another chair, one that's a bit closer to the desk, with my bag, parka and scarf clutched in my arms—I'm doing a kind of daft duck waddle so as not to drop all my stuff—when another door flings open and a tall, athletically built man in jeans and a checked shirt backs sideways into the room with his arms full of files

180

and bumps right into me. My nose is eye-level with his bottom as I wobble and sling out a hand to steady myself, but it's no use, and I end up toppling sideways onto the floor, landing in a heap with the fur-trimmed hood of my parka stuffed in my face. Oh God. I quickly fling the coat off and attempt to scrabble back up into a standing position, but it's hopeless as the Dolly boots keep slip-sliding all over the place on the cream folders which have suddenly transformed into slippery little fuckers against the super shiny tiled floor.

"Ah, for fecks sake! Oh, I'm sorry, I, um . . ." The man quickly dumps the files on the nearest chair. "Jesus, here, let me help you up—I'm so sorry," a deep, lilting and very lovely Irish voice says, followed by a solid-looking hand that reaches down to help me. After grabbing it like a lifebuoy, I glance up.

And that's when I see his face.

Dark curly hair, emerald-green eyes behind black-framed glasses, stubbly chin . . . It's him. The man from the train. And he's not that shouty Adam from the book-shop at all! And he's certainly not the old, traditional, country doctor in a tweedy suit that I had in mind. No, he most definitely isn't. He's young. And he's hot. Fit, in fact, in a big, teddy bear kind of a way. And I don't know whether to cringe or laugh like a looper.

"I'm Dr. Darcy. And I really am so very sorry." He helps

me back to a standing position before pushing a hand through his messy hair.

"And I'm Sybs! But I guess you already know that," I say, picking a stray strand of faux fur from my tongue as I will my cheeks to stop flaming red like a pair of plum tomatoes.

It turns out that Dr. Darcy's first name is Ben. Short for, and get this, Benedict, as in Cumberbatch! For real—I spied it on one of his medical certificates hanging in a frame on the wall behind his desk. And he graduated as a doctor from Trinity College in Dublin in 2002, so I reckon he must be in his late thirties at least, given that it takes years and years at university to learn to be a doctor, then there's the GP training. And he's now sitting opposite me with a very concerned look on his beautiful face.

"I must apologize again. The office is about to have an overhaul, which is why we're sorting out these files." He gestures to the jumbled heap of paperwork strewn all over the floor. "We're in the process of being computerized." And I'm sure I spot a glimmer of an eye roll behind the lenses of his glasses. No wonder the computer has been pushed away in disgust. He's clearly not a fan of technology at all.

"Oh, I see." I do a half-smile and nod politely.

"Are you sure you're OK?" His forehead furrows. I nod again, gathering my parka, scarf and bag into me like some kind of comfort blanket because he may be very lovely looking, and quite unassuming, and seemingly completely unlike Jane Austen's dastardly Darcy—no, that's more Adam's style—but that doesn't change the fact that he's the doctor and well, there must be some kind of protocol that rules against having the hots for your GP. Plus, not forgetting, the message he left on the newspaper. Because why would he deliberately want to make a fool of me? And to be honest, I've had just about enough of men doing that recently. I cross my arms around the bundle of stuff piled up on my lap.

"Yes, I'm fine," I mumble, unable to make proper eye contact.

"Are you sure?" he says, sounding concerned. "You didn't hit your head on the floor did you?" The furrow deepens.

"Oh, no, I'm sure I didn't. My coat kind of saved me," I say, quickly extracting the fur-trimmed hood from my clutch and waggling it in the air as some kind of proof of its crash-prevention qualities. There's an ominous silence.

"Only you seem a bit distant." He picks up a pen and appears to study it, rolling it between his thumb and index finger. *Is he nervous? I'm not sure.*

"Well, that's probably because I haven't slept properly in ages. It's why I'm here, actually," I begin, instantly wondering why I don't just ask him about the message, but he hasn't mentioned it so maybe it's best that I don't, especially after what happened the last time I did over at the bookshop—or perhaps there's a protocol about that kind of thing too, like, doctors shouldn't leave flirty, misleading messages on newspapers for total strangers! I will myself to get a grip and calm down, but it's not easy, especially after what Adam said earlier. Desperate! And despite Lawrence's pep talk, which did help enormously, that ugly word is still swirling round and round inside my head. I momentarily squeeze my eyes tight shut as if to banish the dark thoughts, because I can hardly whip out my knitting in here and do a few rows now, can I?

"I forgot to bring my sleeping pills with me," I say, "so if you can let me have a couple just to tide me over until I get home on Sunday . . ." I stop talking as he's leaning forward now, even closer to me with his elbows resting on his knees, scrutinizing me almost. I lean back, and plaster what I hope is a laid-back and very "undesperate" look on my face.

"Oh, I see," he pauses and if I'm not mistaken, I think there's a hint of disappointment in his voice, "and can you tell me why you're having difficulty sleeping?" He clears his throat and starts shuffling stuff around his desk. How strange; all the doctors I've ever met have seemed far more self-assured than he appears to be.

"I'd rather not," I reply, not wanting to go into all that again, and certainly not with him, that would just be too awkward, but then I quickly add, "If you don't mind." He is a doctor after all, even if he does seem a bit untypical. And I guess I have more in common with my mother than I ever realized—she's very reverent when it comes to "professionals," and almost fainted from sheer ecstasy when Mr. Manningtree, the heart surgeon, moved into the "big house' behind ours. I remember getting home from school one time just as he came flying across our shared gravel driveway with wild eyes, his waxy Barbour jacket flapping around in the wind, swinging a shotgun under his arm and performing a dramatic lock-and-load action. Sasha and I were rooted to the spot behind the water feature underneath the Victoriana lamp-post while Mr. Manningtree hunted for the fox that had ruined his lawn. And Mum had just swooned and proclaimed that we must excuse his eccentricities for the greater good as there are "people all over the world with beating hearts and it's all thanks to Mr Manningtree." Hmm, on second thought, maybe Dr. Darcy isn't so untypical after all. Maybe it's a prerequisite these days for doctors to be a bit alternative: less stuffy, and more casual—I mean, he's wearing faded jeans, a washed-out Fat Face sweatshirt and trainers, nice ones, but still . . .

"Oh, I see. Um, well, in that case it's a bit tricky." *Tricky?*

What does he mean, tricky? I've never heard a doctor talk like this before, not even on *Casualty* or *ER*, and they're pure fiction.

"Oh," I mumble, unsure of what else to say.

"I can't really—" He stops abruptly when there's a knock on the door.

"Sorry, Doctor, I forgot to give you Sybil's paperwork." The receptionist darts into the room and quickly hands Dr. Darcy my form.

"Thanks, Pam," he smiles (a very nice smile indeed). And she backs out reverently, closing the door discreetly behind her. Dr. Darcy studies my details before glancing back up at me.

"So, Sybil, how long have you been taking the sleeping tablets for?" he asks, sounding more professional now.

"About six months."

"I see. And how do they make you feel?"

"Sleepy?" I venture, attempting a joke, and he definitely gets it as his mouth curls at the corners, almost into a smile.

"And do they help you to sleep right through the night?"

"Um, not always," I say, wishing he'd just give me the pills. Two tablets, that's all I need. And my own doctor has already prescribed them so I don't see why he's grilling me. Surely he can just call my GP to check, or brace himself to tackle the computer to access my NHS records and then give me a prescription. I spotted a chemist in the High Street, so I'll shoot straight over there and everything will be fine for a good night's sleep tonight, with a bit of luck."

"I see. And what about during the day?"

"Well, I don't sleep during the day, if that's what you mean." I grin, but he seems to be engrossed in my paperwork now.

"Sure," he says patiently, not looking up. "But how do you feel during the day?"

"Bored mostly." And he does a surreptitious laugh, attempting to hide it behind his hand, but I spot it nonetheless. "Not at the moment, obviously, I mean being here in Tindledale is brilliant, and everyone is so lovely and friendly. Well, nearly everyone . . ." My voice trails off as I think of Hettie's awful nephew, and bossy Mrs. Pocket, and Dr. Darcy could be best friends with Adam for all I know, but he doesn't react.

"But in general, when you're at work." He pauses to scan the form. "Lewisham council—what do you do there?" He glances at me, blinks behind his glasses and I manage to make eye contact. He really does have the most amazing emerald-green eyes, nestling in long, velvety dark lashes. I take a deep breath and look away to concentrate on the pattern of my patchwork handbag instead.

188

"Oh, I'm a housing officer." I wish I hadn't come here now, it's clear that he isn't going to give me the pills, and I feel ridiculous, sitting here, fidgeting like a bashful schoolgirl, barely able to look him in the eye.

"But? I sense there's something else?" He raises his eyebrows and I cough to clear my throat, shifting in my seat. There's another short silence.

"Well, there is something. Quite a few things, actually." I fiddle with the tassels on my scarf, figuring it best to say something as he's clearly not going to stop with the interrogation unless I do.

"Go on," he says, nodding encouragingly and staring right at me now.

"I've made some mistakes, taken my eye off the ball as it were." I shrug sheepishly, really wishing he wouldn't look at me that way, as if analyzing, I know it's his job and all that, but still . . . And why is it so hot in here? I tug at the neckline of my Ho Ho Ho sweater—I put it on before I came out as it's perishing cold this evening, and I have my own jeans on too, after Lawrence kindly tumble-dried them while I was down at Hettie's. It might even be below zero degrees already outside and it's snowing hard. I glance at the window and see that it's a sheet of fuzzy white fluff.

"Would you say this is due to lack of concentration?"

"Oh definitely—and dark thoughts, I get them a lot of

189

the time because I feel so fed up," I tell him, remembering how hard it is to feel motivated at work, and I know I could so easily have added those zeroes on to Jennifer Ford's benefit payment. I really enjoyed today with Hettie—life would be so much better if I could do that every day—and I didn't make any mistakes at the House of Haberdashery. Then I realize: I didn't feel tired either, that fuggy feeling I've had for months now wasn't there and I felt alive, alert, interested for a change. "It's like I'm sleepwalking through my own life when I'm at work." I concentrate on the snow, swirling all around right outside the office window. I can see the twinkling lights of the High Street too, which reminds me, I must go and pick up Basil before it gets late. I mustn't take advantage of Lawrence's hospitality. He's already babysat me enough this weekend.

"Hmm, I've seen this a few times with these particular sleeping pills: mild to moderate depression. A mind fog, or wading through treacle, is how some of my other patients describe it."

"Oh, I see," I say, my heart sinking at the prospect of another sleepless night, as it's obvious he isn't giving me the prescription.

"It could explain the problems you're having at work too, if you're experiencing side effects of this kind; you might find they lessen if you stop taking the sleeping tablets and that, in turn, might make you feel . . ." he picks his words carefully, "more relaxed, which will help you to sleep." It's his turn to glance away now. "There really are some alternative treatments that help," he quickly adds. "I've had remarkable results with hypnotherapy—it's very good in treating the cause of the insomnia." Oh no, I can't sit here in a trance and tell him all about being jilted, he'll just think I'm some kind of freak. "How long are you here for?" he smiles.

"Only until Sunday," I say, sighing inwardly with relief at having the perfect excuse to not have to do a tell-all with him, but there's disappointment too, at having to return to my dull, nondescript life.

"I see, well that's a shame. Sometimes a break, a proper rest, really helps. I could sign you off work for a week or so? You may find it'll help get your mojo back, rather than continuing with the sleeping pills. They do have a tendency to mask the real problem." He starts riffling through the clutter on his desk. "Can't you stay longer?" he then adds, sounding disappointed, and then actually looks a bit flustered, as if he's overstepped some kind of imaginary line.

"I'd love to, but . . ."

Silence follows.

"Ah, here it is." He plucks a leather-strapped watch from inside a brochure about breastfeeding and holds it up in the air, "Jesus, is that the time already? Nearly seven, so there's no point me giving you a prescription even if I wanted to—which I don't, for the record—the chemist is closed now." He sweeps a hand through his thick curls, stops talking and buckles the watch around his wrist, seemingly engrossed and perhaps relieved at having a task to occupy himself with, but I can't be sure.

"OK, well, um, er, thanks anyway." I stand up and pull on my parka. A night of knitting it is, then. I've just reached the door when he coughs as if to clear his throat.

"But there is another option, something else. Something I probably shouldn't recommend at all," Dr. Darcy says too quickly, as if he needs to get the words out before I leave and he misses his chance, or he changes his mind, maybe . . . perhaps. I can't really tell for sure; my flirtometer gauge seems to be completely askew.

"What's that then?" I say over my shoulder, and he's standing up now with one hand pushed into his jeans pocket and the other batting his curls away from his face.

"Brandy!"

"Brandy?" I blink.

"Um, yes. That's right. Er, purely for medicinal purposes," he adds, pushing his glasses farther up his nose and averting his eyes. He *is* nervous! Oh my God. And it's very endearing. And appealing. My plum tomato cheeks make a rapid return.

192

"OKaaaaay," I say slowly, smiling and thinking this is very unorthodox for a doctor.

"My old Irish granny swears by it." And he actually grins, his shoulders visibly relaxing as he places both hands on his hips in a much more confident stance, like he's getting into his stride now. "What do you say to a quick drink in the pub? On me! Um, well, what I really mean is, *with* me. If you'd like to . . ." And he quickly busies himself by trying to pull his duffel coat off the coat stand, but it gets tangled and ends up toppling over—he rescues it just in time, "to apologize for knocking you over earlier. I really am very sorry about that. Just so you know, I don't make a habit of flooring my patients. Honestly, I really don't." And I get the feeling that this is also his way of saying he doesn't ask all his patients to join him in the pub either, after office hours. "And I'll try really hard not to knock anything over." He shakes his head, gesturing to the coat stand. I look him in the eye; and that fluttery flattering feeling on first seeing the message in Lawrence's breakfast room makes a rapid return.

"Well, if your old Irish granny swears by it," I lift my eyebrows, "then how can I refuse?" And his smile widens. I smile too, figuring it'll also be a very good opportunity to ask about the newspaper message, because something I have learned from the fiasco that

193

was my last relationship is that it is far better to tackle things head-on, rather than ignore them and hope they'll go away. If I had done that, then I wouldn't have floated all the way to the altar on a cloud of oblivion. Besides, this is intriguing, and now that I've met Dr. Darcy he really doesn't seem like the type of man that goes around leaving flirty messages for strangers on trains just for belly laughs.

"Grand." He finally manages to extrapolate his coat from the hook on the coat stand and pushes his arms into the sleeves.

"Oh, but I must collect my dog first."

"Is that Basil? The one who tried to swipe my muffin?" he laughs.

"Um, yes, that's the one. Sorry again about that." I roll my eyes and shrug, thinking, *ahh, so he does remember our meeting on the train.*

"Where is he?" he asks.

"At the pet parlor in the High Street."

"Well, that's on the way so I can come with you, if you like . . ." he pauses, and the apparent nervousness from earlier momentarily returns ". . . to pick him up," he clarifies.

"Sure, that would be great," I say, feeling equally nervous, but rather excited too.

With Basil bouncing along in front of us, we walk past the village hall where the pantomime rehearsal is obviously in full swing. A hearty rendition of "We Wish You a Merry Christmas" is belting out and they've just got to the figgy pudding part as we pass Ruby's shop and head along the High Street.

"So, what brings you to Tindledale?" Dr. Darcy asks, still sounding like a doctor, and not a man who's just asked me out for a drink. Hmm, maybe he'll relax when we get to the pub.

"I came to see Cher, the new pub landlady—we're old friends. But I'm surprised you don't already know that," I laugh to lighten the mood as I glance at him sideways.

"Ah, yes, it can be a bit like that in the village." He looks at me and laughs too. "It took me awhile to get used to it when I first arrived in Tindledale to take over from old Dr. Donnelly when he retired."

"Was that very long ago?"

"Three years this Christmas, so I'm still very much considered a newcomer. I think you have to be here for at least fifty years before you can class yourself as a local." We both laugh some more.

"So what brought you to Tindledale?" I ask.

"Dr. Donnelly is my uncle, and I was looking for a fresh start, so it made sense . . ." His voice trails off and a short silence follows as we carry on walking side by side, kicking the snow up into little flurries as we go. I'm wondering if it's OK to ask why he wanted a fresh start, when he adds, "I had just been dumped. For a surgeon." His shoulders drop slightly.

"That's a shame. Sorry," I sympathize.

"Shit happens," he says by way of explanation, and then suddenly flips back to the start of our conversation. "But the villagers mean well, I find. They're very welcoming and friendly." He pats Basil's head as he body-slams into the side of his left leg before scampering off to bite more snow. "He's a live wire. How old is he?"

"Six!" I shrug, shaking my head. "So he really should know better, but I'm still training him."

"Well, maybe he's just a slow learner. Young at heart." He grins.

"Maybe. Or just a bit cheeky." I say, remembering the first time I met Basil. "He's been like it from the start.

196

He was in a huge crate with the rest of the litter, eight puppies in total, and I bent down intending to pet each of them in turn as I wasn't sure which one to go for, when a black bundle of fluff barged the other pups out of the way to get to my hand first."

"That's cute," Dr. Darcy says, giving Basil another stroke as he does a flyby circle of our legs before bouncing back off into the snow again.

"He wouldn't let the other puppies get a look-in, so I guess he chose me, in a way."

"Well, he has very good taste," Dr. Darcy says, making me glow as we reach the end of the High Street and walk onto the snow-covered village green, heading around the edge of the pond toward the Duck & Puddle pub. And it looks so pretty, the Christmas tree in the center, all twinkly and festive in the silent snowy night. I glance up at the star-studded black sky—this place is so perfect.

And suddenly, I can feel myself falling, skidding on a patch of black ice. Instinctively, Dr. Darcy grabs my hand and I manage to avoid ending up on my knees again in front of him.

"Are you OK?" he says, quickly pulling me up and in close.

"I think so. Thank you for catching me in time," I say, stepping back and brushing the snow from the front of my parka with my free hand. Basil darts over to see what's going on, and then hurries away again, when something rustling in the undergrowth catches his attention.

"The black ice can be lethal. Come on, let's get back onto the grass, we're almost there now." Dr. Darcy grips my hand a little tighter. And it feels nice, sort of warm and cozy and comforting. Strong and re-assuring too, trusty even. Well, he is a doctor after all. I smile to myself, thinking of that line, *trust me, I'm a doctor*, and Mum would probably faint with joy if she could see me now. Sauntering, hand in hand through a magical, romantic, olde-worlde village with a very appealing doctor; it's just like something from a rom-com film.

We reach the pub and I realize that we're still holding hands when I go to pick Basil up.

"Oh, um, sorry," Dr. Darcy says, gently letting my hand go.

"Don't be," I grin, but the moment fades as a rotund woman wearing a tartan blanket around her shoulders and a man's battered old Trilby hat on her head comes hurtling through the pub door with a pint of Guinness in one hand and a box of firelighters in the other.

"Got the last lot from the pub shop," she bellows, waggling the box in the air with glee, before downing her pint in one and burping. "Oops, sorry, doc, didn't see you there," she adds, giving him a sheepish look. "Only the one tonight." The woman pushes the empty glass toward Dr. Darcy by way of proof.

"I'm glad to hear it," he says diplomatically. The woman offloads the glass onto one of the wooden bench tables outside the pub and sways off up the lane, laughing and swearing to herself.

"One of your patients?" I smile at him over my shoulder as we go into the pub.

"How did you guess?" He shakes his head and glances heavenward.

And the minute we walk through the inner door, the villagers are on him. I've never seen anything like it. Anyone would think he was a celebrity, or a member of a boy band, or maybe a man band, because he's hardly a boy, but still, they're actually mobbing him. Well, shaking his hand and slapping him on the back at least. It's strange, but lovely too, in a crazy, old-fashioned way that the village doctor is so clearly revered.

"Dr. Ben!" a man wearing wellies and denim dungarees over a chunky cable-stitch sweater (hand-knitted) yells from the bar. "Over here. Let me get you a brandy? Least I can do. That cream you gave me has worked wonder."

"Sorry," Dr. Darcy mouths to me looking a bit

199

embarrassed as I settle Basil on the blanket by the blazing fire.

"You're very popular, I see." I pull off my coat and glance around the pub; it's packed. I do a quick fingers crossed in my head that none of the crowd mentions my face plant in the snow earlier on. Dr. Darcy (or maybe it's Dr. Ben, as that's what they're all calling him and he doesn't seem to mind) takes my coat and hangs it with his on the back of a chair. By the time we reach the bar, a crowd has formed, all of them wanting to chat to the doctor, thank him, and tell him about their various ailments. I stand next to him and grin, unsure really of what else to do.

Clive spots me and after we've hugged he glances at Dr. Darcy and then winks at me as if to say, nice work Sybs. I grin.

"Are you hungry, love, I've got some sticky toffee pudding left if you fancy a wedge? Steak and ale pie is all gone, I'm afraid," Clive shrugs.

"Ah, no thanks." I shake my head, not really wanting to get stuck into a big pudding in front of everyone here at the bar.

"Can I have it then?" the guy in dungarees pipes up. "Be a shame to waste it." He rolls up his sleeves in anticipation.

"But you've already had a wedge," another man yells

from the end of the bar, "give it to me, Sonny. Only fair." And Clive, aka Sonny, holds up his palms to quieten the pair.

"All right, fellas, no need to fight over it, it's the size of a house brick so I'll bring it with two spoons and you can share." Clive turns to me. "Can I put your name down for the karaoke?" he asks keenly. I open my mouth to reply, but Dr. Darcy talks instead.

"No, you can't leave me on my own." He looks at the bar and I immediately see why—there are already four glasses lined up in a row, each of them three fingers full of brandy. Taking two of the tumblers, he places them in front of me. "Please, I'm begging you to help me out. It's like this every time I come in here and it'd be rude not to." He pulls a face and laughs. "For the sake of my liver, before it packs up and I'm carted back to Dublin in a box," he pleads. "And I guarantee you'll sleep well tonight." He lifts a glass and knocks it back.

"Are you sure you're a proper doctor?" I laugh too, lifting one of the glasses, "because this is very unorthodox." And I down the warm liquid, instantly feeling relaxed as it radiates through my body.

"Yes, I really am a proper doctor," he grins, "but you can call me Ben, seeing as we're drinking buddies now." He pulls out a bar stool for me to sit on.

"Thanks." I sit down and rest one elbow on the bar, turning to face him. Then I take a deep breath and say, "So, Ben, tell me why you left the message on the newspaper for me."

"Well, I probably shouldn't have been listening in on your conversation, but before I got off the train, one stop before Tindledale, I had to call a friend's house to collect my car—he was servicing it for me—I overheard you asking about somewhere to buy a gift for your friend, who I now know is our very own pub landlady, Cher." He takes another mouthful of brandy before adjusting his glasses and glancing away as if he's nervous again. "I thought it might help you out. Pam, my receptionist, had mentioned that Tindledale Books is now stocking a range of scented candles—she was very excited. They're part of a new gift line that Adam is trying out, much to Mrs. Pocket's disdain, apparently." And I swear he rolls his eyes, which as the village GP he probably isn't really allowed to do as I bet she's one of his patients. There's bound to be special doctor protocol about that kind of thing. But I can't help thinking, Ha! so he knows what a dragon she is then.

"Ah, I see." I contemplate telling him what happened when I met Adam, but a guy comes over and, after buying Ben yet another brandy, he thanks him for looking after his wife last week when she had a nasty bout of morning sickness.

After the second, or maybe it's the third drink—I've lost count now—but my fears of rejection and humiliation or a repeat performance of my showdown with Adam have definitely floated away on a big brandy boat, so I decide to cut to the chase and go for it when the man wanders away to join his friends by the dartboard in the corner.

"And the smiley face emoticon?" I ask, raising an eyebrow at Ben.

"Oh, um, well, I didn't want you thinking I was some kind of weirdo—a stalker," he laughs, resting sideways on the bar, seemingly more relaxed as well now. Hmm, it's a nice answer, but it doesn't really tell me very much. I know my flirtometer is a bit off-kilter, but he must be interested. Why else would he have asked me to come to the pub with him? And held my hand on the way over here? I take a deep breath.

"So is that why you added a kiss as well?" I swallow the last of my brandy and will my cheeks to stop flushing. Ben opens his mouth; he closes it again, and downs another brandy before looking directly at me with a slightly awkward, but very endearing grin on his face. He's just about to reply, I'm convinced of it, when Clive flicks the switch on the karaoke machine and Pete leaps onto the stage, singing a very loud and very tongue-in-cheek version of Madonna's "Like a Virgin." Ben hesitates.

"Sorry, I can't hear you."

I open my mouth to try again, but another villager comes over, desperate for the doctor's opinion on his suspected hernia, and the moment is lost.

16

It's Saturday afternoon and I'm in Hettie's House of Haberdashery with the granddaddy of all hangovers, but Ben was right, I had a brilliant night's sleep, the best I've had in ages.

My hair is scooped up into a big ponytail and I've opted for the fresh, natural countryside look, kind of; the lashes are still in place, so with a hint of tint on my cheeks and a slick of clear lip gloss that I found in the bottom of my handbag, I look OK. I didn't want to bother Lawrence by using his makeup again, and besides, there really is no need as I've noticed that none of the women here in Tindledale seem to wear very much makeup at all, apart from Ruby—but then, she is a bona fide burlesque dancer; she told me all about it in the pub last night. Pete was halfway through his third, or maybe fourth song when she arrived. She even asked if I had ever danced inside a giant martini glass, or perhaps I imagined that bit, to be honest it's all a bit of a blur now.

I take a sip of the super-sugary hot tea that Marigold made for me. And they're all here—Hettie of course, and Marigold's friends Louise, Edie, Sarah and Vi. Cooper's wife, Molly (who thankfully left the ferret at home today, but that hasn't stopped Basil from sniffing and foraging through her handbag on the scent of him), Beth, a teacher at the village school, and her friend Leo from university days who's staying with her over the Christmas holidays while his boyfriend is trekking in Nepal (he didn't fancy it). Pam from the office is here, and Taylor. She had heard about the knit and natter group on the village grapevine, no surprise there, and was keen to join in too. Especially after having seen a picture in a magazine of the model, Cara Delevingne, knitting backstage at a fashion show! Taylor had got straight on to YouTube and watched lots of knitting know-how films covering the basics through to more complicated stuff like turning corners, rib stitch, moss, basket weave and stocking. And she now knows that knitting is, "Sick! Unless you live in smallsville Tindledale, which is like a whole *century* behind the rest of the *entire* world" (followed by a sulky teenage pout). So she got the bus down here and was standing outside when Hettie opened up this morning. I've already shown her how to cast on and do a basic knit stitch so she's now busy knitting a dog blanket to use in the pet parlor. And thoroughly enjoying it she is too, I even spotted her iMessaging her mates, telling them knitting is like loom bands for adults and to see if they wanted to come and join in as well. And they're planning to yarn-bomb Tindledale, Stoneley *and* Market Briar, just as soon as their knitting skills are up to it.

Between us all we managed to lug a couple more armchairs in from Hettie's oast house next door and then Lord Lucan turned up with an extremely comfy, faded floral sofa from the Blackwood House orangery piled into his sheep trailer with a couple of the farm laborers to help unload it. So now, with the extra tables dotted around, Hettie's House of Haberdashery looks more like a trendy shabby chic coffeehouse that you might find in somewhere like Shoreditch, instead of this quaint little village deep in the English countryside. And we even have music—Hettie brought an old cassette player in from next door so we're now working our way through an entire collection of rock 'n' roll Christmas hits. Brenda Lee is belting out a tune about rocking around the Christmas tree with pumpkin pie and doing some carolling, creating a gorgeous cozy Christmas atmosphere, and despite my fragile state I feel really happy and content right now. Perhaps my broken heart is finally on the mend.

I cough. Ouch. I really need to keep my head still

now that the last dose of paracetamol and Diet Coke has worn off.

"Finished!" I yell excitedly, holding Ruby's Christmas pudding sweater up in the air, and instantly regretting it when the pneumatic drill that's currently hanging out inside my head starts hammering again. I groan as I reach across for the scissors to snip the end of the wool used to sew up the seams. Hettie certainly is a fast knitter—she had finished the back and made a start on the front by the time I had dragged myself out of bed and got myself here, after wolfing down Lawrence's full English breakfast complete with extra fried bread to soak up all the alcohol (in theory).

"Ooh, now that *is* a beauty!" It's Marigold who takes it from me to have a closer look before passing it around the group. "But I'm surprised you have the energy to knit after your romantic rendezvous wandering around the village green with our dashing doctor last night!" She smiles, digging me in the ribs. I try not to smile as I marvel at how, yet again, word sure gets around quickly here in Tindledale.

"Mmm, it wasn't really like that. We just had a few drinks, that's all!" I will my cheeks to stop reddening as they're all leaning forward, eager to hear the gossip about their doctor firsthand.

"And the rest." It's Leo now. He stops knitting his

snowflake-patterned beanie and takes the pudding sweater from Marigold; he turns it inside out to study the back of the pudding design. "So, did he move in for a kiss?"

"Leo!" Edie says, patting her gray bob. "You mustn't ask a lady such things."

"Hmm, well I bet he did, it's always the shy ones," Leo quips, before turning his attentions back to the sweater. "I'm impressed, sweetie. Someone will pay top dollar for this online, guaranteed," he adds, nodding in my direction.

"I can't take the credit. Hettie here did all the hard work." She's sitting beside me on the sofa, so I turn my head toward her. "Thanks so much." She nods and pats my arm before popping a square of peppermint cream into her mouth—I picked up a few bars, along with some chocolate chip cookies, a tin of Roses and a couple of Terry's Chocolate Oranges from the village store for us all to nibble on while we knit. "And for everything else," I add, so wishing I could stay here with her forever.

"And thank *you* my dear. You certainly had your hands full this morning transforming this place, I hardly recognize it." She casts her eyes around the shop, which is shaping up very nicely now. I made a start right away despite my poor head, buoyed up by my big breakfast, and Marigold helped me clear all the old, musty, damaged stock into an empty bedroom in the oast house, and then we artfully reorganized the display tables so there are now defined sections for knitting, needlecraft, quilting, crocheting and general crafting. The floor was swept and the old Silver Cross pram stored in one of the outbuildings and then we replaced the old-fashioned sun-damaged wool with the beautiful rainbow assortment of lovely new yarn from the stock cupboard.

I take a moment to admire the now gleaming, shabby chic interior of Hettie's House of Haberdashery. Lawrence let me bring his laptop, explaining that it's already hooked up to the village broadband hub so should work fine in here, and it does, so after taking some pictures using Marigold's iPad, I emailed them to myself so I could access them from the laptop and then Taylor utilized her degree in computer studies and created a three-page website called www.hettieshouseofhaberdashery.co.uk.

"And you know what?" Taylor stops knitting and we all turn to look at her. "I reckon we should knit a whole stack of sweaters for Hettie to sell online."

"Now that is very good idea young lady," Hettie says to Taylor before leaning forward and addressing Leo directly. "Do you really think someone will pay 'top dollar' as you say?" She scrutinizes his manscaped face.

"Deffo. Honestly, honey, trust me," he says flirtatiously, clasping a dramatic hand to his chest. Hettie pats her bun before doing a very girlish giggle. I nod in agreement, and smile; it's so nice to see her looking relaxed and far less anxious.

"In that case," she turns back to look at me, "take it off!"

"Pardon?"

"You heard. Take off your sweater."

"Oh," I manage, wondering where she's going with this.

"Well, if Ruby is having a sweater in her window display then I need one too. Right away. And that Ho Ho Ho sweater is just the thing!" Hettie points a bony finger at my chest before leaping up and dashing across the shop floor to the table nearest the roaring log fire. Basil stirs from his bed—a pile of granny patch blankets that Hettie stacked inside an old wooden fruit crate—and wags his tail at her, knowing it must be playtime or petting time; they clearly adore each other. After giving Basil a long, lingering stroke, Hettie gestures to a beaten-up old brown suitcase on the table.

"Here, I have a whole trunk of those vintage blouses that you like. Dresses too. Pick one to put on and then give me the pullover. And don't dilly-dally. I want to get it in my window before you take the Christmas pudding one up to Ruby." And she flings open the lid of the suitcase revealing a Taylor Utility stamp in old-fashioned gold swirly letters on the inside. The scent of sandalwood and stale perfume bursts into the air all around us as I giggle inwardly at this, as yet unseen, side of Hettie. Competitive entrepreneur. How amazing, and in her twilight years too.

I jump up from the sofa, closely followed by Leo and Beth, and we all race over to see inside the suitcase, me clutching my head, but I don't care, I'm not missing out on this opportunity. Everyone loves vintage clothes.

"Ooh, did you used to wear these?" I ask, rummaging through the contents—exquisite floaty silks, tailored cotton shirts and a beautiful red gingham fifties off-the-shoulder dress with a wide black belt and the biggest, swirly, whirly, froufrou net petticoat I think I've ever seen.

"Yes, most of the clothes came back with me from America." And for some reason, Hettie drops her voice and casts a furtive glance in Marigold's direction, but she's busy chatting to Edie, so doesn't appear to notice. How strange. But there's no time to ponder as Leo is now holding up a gorgeous pair of silk stockings that have an actual seam down the back.

"You can't have those." Hettie blushes and swipes them from his hand, quickly tucking them into her cardigan pocket.

"What about these? Name your price, Hettie," Leo swoons, happily swapping the stockings for a pair of beautiful mink-suede Roger Vivier stiletto heels. Hettie touches the tip of her left index finger to the toe of one of the shoes and then lets out a long sigh.

"I loved those heels, and there are so many memories attached to them—dancing, dating, doing all the things that young girls love to do . . ." Her voice trails away. "But you can have them," she then adds briskly, and in a very matter-of-fact, almost cold, way.

"Oh my God! Are you sure?" Leo can barely contain himself and hugs the shoes to his chest as if they're price-less diamonds.

"I'm sure. But you must promise to cherish them," Hettie smiles wistfully.

"In that case, I've died and gone to heaven. Let me find out how much to pay you for them, I wouldn't dream of just taking them." Hettie looks surprised, as if she hadn't even considered actually selling the contents of the suitcase. "Marigooooold, can I use your iPad to see how much these shoes are worth please?" And Leo runs off with his treasure.

"Ahh, look at this," I say to Beth, lifting up an intricately embroidered hanky with the initials GHM on.

"Gosh, it's exquisite. Silk too by the looks of it," she coos, touching the corner.

"Gorgeous, isn't it," I say, admiring the detail and effort that have obviously gone into creating it.

"Put it back!" Hettie swipes the hanky from my hands and snaps the case shut, before bowing her head and rushing out the back to the kitchen-cum-sitting-room. I'm shocked, Beth too. She gives me a look before running off to rejoin the others. I dash after Hettie, but when I pop my head around the curtain, she's staring at the photo frame with a papery hand clasped at her neck, and I sense right away that she wants to be alone. I let the curtain sweep silently back into place and leave her be.

A few minutes later and Hettie returns to the shop floor, seemingly composed and stoic as always—as if nothing had just happened.

"And make sure you put a picture of the Christmas pudding sweater in the online shop," she instructs sharply. "If Ruby sells it then I want to too—not that exact one, clearly, but I can easily make some more to order."

"Yes, yes, of course, no problem, I'll make sure it's there," I say, feeling a little taken aback. I smile gently and try to make eye contact but she flicks her eyes down and focuses on the pattern of the rug instead.

"Right you are." Hettie glances back up and stares at the dress still clutched in my hands. "Well, are you going to put it on then?"

"If that's OK?" I say, not daring to disagree with her,

even though my legs will freeze when I go out in the snow to take the sweater up to Ruby's shop.

"Of course it is, dear," Hettie says in a very pleasant voice now, and it throws me, the complete contrast in her manner from just a few seconds ago, and as if reading my mind, she adds, "And you can keep your jeans and plimsolls on. Just put the dress on over the top." She points to my fetid Converses. "You'll catch your death of cold otherwise."

So that told me!

"Um. Great," I mutter. "And thank you."

"And you can take the suitcase up to Ruby too. See if she'll buy the contents for her shop," Hettie says with a determined look on her face now.

"Are you sure? Hettie, you don't need to do that," I say softly. "You'll have online orders in no time. Honestly, there really is no need. Your mother's bone knitting needles have already exceeded the reserve on eBay."

"I've made up my mind. Take the case."

"OK. If you're absolutely sure." She nods, but I notice her hand-wringing starts up again.

"I am. Now will you please put that pullover in the window! I'm off next door to hunt for the box of Christmas decorations in my back bedroom. I'm sure that's where they're stored." And she pads off to go in search.

Marigold comes over to me.

"You OK?" she asks, kindly. "She doesn't mean to be . . ."

"Oh, I know," I shrug, "but I'm worried about her."

"We all are." Marigold shakes her head in concern. "There's some gaffer tape in the glove box," she adds, dangling the key for the Land Rover in front of me. "For the suitcase."

"Ahh, yes, it is a bit battered, I'll bind it up," I say, taking the key. "Thank you."

*

I've just found the gaffer tape and closed the car door behind me, when a white van swerves up at the curb on the other side of the lane and two men in black bomber jackets and Doc Marten boots jump out and stride toward the shop.

"Oh, hello. Can I help you?" I ask, quickly stuffing the gaffer tape into my jeans pocket. I can't imagine they're here for some yarn and a nice pattern or two. They look very menacing. "Who are you?" I add, more forcefully.

"We're here to see the owner of this establishment," one of them growls as they march past me.

"Um," I open my mouth, but they keep on going. Pushing my elbows out, I immediately charge after them, catching up just as the meanest-looking one of the pair pushes a hand out to open the door to Hettie's shop. "Can I help you?" I blurt again, swiftly pinning my body between them and the door.

"Not unless you are," the one with a clipboard snarls, before pausing to scan his list, "Henrietta Honey!" he announces.

"Gentlemen!" Marigold suddenly appears at the door behind me. I swivel my head and see that she has an extremely gracious smile on her flushed face. "How may I help you?" she says with impeccable diction, shooting me a look and offering a regal hand to one of the men who, after staring at his mate, shakes her hand so gingerly, anyone would think it was coated in arsenic.

"Are you Henrietta Honey?"

"Would you mind if we discuss this matter away from the shop? Bad for business, you see. And with all these customers? Oh now, that would never do." Marigold shakes her head and gestures to the window where Louise, Taylor, Edie and the rest of the gang are busy knitting and nattering away, totally oblivious to whatever it is that's going on out here. She steers the two men toward the bus shelter just along the lane and I go with her, wondering if it's something to do with Hettie's horrible nephew—could they have come to haul her off to an old people's home or something? Surely not—wouldn't they send nurses? Or at least kindly men in white uniforms with soft voices and a blanket or a wheelchair, perhaps, not that Hettie needs one, far from it, but these two look like total thugs. The one with the clipboard has H-A-T-E stamped across his knuckles. "That's better," Marigold says, sounding like a mother placating a pair of whiny toddlers. The two men stare at her, both breathing heavily through their slack-jawed open mouths. "Now, what's this all about?" Marigold tilts her head to one side and I stare at the ground, thinking she's good, very convincing. Lawrence needs to sign her up to the Tindledale Players right away, as she's an exceptionally talented actress. These two thugs are totally buying it that she's Henrietta Honey.

"The arrears on your secured loan—we have a warrant to seize goods to the value of . . ." the clipboard one says, sounding like a recording, having clearly practiced the words beforehand. He checks his list and my heart sinks. I clasp my hands up under my chin. Poor Hettie. "Four thousand, seven hundred and fifty-two pounds and sixteen pence."

"Whaaaat?" I gasp.

"It's OK, I'll take care of this," Marigold breathes, not missing a beat and placing a steadying hand on my arm. "There's obviously some kind of mix-up." One of the guys clears his throat before doing a phlegmy spit on the pavement. Jesus Christ. I turn away, trying not to heave.

"Nope. No mix-up. If you can escort us in so we can get it over with you'll be given a full inventory of the seized goods." And the two men go to walk off.

"Hold on!" I whisper-yell so as not to alert Hettie or the others, my hackles well and truly raised, making my voice sound shrill. "You can't do that." But the two men just keep on walking toward Hettie's lovely House of Haberdashery.

"You heard the lady." Marigold marches forward and stands firmly in front of them with her hands on her hips, blocking their path. One of the men goes to barge past her but she grabs the sleeve of his jacket.

"I wouldn't advise that, madam." The guy lifts her hand away with an extra-menacing look on his greasy, blackhead-covered face.

"Then what would you advise, young man, because I am telling you that there isn't anything worth that kind of money inside the shop?" Marigold folds her arms underneath her ample bosoms, sounding even more "Lady of the Manor" now. I glance away, knowing that what she's saying isn't strictly true. I reckon Hettie's mother's old Singer machine is probably worth quite a bit—it's in exceptional condition—but I just know that it would break Hettie's heart if these two were to cart it away like a piece of old junk. We can't let that happen.

"The loan is secured on the house and the warrant covers all the contents, so we'll clear the lot—TVs, washing machine, jewelery—if that's what it takes to recover the arrears." A stunned silence follows while the two men try to stare us out.

"So, let me get this clear: if the arrears are cleared then this all goes away?" I ask, sweeping a hand through the air and shaking my head as if to gain some clarity on the situation.

"Nice try, sweetheart, but nah! It don't work like that. The arrears need to be cleared and then the rest of the payments have to be made on time, every month, or we come back and take the lot—TVs, washing mach—"

"Yep, I get it—TVs, washing machine, jewelery, etc. You said that already." The guy doing the talking gives me a sarcastic smile, which I promptly replicate.

"And the house and the shop if necessary," the phlegmy man grunts.

"You will certainly do no such thing. This is outrageous," Marigold hisses. There's a short silence. I rack my brains desperately searching for a solution, anything to stop them from going inside and upsetting Hettie. She'll be absolutely devastated, mortified with embarrassment too, especially if they do this in front of the others. And what will the rest of the villagers think? They'll all be upset for her, I reckon, and it'll take about two seconds for word to get round, not in a gossipy way, as they don't strike me as the type of people to be like that, the ones I've met anyway—apart from Adam, of course, and that bossy witch, Mrs. Pocket.

A plan starts to hatch. I step forward until I'm standing adjacent to Marigold, and square on to the thugs hired by the bank or the dodgy finance company or whatever Hettie's nephew has roped in to scare old ladies living in rural little villages. Well, they don't scare me! I see their type every day, hanging out on the corner of my street thinking they're the greatest with their guard dogs in stupid, oversize studded collars, *cos that makes them look hard-ass*, not.

"How much?" I keep my voice steady and strong. I can see Marigold in my peripheral vision. The men stare at me.

"Yes, how much?" Marigold joins in. "How much for this horrible misunderstanding to go away?"

"Oh, it ain't going away, lady," the clipboard guy says, with added snark.

"We get that, but I've seen the programs on TV and bailiffs doing deals. Surely you can take a partial payment?" I say, unflinching and looking them right in the eyes. I've had just about enough of men thinking they can push women around. Luke did that, but I survived; I didn't shrivel up and die, so no! This worm has turned. "Come on. I'm waiting for an answer." I'm on a roll now. "Ten percent should do it and the rest in—"

"Five hundred might buy you some time," Clipboard says begrudgingly in Marigold's direction. "I'll call the guvnor." And he pulls out a mobile. I surreptitiously cross my fingers and do a silent prayer—let's hope he gets a signal.

"Yep." He's through! Thank God. He must have that one bar that Dr. Ben gets when leaning out of his skylight window. "Nah. Yep. Yep. Nah. Yep. OK, boss." And he ends the call. "Five hundred now and the balance in full within two weeks."

But that's right before Christmas! It could even *be* Christmas Eve! What happened to the season of good-will? Hettie's an old lady who's been duped by her only living relative and it's just so unfair. I've a good mind to hunt the nephew down and force him to cough up the money to pay off the loan that he tricked her into signing up for in the first place. I bet he knew this would happen and it's all part of some hideous plan to get her out of the house and off the land so he can then buy it back at a rock-bottom price when it goes to auction following repossession.

The bailiff unzips his jacket and stuffs the mobile

away—and oh my God, he's wearing a bulletproof vest. Sweet Jesus, what did he think was going to happen here today? That Hettie might attack him with a fistful of knitting needles?

"Perfect!" Marigold claps her hands together in glee and I glance at her sideways in horror, praying they don't cotton on to her not being the real Henrietta Honey. "Oh, um, sorry, I'm just so relieved." She fiddles with her hair and smiles sheepishly before hugging her arms around her body, shivering in the subzero wintery air. I hadn't even noticed how cold it is out here; it's weird how a rush of adrenaline does that to a person. And how the hell are we going to scrape together that amount of money with literally no notice? Perhaps the village store has a cash machine; I could probably do it, if the direct debit for this month's rent hasn't left my account yet. It's Marigold who saves the day. "I'll get my purse. Do you take Amex?" she says, in a very breezy voice. The two men stare at her, goggle-eyed and speechless, both doing the stupid breathy thing again. Maybe they are genuinely stupid, because they haven't even asked for Marigold, aka Henrietta Honey's, ID or anything—but then if they get the money, even just some of it, then what do they care?

"Sorry, what, um, er, Hettie really meant was, do you take cards or does it actually have to be hard cash?" I squirm, but to my utter surprise he replies.

"Debit cards only." And whips out a handheld card machine.

"Hurrah! How very civilized!" roars Marigold, making me want to shrivel up in the corner of the bus shelter and quietly evaporate.

"Hey, Sybs. Come on in honey." Ruby is at the back of the shop, a gorgeous little boutique crammed full of all kinds of goodies. Frank Sinatra is singing "Have Yourself a Merry Little Christmas" from a red Dansette record player, creating a cozy, nostalgic feel. A rainbow of old-fashioned paper chains are looped from a chandelier in the center of the ceiling, cascading out to each corner of the shop. Red crepe Santa lanterns are swinging in a row on one wall that's papered in Elvis Presley print, the iconic black-and-white *Jailhouse Rock* image. It's so kitsch and fascinating; like stepping back in time to another era. There's even a shelf with a row of old-fashioned sweet jars with cola cubes and pear drops. Blimey, there's even one stuffed full of Parma Violets. I haven't had those in years.

I weave my way through, in between the racks and racks of vintage clothes. The suitcase is in my arms as the handle is broken and no amount of gaffer tape was going to keep it all together. A festive red poinsettia plant is perched on top—I bought it from the florist three doors along—and Ruby's jeans and blouse, together with the Christmas pudding sweater, matching mittens and a long, crimson-colored scarf are nestling inside a paper Hettie's House of Haberdashery shopping bag looped over my left wrist. I'd found a stack of bags languishing under the counter. So with my handbag swinging precariously from my shoulder and Basil bouncing beside me on his lead looped over my right wrist, I have to be extra careful not to bump into the mannequins. Each one is dressed in a pretty dress: short and fitted, classic designer, long and floaty, and all with coordinating accessories like big hats, beady necklaces. One even has a swingy black bob and aviator shades on and is definitely a favorite; it's wearing a glorious fuchsia pink patterned Pucci maxi dress with a matching resin wrist cuff.

"Wow, your shop is fantastic!" I say, ducking down into Ruby's little office, which is cleverly concealed under the staircase, the banister of which is adorned with twinkling Christmas tree lights, and they're woven in and out of the spindles too, creating a magical Santa's grotto effect. There's a miniature Christmas tree and even a kitsch little nativity scene with plastic figurines and a manger.

"The kids love it," Ruby explains, seeing me looking. "Keeps them amused while the mums shop."

Ruby looks effortlessly chic in navy silk palazzo pants, teamed with a white cotton wrap top that she's tied into a huge floppy bow that trails elegantly from her hip.

"And you look amazing," I say, trying to sound breezy—can't let my girl crush completely ruin me.

"Thanks, lady," she mumbles, through a couple of dressmaking pins that are poking out from the corner of her mouth. "Dump your load down there." Ruby points to a dusty-pink crushed velvet armchair over by a window that looks out onto a pretty courtyard garden that's covered in snow with just the twigs of a few bushy potted plants peeping through at the borders. I do as I'm told before handing her the plant.

"To say thank you," I beam.

"Oh, how sweet. And *thank you*." She carefully presses her cheek against mine so the pins don't catch my face. "But what for?" she asks, turning back to check the hemline on a gorgeous Japanese silk kimono.

"For, well . . . for everything. For lending me the clothes."

"Ah, don't be daft, it was my pleasure." Ruby pulls a vague face and wafts a dismissive hand in the air, making me smile.

"Oh, and there's this for you too." I point to Hettie's suitcase. "'It's crammed full of vintage clothes, shoes, stockings, that kind of thing. Hettie wondered if you might want to buy some, or all of it, to sell on in your shop."

"Ooh, how exciting," Ruby says, eagerly dropping the hem of the kimono to pull the gaffer tape from the suitcase instead. She riffles through. "I'll take a proper look later, but on first glance, some of these items are American couture—see here." And she shows me the label inside a lovely salmon-pink satin sheath dress. "*Very* nice. This is from a boutique on Fifth Avenue in Manhattan—it opened in the fifties and is still there, I think—very exclusive." Ruby does big eyes. "This dress probably cost a fortune back in the day." She nods her head, clearly impressed.

"Ah, well that makes sense, Hettie did tell me that she lived in America for a while."

"There you go—I'm an expert when it comes to vintage couture," Ruby says in her usual self-assured way. "Tell Hettie I'll catalog the contents and put them on my website; I think my overseas customers are going to love this collection. I'll just deduct an amount for shipping and she can have the rest of the revenue. I know she struggles financially," she adds matter-of-factly.

"That's kind of you," I beam.

"Pah, it's nothing. If I can't help an old lady, then there's something seriously wrong in this world. It's just a shame that she won't let us help her more."

"What do you mean?" I crease my forehead in concern; hoping word of the bailiffs calling hasn't gone around already.

"Oh, the whole village knows that she's struggling to make ends meet, but she won't take so much as a sticky bun. Kitty in the Spotted Pig offered her one, even pretended it was a leftover from the day before, but Hettie still insisted on paying for it. I'd have ripped Kitty's arm off—I love a nice gooey cake—and even better if it's free." Ruby nods her head as if to confirm her stance on the matter.

"I guess Hettie is just a bit proud. Probably a generational thing," I say tactfully, not wanting to be seen to be gossiping; I get enough of that about me at work, so I know what it feels like. Marigold had a debit card in the glove box of her car (I know! You'd never risk that in London) and she got a receipt—the bailiffs barely glanced at the card, which was a massive relief as they'd soon have seen Marigold's name on it and not Hettie's, but I guess as long as they're getting paid, then what does it matter to them? After they'd left, we went into the oast house and found Hettie in the bedroom, still rummaging for the decorations. Marigold explained what had happened, we'd figured it was for the best, and she even offered to clear the rest of the balance, but Hettie, panic-stricken and thoroughly humiliated that her debt problem had been publicly revealed, flatly refused, so we're now hoping to raise the funds through the online shop. Quickly. The bone knitting needles are up to four hundred pounds now, so that's a start, and I've listed practically everything else in the shop on eBay. Hopefully, the contents of Hettie's suitcase will fetch a good price too.

"I'm sure you're right," Ruby says. "So, changing topic entirely, did you get it on with our gorgeous-but-doesn't-know-it Dr. Ben?" She plants both hands on her hips, clearly impatient for an answer. "He is one hot dude. Lady boner alert." She does kissy lips in the air.

"Ruby!" I snigger, diving into a nearby rail of gorgeous tops and blouses to hide my flaming cheeks.

"Well, he is! Why deny it? And I saw you holding hands as you walked around the duck pond." She laughs too. "A date is a date, and trust me, the good ones are few and far between, so you need to catch Cupid's arrow while you can," she sighs.

"It wasn't really like that," I protest, trying not to smile as I select a sumptuously soft pastel-pink cashmere polo-neck sweater for closer inspection, but instantly wonder: then what *was* it really like? Is it too soon to meet someone else? Is my trampled-on heart up to it? I am only just over halfway through my year of heartache—and then I realize that I'm getting way ahead of myself. He probably felt sorry for me, thought I needed cheering up, and a good night's sleep. That's all. Who knows? And I have to go home tomorrow, so there's a high chance I'll never find out.

"Trust me, it's *always* like that!" Ruby says.

"Hmm, maybe. How much is this?" I ask holding up the sweater and not seeing a price tag.

"Everything on that rack is thirty pounds, but if you want two then you can have them for fifty."

"Ooh, in that case, I'll have this one as well," I say, performing a pincer movement on a gorgeous navy sailor top; it even has the big boat collar and puffy short sleeves with little gold anchor detailing at the edge.

"Good choice. Come on, follow me to the changing room and then I've got a surprise lined up for you. Want to have some fun?" She tilts her head to one side, her eyes sparkling.

"Maybe . . . it depends," I say warily, not wanting to commit until I know what she has in mind.

"Burlesque. You told me last night that you would love to give it a go," Ruby says casually, giving me a sweet smile. I open my mouth and quickly close it after a

231

ridiculous Scooby Doo ruh-roh sound comes tumbling out. Major cringe. "Yep. Admittedly, when I made it over to the Duck & Puddle pub, you had already downed several brandies, but you definitely said it. Don't you remember? Dr. Ben was busy pretending to be interested in old Tommy Prendergast's totally imagined hernia—last week he was convinced he was having a heart attack because his pulse wouldn't stop racing but it turned out he was sugar rushing, having scoffed his way through a whole Christmas chocolate selection box. But yep, you definitely said it." She shakes her head in amusement.

"Um, well, I do remember you telling me that you dance burlesque, but I was joking about actually having a go myself. Really, I couldn't." I hold my palms up in protest, panic tearing through me. OK, I may have gushed out something about wishing I had the guts to try it; funny what you say after a few too many brandies, isn't it? But with a hangover head in the cold light of day, no way. I'll look ridiculous. Ruby's staring at me now, doing a snorty, flared-nostril thing. "Anyway, I haven't even shown you the sweater or the matching mittens and scarf yet. Don't you want to put it in your window display right away? Look!" I grab the carrier bag, pull out the sweater and hold it up to show her as a distraction. She gently takes it from me.

"Wow. Thank you. It's gorgeous and just what I had in

mind," she says, taking a good look, before placing it on a nearby chair.

"You're welcome," I say, not daring to meet her gaze. A short silence follows.

"You don't have to go for the nipple tassels. Just try on an outfit, trust me . . . you'll love it," she says excitedly, clapping her hands together in glee.

"But what about the customers, what if someone comes in?" I gulp, just about managing to avoid a repeat Scooby performance; she's clearly not taking no for an answer.

"Darling, I'm not expecting a stampede of customers; this is hardly Oxford Street, now is it?" She casts a regal hand toward the front window overlooking the little snow-covered village High Street with the olde-worlde shops and no one around. It makes me laugh. "Come on. It's the perfect lift; you'll be flying high afterward with no memory of ever having been betrayed by your own sister—the one who organizes foxhunts! Can't say I really agree with all that. And I grew up in the countryside so I know what a nuisance foxes can be, but still . . ." She rolls her eyes and shakes her head in disgust. Hmm, I think I may have said something about Sasha too, last night. "And that . . . whatever his name is." She pulls a face as if Luke isn't even worth mentioning, which is a bit harsh as I did love him, I truly did, of course I did, once upon a time. Didn't I? Oh well! And then it hits me. I've just thought about Luke, but with absolutely no physical or emotional reaction attached. No ice-cold swirl in the pit of my stomach, or tearing, searing, tight band of brokenness wrapped around my heart. Wow! I actually think I might be getting over him. Hallelujah!

Taking a big breath as if to clear my head, I ponder for a moment. I know there's no escape once Ruby has made up her mind; she's very tenacious, look what happened with the Dolly boots. So I'd best just get it over with. Gingerly, I nod my head, a secret part of me warming to the idea; nobody will see me, and you never know, it might be fun, in a mad, kookie cuckoo, liberating kind of way, and certainly the perfect opportunity to celebrate me having reached a momentous milestone in my predicted year of heartache.

"OK, I'll give it a go—but I'm not coming out of the changing room."

Laughing and shaking her head, Ruby lets the curtain swing closed. "Brilliant. And I have just the costume for you. It's a new Christmassy-themed one and, to be honest, I really could do with seeing how it looks on someone else, so now is the perfect moment. I'll get it while you try on those two tops."

*

I've just about managed to cram myself into a crimson satin corset with matching frilly knickers that has a white lacy trim around the cleavage part and fluffy feathers fluting around the tops of my thighs. I've also managed to bury my stinky Converse trainers under my jeans; I didn't want to inflict them on Ruby again.

"How do you feel?" She pokes her head around the curtain. "Wow, look at you! Sally Rand, eat your heart out," she adds on seeing me.

"Who?"

"Oh, she was a famous burlesque dancer in the thirties and quite beautiful," Ruby smiles, "just like you."

"Aw, thank you," I grin. "I do feel pretty good, actually." It's amazing how it gives me a lovely hourglass figure. Feeling pleased with myself and a bit daring, I put my hands on my hips and twist my body from side to side. Not bad, even if I do say so myself.

"Try these." Ruby hands me a pair of fishnet stockings. They have snow-white and scarlet satin rosebuds stitched around the top with black frizzy tassels dangling down from each side.

"I can't wear those. I'll get arrested," I say, in a very breathy voice, as the corset is so tight it's making me feel giddy. I make big eyes at her and pull a pretend outraged face.

"Of course you can. It's just for fun. Don't worry, I'm

not going to make you dance or anything . . . unless you want to." Ruby smiles eagerly. "I'd be happy to show you some moves."

"Er, no, I don't think so." Smiling and puffing, I hold up a finger, my miraculously enhanced cleavage practically bursting up to greet my chin as I attempt to bend over and swing a foot up onto a stool in preparation for a stocking. "Can you imagine me shimmying and bouncing on the back of my heels? Hmm, I don't think so; I may have to build up to that part of my burlesque experience."

"OK, calm down. You have to be ready. Hang on, I'll find you a wig! Ooh, I've got just the thing." Her eyes light up. "And some Mary Janes and a choker. You *have* to have a choker." She darts off excitedly, and I admire myself in the mirror until she returns a few minutes later with a shoe box under one arm, a long blond plaited wig over the other and a matching crimson velvet choker in her hand.

Once I have the rest of the costume on, and now with my confidence soaring, I swing the curtain back and kick a stocking-clad leg out of the changing room. Ruby claps her hands together. She's reclining on the chaise longue, and I feel euphoric now, so I kick my other leg, place a hand on my hip and sashay out into the back of the shop.

"See? What a transformation. You're flying now, aren't you?" Ruby laughs.

"Oh yes," I purr, in a way that hopefully sounds sexy and not too much like a chain smoker heavy breathing down a phone line looking for a cheap thrill.

"You could do a turn at my next burlesque event; I'm hosting a Christmas special at the Picture House—that's the old cinema building in Market Briar. Think gold satin swishy curtains and a cocktail bar *on the stage*. Perfect. I'm sure I could find a spot for you," Ruby laughs throatily, but with a deadly serious look on her face. *Is she mad? I can't dance burlesque in public. On a stage, in an old cinema with all those people watching? Oh no!*

"Steady on," I laugh. "I'm just a beginner."

Unperturbed, I press on, arching my back as I stick my bottom out and rest my hands down on the chaise. Ruby has switched off the record player now and turned her iPod on instead. She swipes the screen a few times until Mariah Carey starts singing "All I Want for Christmas Is You," so I strut around in front of her, flinging my arms out high and wide before doing a big air grab on the "yoooooooou" bit, which I then draw in, clasping my left fist against my chest in an exceedingly overdramatic way, all the while strutting up and down, tossing my long blond plaited wig around with lots of attitude and loads of twerking action going on.

"Yes, Sybs. You go, girl. I see you, shaking that arse!" Ruby whistles, and we're both laughing like a pair of nuts when the bell jangles and the door flies open.

With my pointy finger suspended in mid-air, my backside still sticking right out and my mouth agape, I freeze.

"Oh, er . . . sorry. Um, perhaps I should go."

It's Dr. Ben, aka Dr. Darcy, aka Dr. Benedict Darcy, aka utterly hot man in a very unassuming way who doesn't even know it—which just makes him all the more fanciable. *And I'm squatting here like a constipated duck.* Aaarggghhh!

The floor sways.

What the bloody hell is he doing here? Is this some kind of home visit? Because that would never happen in London. Oh no.

I want to evaporate. Right here on the fluffy carpet of Ruby's lovely little shop. So much for feeling sassy! Right now I just feel like a massive quivering jellyfish. My mouth drains of saliva. I try to swallow but end up doing an impression of a python devouring an egg instead. Whole. This has to be the most embarrassing moment of my whole life—apart from that time in the church, of course. Oh God.

Looking flustered, distracted, who knows what? But most definitely surprised and quite possibly horrified, Dr.

Darcy turns and walks straight into the Pucci mannequin, making its wig swing furiously from side to side.

"Ah, Jesus, I'm so sorry, I um," he apologizes to the mannequin, before pushing a hand through his curly hair and quickly adjusting his glasses. Ruby whips a pashmina out from somewhere and hands it to me. I grab it gratefully and swing it around my shoulders.

"We, er, were, just, um . . . testing out a . . . new costume," I splutter, swiveling my head toward a stack of unopened cardboard boxes as some kind of proof, still whirling my pointy finger around like the blade of a helicopter spiraling in for a catastrophic crash landing. "Um, yes that's it." I bob from one foot to the other with a crazy cow smile plastered all over my face.

"I saw you coming in here," Dr. Darcy tries to explain, doing a half-grin and making big saucer eyes. A mixture of embarrassment and amusement, I think, hope, not . . . oh, I don't know. I'm so flustered.

"Yes. That's right. I came in here." I cringe all over. Of course I bloody did. I gulp. Big mistake, as it makes my neck expand and the choker pings right off. For crying out loud! The choker lands among the tassels at the top of my stockings and then just hangs by the Velcro fastener, like a spare appendage. Basil, not missing a trick, does a running body slam, bringing

239

himself to a halt beside my thigh to play with the tassel. I attempt to shoo him away, but it's no use, he just gets even more excited and spins in a circle instead, his little fluffy tail batting the tassel back and forth like a pendulum.

"Yes. Er, well I thought I'd," Dr. Ben coughs and quickly flicks his eyes to Basil and the bouncing choker, "bring this back." And he pulls my Kermit green scarf from his duffel coat pocket. Ruby clears her throat.

"Oh, right. Thank you," I say, taking it from him and then, for some utterly inane reason, I wind the super-chunky knitted scarf around my neck. Not once, not twice, but three flaming times, as if I'm about to step outside into the chilly white snow. I stop winding and fold my arms instead.

"You left it at the office. I, um, found it earlier when I was trying to get a head start on sorting through the mountain of files." Mirroring my stance, he crosses his arms too and then seems to think better of it, as he quickly unfolds them and shoves his hands in his pockets instead, before changing his mind again and, pulling his left hand out, runs it over his stubbly beard.

"Er, excuse me, you two. I'm really sorry to interrupt," Ruby says, leaping up from the chaise, "but I just need to dash over to the village store before it closes. To get some, um, milk. Yes, that's it. Milk." She sticks an index finger in the air as if to confirm the perceived sudden urgency. "Won't be long." And she practically hurls herself at the shop door, flicking the closed sign over as she scarpers.

The sound of a pony whinnying in the distance stirs me and for a blissful moment before the synapses of my brain kick in I'm a nine-year-old again on holiday at Brownie camp. I stretch out like a starfish, relaxed and carefree, happy after another glorious night's sleep. And without a hangover, which is actually a bit of a miracle—or perhaps I'm just getting used to the merry amounts of alcohol consumed here in the countryside, as I did have rather a lot of deliciously fruity mulled wine last night, with several brandy chasers. Yep, I ended up going to the Duck & Puddle again with Dr. Ben; well, not exactly with him, as in just the two of us, but he invited me to join him. And I was very happy to.

After Ruby fled on the pretext of getting milk, Dr. Ben said that he planned on having dinner in the pub later, seeing as it was curry-and-quiz night, and that if I wasn't already booked (hardly!), then I was more than welcome to join him. So I did. And just as it played out on Friday evening, his time was monopolized by several of the villagers wanting advice on a variety of ailments, so we didn't get any proper time together alone—I spent most of the night helping Clive to facilitate the quiz, which I actually thought was going to end in disaster at one point as Cooper could have sworn blind that the official language of Togo was Dutch, when in fact it's French. Molly was on the opposing team, which got it right, which didn't help matters at all, especially as she had the ferret with her and it nipped Cooper's thumb during the debacle.

There's a knock on the door so I fling back the duvet and get out of bed, much to Basil's dismay—he does a grumbly growl at having to galvanize himself into action and move from the snuggly nest he's made at the end of the bed. I pull on a robe and answer the door.

"So sorry to wake you, Sybs." It's Lawrence.

"It's OK, I was just languishing." I smile, attempting to smooth my tangled knot of curls into something resembling normal.

"Jolly good. Only there's someone here to see you."

"Me?" I instinctively pull the robe in tighter, really hoping it isn't Ben doing another one of his impromptu home visits—I'm still cringing from him inadvertently witnessing my first-ever burlesque moment, even though he was incredibly polite and didn't mention it at all when we met up later in the pub.

"That's right. Here she is." Lawrence steps aside.

"CHER!" I scream, flinging my arms around her shoulders, taking care not to squash her magnificent treacle-colored beehive (she hates it when people do that). And she looks amazing in giraffe-print leggings teamed with black suede knee-high wedge boots and a gorgeous leather and shearling aviator jacket. Very rock chick, as always.

"I'll put the breakfast on, will you be joining us?" Lawrence asks, turning to Cher.

"Ooh, yes please. I could murder a good breakfast and I've heard on the village grapevine that yours are legendary," Cher says eagerly, in her cracking cockney accent—still there even though she left London's East End when she was just a girl, but both her parents are cockneys, her grandparents too. "If you're sure that's OK?" she quickly adds, beaming at Lawrence.

"It most certainly is—the more the merrier. And I'll take this little fella downstairs with me, he seems eager for his breakfast too," he laughs as Basil plonks his bottom on Lawrence's left shoe, tilts his black whiskery head up and does his usual "feed-me-because-I'm-starving" (not) look.

With Basil under one arm, Lawrence waves a cheery hand over his shoulder and heads off down the corridor, leaving us to it.

"Babe, I'm so sorry I wasn't here when you arrived," Cher turns to me. "How are you? I could have killed Clive when he casually mentioned that you had helped him with the quiz last night. That was the first I even knew you were here." She pauses to draw breath and roll her eyes.

"Oh, never mind. I've had a fantastic time, honestly," I say, squeezing her hand. "Come inside while I get changed."

"Thanks, babe. But are you sure you're OK?" She twiddles a finger around the inside of her massive gold hoop earring.

"Absolutely. It's been brilliant. Just what I needed—to get away, a change of scenery sure puts lots of things into perspective," I say, closing the bedroom door behind us while trying not to think about Jennifer Ford and Mr. Banerjee and having to face the fallout of all that tomorrow morning at work. I may have eased my broken heart here in Tindledale but there's still the not-so-small matter of £42,000 of taxpayers' money to account for. *Eeep.* And the really lovely thing is that being here in Tindledale, I have felt protected, insulated almost, from it all. "And it's like another world here, and everyone is so friendly," I say quietly, and then, letting my voice trail off, "I really wish I didn't have to go home."

"I wish you didn't have to either," Cher says and I

245

realize that I actually said the words out loud, but before I can tell her all about it, Cher carries on talking.

"Oh God, come here, and give me another hug. I'm so pleased to see you." She gives me a squeeze. "As soon as Clive said you were here, and I'd had a go at him for not ringing me the very minute you walked into the bar, I was out of that dump of a hotel—a shack on the side of a highway, more like. You know, I got woken up at four this morning when one of the druggies in the crack house opposite decided to play silly buggers and call out the fire brigade. And they don't come quietly!" She waggles a sparkly tipped finger in the air. "Oh no, blues and twos, the works. And then they left the lights on for the whole duration of their visit. Spinning round and round and round and round," she loops the finger in a circle to emphasize the spinning motion, "for at least an hour! How am I supposed to sleep with all that going on? I'm telling you, it was like a flaming theme park in that shit-hole of a bedroom." She shakes her head in disgust and I have to stifle a giggle. Typical Cher, always outraged. And always tells it like it really is. "So, have you had any more calls from that sneaky sod of a sister of yours?"

"No. Well, not since I arrived here. I don't have a mobile, remember, so I've been totally incommunicado, which is actually a whole lot better than you might imagine," I say, taking a hairband and scooping my curls up into a messy bun, making a mental note to pop in and see how Poppy is when I get home—I'll call the others too, although I don't fancy going to Zumba again.

"Hmm, mobiles don't work in Tindledale any case," Cher shrugs, "and a good thing too. Maybe Sasha will have got the message by now and stop with all those 'poor me' calls. You're the injured party here, remember." She sniffs in solidarity. "No, those two deserve each other. I never liked Luke in any case," she adds ominously, while flicking a stray lock of hair away from her face.

"Oh?" I crease my forehead in surprise. "You never said."

"Hmm, well, how could I? When we all thought he was going to be your husband. You wouldn't have wanted to hear it, and I wasn't going to risk ruining our friendship over it. How would it have been if you had never have spoken to me again? No, I wasn't taking that chance." Cher bounces down on the bed while I wander into the bathroom, leaving the door ajar, to get changed into my jeans and the gorgeous cashmere sweater that I bought in Ruby's shop yesterday.

"Maybe you have a point. I was a bit oblivious," I call out.

"A bit?" Cher teases.

"OK. A lot. But let's suppose you had said something and I *had* listened like a mature, sensible, grown-up adult," I do a cross-eyed funny face and Cher giggles, "what would you have said to me?"

"That he didn't adore you. That you could do better. That I didn't trust him as far as I could throw him." Cher reels the reasons off on her fingers one by one. "You know, he came on to me once, and—"

"He did?" I jump in, utterly shocked. God, how sordid! My boyfriend trying it on with my own best friend—it's embarrassing, creepy too. With my jeans half up, I shuffle out of the bathroom until I'm standing square in front of her, hands on hips and jeans dropped around my ankles.

"Yep. Don't worry, nothing happened, I'd never do that." Cher holds up her palms in protest and shakes her head vigorously, causing a lock of hair to bounce out of her beehive and plop over the left side of her face. She tucks it behind her ear and leans back on the bed. "Nice knickers, by the way."

"Thanks. They're real silk."

"Classy." She nods and I nod back, reveling in the moment of light relief. And why not? Decent knickers are important, even more so when your ex is clearly a proper shit.

"And?" I say, keen for her to elaborate on Luke's tragic

248

inability to understand that cheating is out of order, and especially with sisters and friends of your girlfriend being totally off-limits.

"Oh, yes, it was ridiculous really—he said that he'd always fancied me and that if I ever wanted to give him a try then to just let him know, or something like that. I just laughed it off as we had all been drinking—it was at that music festival we went to that time. I don't know where you were, queuing up to use one of the rankest bogs in the universe, I think. I was in the tent when he turned up and creeped me out." She grimaces. "Clive wanted to batter him."

"Oh my God, *Clive knew about it*?" I say, aghast. How humiliating! But weirdly, I don't feel anything very much toward Luke. Hurt, a bit, I suppose, but it's more of a stunned numbness to be honest. I pull up my jeans and fasten the button.

"Ah, Clive was fine and we actually laughed it off, once he had calmed down; you know what he's like, and how he goes off the deep end without thinking things through. But he had a word with Luke and told him to show me, *and you*, a bit more respect." She sits back upright and pulls off her jacket. "Blimey, it's hot in here." She dumps her jacket on the carpet. "I'm so sorry babe."

"What for? It wasn't your fault," I say, pushing my head through the neck of the cashmere top.

"Well, for not saying anything before; but I didn't really know what to do for the best. Clive said to forget it and that it would only hurt you and that there was a chance you might not even believe me in any case—plus Luke told me that he'd say that I had come on to him, if you ever found out." She bows her head and lets out a deep breath.

"Hey, it's fine. Honestly, he did me a favor, not turning up at the church, we can all see that now. Lucky escape and all that." I smile wryly. "If he was trying it on with my bestie, and at it with my sister before we were even married, imagine what it would have been like after the wedding, if I had found out about his philandering a few years down the line—a whole lot worse, especially if we had gone on to have children. You can't mess around when it gets serious like that, with responsibilities, it's just not fair," I say, patting her arm. And then it comes to me—what if he does the same thing to Sasha? She is my twin sister after all, and I know we've never had that "twin" connection, sixth-sense bond that people talk about; we don't finish each other's sentences and all that, but I do still love her. The trust has gone, obviously, but I care about her, and we have a shared history from growing up together, which bonds us no matter what, I guess. I wonder if I should talk to her, get it over with and at least hear her out. Hmm, the thought lingers.

"Do you wish I had told you?" Cher says, twiddling her earring again.

"I'm not sure." I shrug. And I'm really not. "Anyway, it's all in the past now. Something I do know is that hindsight may be a wonderful thing at times, but is it always a benefit?" I raise an eyebrow in what I hope is a very profound way and swiftly decide against telling Cher that Luke was never keen on her; he'd always try to stop me going to visit her, claiming she was either using me, because, "How come she never bothers to make an effort to travel to you?" It didn't matter to him that she had a pub to run, he didn't get that, or he'd call her trashy because of the way she dressed. And now I know why. It all fits together; there was a reason why he wanted to keep me away from her—in case she told me all about his pathetic behavior. God, I must have been such an oblivious idiot not to have even had an inkling of what he was really like.

"Indeed," Cher says, jumping up and giving me a hug.

"Come on, let's get some breakfast and have a good catch-up; I want to hear all about the course with the brewery," I say, smiling, not wanting anything to tarnish my last day in Tindledale. I loop my arm through hers as we head downstairs.

*

251

"So you'll at least come and have today's special with me before you go home?" Cher pleads after polishing off the last of an extra-plump pork sausage. She places her knife and fork together on the plate and then dabs the corners of her mouth on the linen napkin. "I won't have seen you at all, hardly, otherwise." She pushes her bottom lip out. "Clive's doing his special mixed roast and all the meat is sourced locally, organic too, I think. Hmm, don't quote on me that as I'm not totally sure, but anyway, there'll be pork with crispy crackling, beef with the biggest Yorkshire puddings you'll ever see, lamb infused with garlic and rosemary, loads of potatoes roasted in goose fat, a vegetable medley pulled from one of the villager's polytunnels mere minutes earlier, stuffing balls—and lashings and lashings of lovely rich gravy," she adds in a silly voice to sound like an Enid Blyton character. And I laugh.

"OK. I promise," I hold up the palms of my hands in protest, but truth be told, I hardly need an excuse to stay a little while longer. And how can I refuse a proper pub Sunday roast lunch?

"Yay!" She claps her hands together in glee.

"But I must pop down to Hettie's first. I need to make sure she's OK, and say goodbye to her properly . . ." My voice trails off. I'm going to worry about her, but she has Marigold, I reassure myself, and make a mental note to call the House of Haberdashery every day to see

252

how she's getting on, and I'll definitely be coming back on weekends, if I can afford to—I could be out of a job by this time tomorrow.

"Why don't you bring her with you?" Cher takes a swig of her tea. "For lunch! And the others, the knit and natter group—the more the merrier. My treat, on the house; my apology for not being in my actual house as it were, when you turned up." She grins.

We've had a lovely catch-up, a gossip and a laugh. I've told her about Ben, and she was very approving, said that he's a far better fit for me than Luke ever was, even if he does seem a bit awkward and inexperienced when it comes to women, at least he won't be thinking he's some kind of super-stud and try it on with my sister and best friend, to which I said, steady on, as absolutely nothing like that has happened between us, apart from him holding my hand, and even that was circumstance rather than a deliberate intention. And I mentioned Adam too, and she said he's out of order for barking at me like that and she has a good mind to bar him if he ever ventures into the Duck & Puddle, which he hasn't done since arriving in Tindledale, and that in itself is odd as far as she's concerned, because everyone who comes to the village ends up in the pub, as I well know.

Hettie was very reluctant at first to join us for lunch so I'm glad Marigold took charge, practically pushing Hettie's spindly arms into the sleeves of her good winter coat—Marigold had mistakenly chosen the thick wool coat at first, only to be told off by Hettie insisting that it wouldn't do to wear "that old thing' to the village pub. Marigold then bundled Hettie into the passenger seat of the Land Rover and chugged us all the way up the grit-covered lane and through the village before abandoning the car right outside the Duck & Puddle's solid oak front door, so Hettie literally had no time to protest further. And it's now a wonderful sight to see her tucking into the mixed roast with all the trimmings—she's sitting beside me at a long scrubbed pine table in the best spot next to the roaring fire in the inglenook surround in the snug. She's still very subdued, worrying about the money and bailiffs coming back, no doubt, but at least she's here among friends.

And I know Marigold and Lawrence will look out for her and I'll be making sure all the eBay stuff gets paid for and posted off right away and Taylor has offered to help out too.

The table is decorated with sparkly wreaths of holly set around crimson-red candles to give it a gloriously homely festive feel, and Michael Bublé is singing "It's Beginning to Look a Lot Like Christmas" through the pub sound system, which I suppose it is. Only seventeen shopping days left! That's what it said on the front page of the *Tindledale Herald* newspaper in the B&B breakfast room this morning. And I haven't really thought about Christmas much this year, having decided a few months ago that Basil and I will just stay at home alone and watch all of the TV while I plunge my face into a tin of Quality Street, lifting it only to swig from the biggest bottle of Baileys that I can find. Talking of which, Cher has just appeared at the table and is now handing out tumblers of the creamy coffee-colored mixture.

"Something to get you all in the Christmassy mood, ladies," she says in a merry voice, giving Leo a wink. He lifts his glass, tilts his head to one side, clicks his tongue on the roof of his mouth and gives her a big wink right back.

They're all here, the knit-and-natter group, plus Lawrence, who's over by the bar chatting to a few of the

Tindledale Players—he's having a rare afternoon off, so I insisted he join us as my guest—I wanted to thank him for being, quite possibly, the best B&B owner in the whole wide world. He's literally moved me on from the perpetual doldrums state that I was in when I came here just a few days ago, and I'm not joking. I can honestly say that I feel as if my life has changed by coming to Tindledale. I look around the table, at all the cheery faces, laughing and toasting each other, chatting about their knitting projects and how the newly formed Tindledale Tappers (the name that Taylor has chosen for the group) could put up a notice in the village store window to see if anyone else would like to join in. The group is thinking of venturing as far as Market Briar too with their invitation—Marigold and Hettie are very keen to get Dolly involved; they're determined to know *exactly* what it was that she was doing up in London when I met her on the train.

It's such a marvelous, close-knit community here, not like the anonymous converted Victorian house I live in at home. Hmm, I wonder if anyone would actually notice if I just never turned up at work again? You hear of it all the time in London—just a few weeks ago there were a few lines in the local paper about the body of a man lying undiscovered for three years before neighbors called the council complaining about the stench—and he had worked for TFL.

I ponder for a bit, daydreaming some more as I immerse myself, watching and listening to the chatter going on around the table, but soon realize that I'm being ridiculous, I can't just leave my life in London behind. Besides, I have a flat with rent and bills to pay for, not to mention the Buy Now Pay Later agreement that I took out with DFS to get a new sofa—I had reached a particularly low point one night soon after the wedding that wasn't, and stabbed apart Luke's old leather two-seater with a crochet hook followed by a pair of size-nine knitting needles. He had brought the sofa from his house share when we first moved in together and was very attached to it, on account of it being his special "gaming" seat. Well, that'll teach him to play games, is what I had thought at the time. Ha! And I have to say that it was pretty satisfying, especially the part where I found a folded-up fifty-pound note wedged inside a crack in the leather. Because as luck would have it, that was the exact same amount the man-with-a-van wanted to take the sofa to the dump. And that's not all, because I also found a pair of Sasha's Jimmy Choo shoes that she had left at my flat one time, then begged me to keep safe as they were limited edition or something—yep, I donated them to the local charity shop.

A woman with fair hair, pale aqua eyes, porcelain skin

and rose-tinted cheeks appears at the table, holding the hand of a very pretty, brown-eyed toddler with a wonky, super-short, Baldrick-from-Blackadder style fringe.

"Kitty!" Lawrence dashes over from the bar and gives her a hug. "And Teddie." He crouches down to smile at the little girl. "Oh dear!" He stands back up and gives Kitty a curious look.

"Mummy got a bit carried away with the fringe trim," Kitty explains with a very regretful look on her face.

"Ah, I see. Want me to even it up sometime?" Lawrence offers jovially.

"Oh, would you mind, please? That would be great," Kitty says, clearly relieved.

"Sure, no problem. So how are you, darling?" Lawrence says, and I scoot along on the bench to make room for them all to sit down.

"Thanks," Kitty says politely, glancing at me then, "Pretty good, thank you," turning to Lawrence, smiling serenely, meeting his gaze then flicking her eyes away. "Yes, we're doing OK, aren't we, petal?" she adds in a kind of dreamy voice, kissing the top of the little girl's head, who's now sitting on her lap snuggling into a fleecy blanket.

"Well done," Lawrence says softly, giving her hand a quick, discreet squeeze before looking at me. He rubs his hands together as if to lighten the mood. "Kitty, did you get to meet Sybs and her dog, Basil?" he says in an extra-cheery voice. Basil, on hearing his name, pops his head up from underneath the table and licks the back of Lawrence's hand. Lawrence gives Basil a piece of pork crackling from his plate. "Shush, don't tell the chef," he jokes. "His crackling is legendary, but you're such a cute dog, plus I'm going to really miss you."

"Oh no, I haven't," Kitty says. "And you're leaving us today, I hear. Have you had a lovely time?" She smiles in my direction as she leans around Lawrence.

"The best, thank you." I grin warmly. "Although I really wish I had made time to pop into the Spotted Pig to try out your panettone bread pudding and rum custard. It sounds truly scrumptious."

"Well, you're in luck because that's why Teddie and I popped in—to deliver a fresh batch to Sonny the chef. He sent the kitchen boy over earlier on the off chance of me making some for today's special," she laughs.

"Ooh," Lawrence and I say in unison, both of us licking our lips in anticipation, not having looked at the pudding menu yet. I've just polished off the mighty mixed roast, which I have to say was just as Cher promised, sterling and superb, and so filling that I can barely move now, but I'm sure I can squeeze in Kitty's pudding too—I'll just propel myself down to the station later, using my wheelie suitcase as a toboggan if I have to.

"And are you OK after your tumble in the village square?" Kitty says softly. My forehead creases and my heart sinks slightly, but it soon lifts when she follows with, "Teddie loves lying in the snow, don't you poppet? It's such fun." The little girl nods and holds out her soft toy cat for me to see. I give it a stroke, feeling relieved and grateful to Kitty for kindly alleviating my potential embarrassment.

"Yes, no physical damage," I say truthfully—only emotional, but I'm dealing with that. I take a big swig of Baileys.

"I wanted to dash out and give you a hug," Kitty continues, lowering her voice and leaning into me, "but I couldn't leave Teddie on her own in the café. I'm so sorry," she adds kindly, and my heart melts; with all that she must be going through, she still has compassion for a total stranger, face planted and bawling in the snow.

"Thank you. You're so kind," I reply, and she simply nods and gives me a gentle look before turning toward Lawrence.

"I was going to call you today, but seeing as you're here I might as well ask you now . . ." Kitty pauses and ruffles Teddie's hair. "I think it's time," she says quietly. "Will you deal with . . . ?"

"Of course I will. No problem at all. I'll call in this evening and take care of it after I've tidied up Teddie's bangs." And whatever it is, makes Kitty let out a long sigh of relief, as if she has been holding it all in and can finally let go. She instantly appears to look lighter, even her shoulders have moved down from the tight position they were in just a few seconds ago at the nape of her neck. The moment changes when Cher darts back over to our table.

"Sybs. So sorry, love, to interrupt your special leaving lunch." She looks really uncomfortable, awkward almost, which is totally unlike her.

"What's up?" I ask, before taking another swig of Baileys.

"Er, there's a phone call for you." And for some reason she looks away.

"Oh?" I lift the linen napkin off my lap, place it on the table and instinctively go to stand up. "Who is it?" I ask. Nobody knows I'm here, apart from Mum. Cher twiddles her earring furiously.

"Please, just come with me out to the back."

"Cher, please, you're scaring me." *God, please don't let something have happened to Mum or Dad.*

"Oh, no, sorry babe, it's nothing like that." A short silence follows. Cher purses her lips, plants a firm hand on her hip and then quickly comes out with it. "It's Luke!"

"I'll be right outside the door if you need me," Cher says kindly, gesturing to the phone on the coffee table in her private lounge behind the bar. I swallow hard and give her a nod before closing the door and lifting the handset to my ear.

"Hello," I say tentatively, my mind already in overdrive, trying to work out why on earth he's calling me now. And here? Surely it can wait until I get back? It's not like he's phoned me at all since the wedding. Apart from one time, which was just full of excuses, so I didn't really listen properly. No, he's left Sasha to make all the calls, claiming that he didn't want to upset me any more than was really necessary. Arrogant, spineless bastard, more like—did I not even deserve an explanation? After he had cleared out his stuff on the day of the wedding, that was that; he cut ties with me, and the flat, not even bothering to inquire about his half of the rent according to the tenancy agreement that he had signed too. Not to mention all the other joint things: utility bills, the massive balance still owed to the wedding venue, the florist, the photographer, the tour bus company. And it didn't all just go away because the wedding didn't happen. It's one thing him not wanting to marry me, but he could have at least mentioned it before the actual day.

"Sybs, it's me!" I close my eyes, momentarily blanching at the presumption that it's OK for him to have retained such familiarity by way of a casual "me."

"Who?" I can't resist making him sweat just a little bit and the hesitation in his voice is palpable.

"Luke."

"Oh, hi," I say as casually as I can possibly muster, followed by a very breezy, "how are you?" And this completely throws him.

"Er, yes, I'm all right." He coughs. A short silence follows. "How about you?" he adds.

"I'm great." And I do the biggest smile ever—so big, I could give Ronald McDonald a run for his money. And because I've been on the telephone techniques course at work and I know that he'll hear it in my voice and, as juvenile and immature as it may seem, I so want him to know that I'm doing fine, *actually*! Just the way I am. I'm not the crumpled mess I was in the weeks after May 4.

"Brilliant," he says in an overly bright fake voice

263

followed by, "I, er, had to call your mum, you know, to like find out where you are," he says, as if it were akin to a waterboarding session. I give him a few more seconds to elaborate further before losing patience.

"Can you get on with it please? Only I'm in the middle of having lunch with friends."

"Friends? What friends?" And there's definitely a hint of surprise, if not suspicion, in his voice.

"Nobody you know." Ha! I catch sight of myself in the mirror above the fireplace and do a very immature smirk. There's a short silence.

"I've been looking everywhere for you. I'm worried about you." Hmm, he hasn't been worried about me for the last six months or so. "Are you OK? Why aren't you at home?" he says, talking too fast.

"I fancied a weekend away," I say.

"I see. I've really missed you." Another silence. "I still care about you, perhaps we could meet up and sort everything out?"

And I'm stunned. Really stunned. Does he have some kind of amnesia? Has he forgotten what he did to me?

"Oh," is all I manage in response.

"What do you reckon?"

"I don't think that's a good idea, right now," I say, knowing if he'd said this a few months ago, then my answer might have been different—I was so desperate for closure, if nothing else, back then, and probably would have leapt at the chance to meet up with him to talk. But not now; I'm in a different place now.

"I see," he says quietly, followed by, "I never meant to hurt you, you know, it just sort of happened—"

"Is that the only reason you called?" I interject. The past is the past and there's no going back, that's what Lawrence helped me realize, and he's right. Besides, I've moved on.

"Yeah," he pauses, "and to say that Mr., er, Mr. Bungee . . ." He stops talking, and sounds distracted, like he's trying to remember the details.

"Banerjee," I correct.

"Yes, that's him. He left a message on Friday afternoon, on my mobile, saying he wants to talk to you urgently. And that he's left loads of messages on your home phone, but you haven't *bothered* to call him back." Hmm, my back constricts. Mr. Banerjee may be a bit traditional in his management style, but he's not rude and I don't believe he'd say I hadn't bothered. Luke has put his spin on it.

"I see." There's no point in pulling him up on it.

"Yeah, so he said that he had no other option than to call the next-of-kin number on your personnel file," he blurts out really fast. "I just picked the message up, we, er, I," he quickly changes, "got back from Dubai this morning and I had my mobile switched off. Didn't want to get stung with a big roaming bill."

"OK." I inhale sharply, immediately parking the "Oh God, Mr. Banerjee must have found out I'm to blame for Jennifer Ford's spending spree" thought that's tearing around inside my head now. Instead, I let out a long silent breath and impulsively decide to go for it, once and for all, remembering my thoughts from yesterday—that she is my sister after all, that everything Lawrence said about letting go of the past and looking forward is right. It's time to draw a line under it. "And how is Sasha?"

"Er, she's . . ." He coughs again and then sounds as if he's clearing his throat in preparation for a big announcement. *Oh God, what's he going to tell me? Surely, they're not getting married, so soon? Or, nooooo! Perhaps she's pregnant?* I place a hand on the mantelpiece as if to anchor myself in readiness. *Keep calm and carry yarn, keep calm and carry yarn.* I say it fast, over and over inside my head like a mantra. "Look, Sybs, this isn't easy for me, you know," he starts, gruffly.

"What isn't?" I ask, making an effort to keep my voice even.

"Well, you know, all this . . ." *Whaaaaat?* "And now, er, well, I've had to move back in with Mum and Dad," he finishes in a decidedly sulky voice.

"Oh?" I say, and an image of him squashed into the single bed of his parents' storeroom springs into my head.

"You might as well know," he says, begrudgingly,

"Sasha never wanted me, not really. I panicked, I felt shit and had to get away, that's why I went with her to Dubai, I needed some space." He can barely contain his perceived sense of injustice from seeping into his voice.

"Oh dear," is the first thing that springs into my head, closely followed by an internal: *awwwww, well cry me a fucking river*, for which I have no shame as he then says,

"So I've got nothing now."

And I end the call.

Ah, now it makes sense. No wonder he's claiming to be missing me. Bullshit! Talk about transparent. He wants to wheedle his way back into the flat. Well, it's tough luck; he clearly doesn't know me at all, if he thinks I'm that daft to not see what his game is. He can stew in his tiny little storeroom while his mummy moans at him for leaving his dirty underwear on the bathroom floor. At least I don't have to step over them any more. Ha!

Moments later, and I'm aware that Cher is in the room.

"You OK, babe?" she asks tentatively, taking the phone from my gripped hand.

"Um, sure . . . yes. That was Luke." The words are coming out of my mouth, but it's as if someone else is saying them; I'm on autopilot. And for a moment, I'm not even sure if the call was real. I take a deep breath and get a grip: it was real all right, and it just goes to show the chasmic difference between Luke and me, what on earth was I thinking? This was the man I had seriously considered marrying, and I realize now that I didn't even know him.

"Yes, I know," she says softly, giving me a look. "What did he want?" Cher cuts to the chase. She's pacing around the room now, twiddling her hoop earing, and with a riotous look on her face.

"I have to call my answering machine at home, Luke said my boss is desperate to get hold of me," I say, still feeling stunned.

"OK," Cher says slowly. "Shall I do that for you?" She has her index finger poised on the keypad.

"No, it's all right. I'll do it, thank you." Cher nods and hands me the phone. "Sasha never wanted him, he said," I say absentmindedly, as I tap out the number.

"Oh!" She hesitates, and then adds a vague, "Good," before letting out a long whistle and shaking her head.

"Are you busy?" I ask. "Only, I could do with . . ." And my voice wobbles slightly. I swallow and try again. "Sorry, it's Sunday lunchtime, of course you are. You're rushed off your feet!"

"Never too busy for you, my friend. I'm sure they can cope without me for a few minutes." She doesn't hesitate, and perches on the arm of the sofa as I lift the phone to my ear.

"Thank you," I mouth as I dial in with my pin number.

A few seconds later, and the automatic voice says there are seven messages. I brace myself and go for it. The first message is from one of the Zumba girls asking if I fancy going again next week, the next four messages are from Gina, starting with a polite "Please can you call the office if you're feeling up to it" through to "Sybil, you need to phone me immediately." Oh crap. The sixth message is from Mr. Banerjee himself.

"Sybil Bloom. This is Mr. Banerjee, senior housing officer, from the housing benefit department," he begins formally—like I don't know who he is already; I've only sat in the end desk three rows behind him for the last nine years. "I'm calling because we're all worried about you, given, your, um, well . . . your track record over the last few months. I'm aware that you've had a difficult personal matter to deal with . . ." He coughs and there's a short pause, followed by the sound of rustling paper-work, as if he's checking his notes. "Maybe you could call me if you're up to it. There's been an incident, which is now under investigation, and we feel it might be wise for you to take a bit of time off while this happens. I under-stand you have a considerable amount of annual leave left still to take before the end of the current year, which will only be lost otherwise, so you could come back to work on . . ." another pause, followed by a woman whis-pering (Gina most likely), "the—oh, the fifth of January."

And the surprise in his voice is palpable. He then goes into a big spiel about my rights and how this will all be put in writing to me, and if I want to talk to someone then that can be arranged too, but a person from HR will be in contact with me in any case. "Good day."

OH. MY. GOD.

I can hear the sound of my own blood pumping in my ears. I feel weird—whoever heard of someone's boss calling to say they can take time off—they must think the cock-up to end all cock-ups is my fault and this is their nice way of saying I'm suspended during the investigation. But I also feel elated too as this means that I can stay off work until after Christmas! And how I feel right now is like nothing I've ever felt before. And you know what? I suddenly realize that I don't actually care what happens to me—just sack me and get it over with already, as I actually hate my job. I do, it's true. Of course, I truly hope I'm not to blame for Jennifer Ford's spending spree; I really do, as I'd never do something like that on purpose. I really wouldn't. I always try to get it right, do the best I can at work. Because I'm not a total idiot or fantasist; I know I have to support myself. As much as I'd love to knit and sew and earn my living that way, it's just not ever been possible. And then it dawns on me! What if I am sacked? It's one thing being all blasé and bold about it, but when it really comes down to it, how the hell will I survive with no income? I'll be evicted if I don't pay the rent and then Basil and I will end up homeless, which would be utterly ironic given that I had worked in the housing office, as there is no way I'm doing a Luke and scuttling back home to my parents' house.

There's one last message.

"Sybil, darling, it's Mum. You'll never guess what, sweetheart?" She pauses to draw breath. "I was in the middle of packing your father's suitcase for the cruise, and the house phone rang. It was Luke! And he wants to talk to you *right away*." And I swear her voice lifts a couple of octaves in sheer exuberance. "He sounded so sad. Maybe he's missing you and wants to make another go of it. That's nice, isn't it? And just before Christmas too. Now don't be worrying about Sasha—I'll talk to her, I'm sure she'll understand." I delete the message before she has time to draw another breath and continue on her merry crusade to pair me off with a man, any man it seems, just to save me from myself.

*

"So that settles it, then. You're staying in Tindledale for Christmas," Cher says, jumping up and giving me a hug after I've brought her up to speed on the Jennifer Ford cock-up and how, as of now, I'm officially on annual leave.

I pull back. "Hey, what's up?" she adds, gently lifting my chin to look me in the eye.

"Oh Cher, I wish it were as simple as that." I chew at a cuticle, my mind racing at this sudden twist of events.

"What do you mean? Why isn't it?" she frowns.

"Well, where I will stay, for starters? Lawrence is fully booked for Christmas with a group of tourists; apparently they come every year from Japan."

"Yes, I heard about that too, Cooper was chatting about it in the bar the other night—said they love the quintessential British countryside. They even have a theme park replica of a traditional English village somewhere near Tokyo—one of the tourists told Cooper all about it on their last trip here."

"Blimey."

"Yep. Fancy that. Anyway, they can't get enough of it, so this group comes every year to experience the real thing—the traditional Tindledale village Christmas. Cooper said it's marvelous, because they spend loads of money in the village shops and go mad for his special hog roast at the annual Christmas Fair, which takes place on Christmas Eve over on the village green. He asked if I was up for supplying a gazillion vats of mulled wine— they get through it like water, apparently."

"Sounds amazing," I say, and much more appealing than my sad, home-alone Baileys and Quality Street combo. But I feel like crap. Crap that I've messed up so royally at work. How can I have been so careless to let something in my personal life affect things so much at work? I should have taken time off and stayed at home as was suggested after the wedding that wasn't, instead of carrying on like a robot, too afraid to stop in case I just broke down and crumbled away into nothing very much at all. I should never have taken the sleeping pills—Ben was right, my head was foggy, I can see that now I've been off them for a while. The clarity that faded away on my so-called wedding day has now returned, but what will Mr. Banerjee discover during the investigation? That £42,000 of taxpayers' money has been squandered on expensive hair extensions and gambled away in Vegas and it's all my fault? Yes, he's being nice about it now, but when it comes to light I'll be sacked for sure. Maybe I should take Ben up on his offer to sign me off work for diminished responsibility or whatever; at least then I'd have an excuse for having cocked up so monumentally. I take a deep breath and will myself to get a grip, as, to be honest, I really don't want to drag Ben into it all. This is baggage, and I'd rather not have it hanging over me—us—if there's a chance of something happening with him. No, when he walked me over to the pub and held my hand so firmly, it was lovely, special, and being here in Tindledale is wonderful; I'll always cherish the memory of this weekend because it's been brilliant, magical even, and I don't want that tarnished in any way. I want Tindledale to be totally separate from the rubbish and heartache associated with work and home.

"Sure does!" says Cher. "And stop being so hard on yourself—if you slink off home like a martyr just to sit on your spike, what will that achieve? You'll just miss out. So what, you cocked up! I'm sure you're not the only person ever to have made a mistake at work. It's not like you stole the money on purpose, and you did have a lot going on, to be fair, mitigating circumstances and all that," she continues, pragmatically.

"Maybe, but it is a pretty big mistake and it'll be near-on impossible for me to find another job if I'm sacked. Of course, I'm delighted at the prospect of staying here for Christmas, but I can't shake off this feeling of failure, of cocking up at work, big-time."

"Ah, I'm sure that's not true. Look, it'll be fine: you never know, it might not be anything you've done in any case. Computer error. Happens all the time, and when they find out, your job will still be there. But until it's all sorted out, you can stay here. I've got beds on order from IKEA, which should arrive tomorrow, so you can give me a hand to put them together, in situ, Clive is hopeless at stuff like that." She grins, having it all worked out.

"Really?"

"Yes, really," Cher laughs.

"And you're sure you wouldn't mind? Basil too?" I grin, warming to the idea.

"Now you're being daft. Of course you and that cheeky mutt, you idiot!" she says kindly.

"I need to go home though, at least to collect clothes and makeup and stuff." I feel excited now, the shock of being asked to take some time off—read, suspended, I'm convinced of it—having sunk in a little.

"Or you could just wear jeans for the duration like everyone else does in Tindledale; I've cut back considerably on makeup since I've been here. All you really need is some wellies and you can easily pick up a pair in Market Briar."

"Hmm, I could certainly do with a pair," I say, hardly bearing to peep down at my fetid Converse.

"Well, I'm heading there tomorrow to bank this weekend's takings, so you can come with me. There's even a cute little Boots just off the market square if you really need a new lipstick." Cher purses her lips and flutters her eyes in a silly way.

"And you know how much I love Boots," I say, my mind in overdrive.

"Well, there you go. Come on, it'll be fun. Dr. Ben will be pleased, that's for sure. He popped in for a pint and

275

a packet of crisps when you were on the phone to Luke and asked if I thought you might be coming back to Tindledale sometime soon. So now you can tell him yourself. I bet he asks you out again." She nudges me gently and I smile. "And your new knitting buddies will be thrilled to have you around for a bit longer, I'm sure. I heard them all chatting, something about an order that had come through. Very excited they were, and poor old Hettie looked near to tears."

"Really?" I say, jumping up, excitement bubbling some more. Poor old Hettie indeed—I'm worrying about losing my job, when it could be much, much worse. At least I'm not on the verge of having my home, my memories and my whole world repossessed. No wonder she's been terse and outspoken, her heart is probably a bit broken too. "Thanks, Cher." I give her a big hug.

"What for?" She scrunches up her face.

"For sticking by me, and for not judging me, and well, for putting everything into perspective."

"Hmm, not sure how I've done that, but it sounds like a compliment so I'll take it," she beams.

"And so you should, my lovely, loyal friend."

"Awwwww, that's what friends are for!"

21

When I make it back out to the pub room, Ben is standing by the bar, and he grins and waves me over.

"Nice to see you're still here," he starts, offering me his packet of crisps, which I wave away after saying a polite, "no thank you." "I thought you were leaving today." He fidgets with his glasses.

"I was, but change of plans—I'm staying for a while longer. For Christmas, in fact," I tell him.

"That's great. So does this mean you have time to try some hypnotherapy then?" he asks eagerly.

"Um, I'd rather not," I smile, and his face drops, "but I could try another brandy some time." I grin, and he nods and smiles.

"I'd like that. I could call you." He pulls an iPhone from the pocket of his jeans as if to store my number.

"Oh, I don't have a mobile."

very wise, damn thing drives me mad." And he shoves his phone away.

"I'm staying with Cher, here at the pub so . . ."

"Perfect. Seeing as I spend most of my time in here, when I'm not at the office or out on house calls, that is."

"OK." I grin, then add, "I had better go as I'm having lunch with . . ." and I gesture over to the table where the Tindledale Tappers are all looking over at us, whispering and nudging each other like a bunch of giggly schoolgirls. "You're welcome to join us if you like?"

"Oh, no, I need to get going, I'm on call later."

"On a Sunday?"

"Yep, I'm part of the rural group that covers Tindledale and all of the surrounding villages," he explains.

"Ah, I see. Well, another time then perhaps," I say, before wandering over to join the others.

Taylor jumps up, and after squeezing around the backs of all the chairs, she eventually makes it to my side of the table with Lawrence's laptop open in her arms.

"You OK?" she asks, bobbing down beside me. "Only you look a bit flushed."

"Oh yes, I'm fine," I say in my best breezy voice.

"You sure?" She nudges me gently and I smile, thinking that she might be a typical, petulant teenage girl at times, but she's also very lovely too.

"Yes, sure. Thank you." I pull a big smile onto my face

and pat her arm fondly. I take a deep breath. "I hear there's an order. Is it for a sweater?" I mentally cross my fingers, knowing this could be the start of things that could make all the difference to Hettie.

"Er, excuse me!" she giggles, casting a glance around the table, and they all lean forward, with enthusiastic looks on their faces, eager for her to share the very exciting news. "Not just one order. Oh no! But a really big order."

"Go on." My heart beats a little faster.

"The Japanese tourists want *fifteen*, that's *one five*," she says cheekily, making us all laugh, "of your Ho Ho Ho sweaters." And everyone claps, even little Teddie, who has no idea why, but joins in anyway, pulling her chubby toddler hands together and giggling at Kitty, who smiles and nods her head.

"Wow! Really?"

"Yes, really." Taylor taps the screen and Amber leans across the table to pat her proudly on the back.

"This is incredible," I say, my heart lifting, especially on seeing Hettie's face; the deep furrow between her eyebrows has softened. I sit down on the nearest chair, my mind instantly in overdrive trying to work out if this, together with the money from the bone knitting needles, is enough to buy Hettie some more time with the bailiffs. I put a price tag of £75 on the sweater, figuring that was about right, after finding a few similar ones for

.parison. Hmm, well over a thousand pounds, which a jolly good start.

"It sure is," Molly heckles from the far end of the table.

"So when do they want them by?" I turn to Taylor.

"Ooh, hang on a minute—I didn't even think to check that, I was so excited to see the first order." She taps the keyboard. "Um, OK, here we go, there's a note next to the payment details and the sizes required—all small, by the way," she grins.

"Jolly good, means we can knit them more quickly," Leo says, thinking practically.

"Does this mean they've already paid?" Hettie asks in a low voice, leaning into me, before glancing in Marigold's direction.

"They pay half up front and the other half on completion," I say quietly, squeezing her hand reassuringly under the table.

"Ah, and it says they'd like the sweaters ready to wear when they arrive," Taylor beams.

"But they're coming on the twentieth of December!" Lawrence exclaims. "Can you knit fifteen sweaters by then?"

"Of course we can," Hettie sniffs. "That's two weeks away. If I can knit a sweater in a weekend, then I'm sure between us, we can knit fifteen in a fortnight. And Japanese people are very petite, not like the lumbering big-chested farmers we have around here. [...] around the group and they nod vehemently in a[...] all determined to knit fifteen small Ho Ho Ho[...] in the allocated time.

I swivel the laptop screen around to check the[...]

"Hang on a minute!"

"What is it?" Marigold says.

"They don't want fifteen sweaters . . ." I hesitate a[...] tap through to the orders page again, just to be sure.

"Oh no, don't tell me it's a hoax, or that I got it wrong,[...] Taylor grumbles, leaning back in her seat, crossing her arms for a sulk.

"Oh. My. God." I fling a hand to my mouth.

"What is it?" Hettie turns to me with a worried look on her face, clasping her hands in her lap. Marigold leans forward, looking concerned.

"Hettie, just how fast can you knit?" I start slowly, keeping my voice even.

"*Very* fast. You know I can," she says proudly, puffing her tiny birdlike chest out a little farther.

"Good. That's very good. Exceedingly good, in fact. Because . . . guess what?" I take a deep breath.

"Whaaaaat?" they all shout out.

"This order, your very first order for Hettie's House of Haberdashery online shop, isn't for fifteen sweaters at all, oh no. This order is for *seventy-five* festive Ho Ho

281

aters!" I yell at the top of my voice,
in my sheer joy. And then comes the
after panic at this revelation. And for
er, I imagine (apart from when I first
door on Thursday night), the exuberant
me crowd of the Duck & Puddle pub in
of Tindledale falls completely silent. Even
iggling and stares openmouthed, swiveling
d around the table, looking at each of us

that case, it's a blooming good thing that
aying with me for Christmas then!" Cher bellows
dly from behind the bar.

Really? Is this true?" Lawrence asks, giving me a big
hug. Hettie is staring at me, barely able to take it all in
and I'm sure there's a glimmer of a tear in her eye.

"Yes!" I nod and grin, before swallowing the last of
my Baileys. And everyone starts cheering, then laughing
and then panicking and talking over each other really
fast.

"But how are we going to do it all?" I hear Marigold
say to Edie.

"Yes, I can knit fast, but not that fast, and what about
the wool? Does Hettie even have enough stock to cover
such a huge project?" Edie then replies, turning to Louise
with a look of sheer panic in her eyes.

"OK, let's all calm down," I interject, flapping my hands around for them to stop—I can see Hettie is getting anxious, she's twisting a hanky around and around her left index finger.

"Don't you mean keep calm and carry yarn?" smiles Leo. "I spotted it on your very gorgeous knitting bag," he explains.

"Ha! Yep, that too." They all quiet down. "OK, it says here," I point to the laptop again, "that only fifteen sweaters need to be ready for when the tourists arrive; they want to wear them to the Christmas Fair on the village green, apparently." A collective "Awwwww, that's nice," goes around the table. I scan the notes on the screen some more. "That'll be why you thought the order was for just fifteen, Taylor."

"Phew. I can read properly after all," she says, inspecting one of her loom bands.

"Of course you can!" I smile at her, before addressing the group again. "And Hettie has more than enough yarn in stock so I really think we can do this," I say, truly hoping they'll help out, and remembering Hettie's stock cupboard under the stairs—even after I had finished filling the display unit, there must have been at least a billion balls still left in there. I'm convinced of it.

"Oh, panic over! That's definitely doable," laughs Marigold, "even with my appallingly slow knitting. I'm sure even I can manage a sleeve or two, if someone casts me on and starts me off."

"But, there is an additional request—very polite it is too," I continue.

"Oh, yes, they're always very polite," Lawrence says proudly.

"Ah, here we go." I scroll farther down the online order form. "They want the other sixty sweaters to arrive at the theme park near Tokyo, by Wednesday, December 24, for the staff to wear over the Christmas period."

Cue another stunned silence.

"In that case, I'd better call the chair of the bridge club, straight away," says Marigold, instantly getting involved, as she did when the bailiffs turned up. "And my friends in the Women's Institute will help too, they owe me a favor after I persuaded Lucan to let them hold what's become an annual summer fete on the estate. And they all love knitting, so I'm sure they'll jump at the chance to help Hettie. And besides, it'll be so much fun."

"But the kids break from school soon, so I'm going to have my hands full with them." Molly sighs. "Oh well, they'll just have to get on with it, the older ones can look after the little one." She puffs and pulls a diary from her bag, flicking through the pages, counting the days off one by one. "This is really important for Hettie's livelihood," she raises her eyebrows to Marigold, who nods surreptitiously before glancing away. Ah, so word of the bailiffs' visit has got around the village already then, I see. Molly continues, "And it's important for Tindledale too, we need our small businesses to thrive or, before we know it, the heart and soul will have been ripped out of the village and replaced with a massive big horrible housing development or supermarket or whatever." Hmm, so they *do* all know about Hettie's nephew's plans. "And we certainly don't want to let our Japanese friends down; their custom has been very good for the village over the years." They all nod.

"Then we'll all chip in and make it work," Lawrence summarizes brightly. "I'll have you know that I'm a very good knitter so I'll gladly help out if I can—I'll be busy with the pantomime but I'm sure I can squeeze in a few sleeves, they don't take long, or I can do some sewing up or whatever. I need to make sure my Japanese guests are well looked after, so they come back next year, and the year after that and so on and so on and so on." He laughs.

"And I could occupy the children for you, Molly," Beth says.

"No, you can't. You're needed for knitting," Hettie jumps in with a panicky look on her face. "But they can join us at the shop. There's plenty of space now that Sybil has kindly cleared out all the rubbish, or there's the garden around the oast if they want to play in the snow. It's a pity

I don't have a TV, children like TV these days." She twists her hanky some more, obviously keen to make this work.

"It'll be fine, Hettie, please don't worry," I say, reassuringly. "I'll draw up a list of knitters, once Marigold has roped everyone in, and then we can plan out the most efficient way to get the sweaters knitted in time. I'll knit day and night if I have to." There's a collective reply of "me too" and lots of nodding around the table. It's wonderful to see how keen they are to pull together and help their neighbor Hettie out.

"And I can help too," Kitty joins in. "I won't be able to leave the Spotted Pig to come and sit with you at Hettie's, but I can knit, and it'll give me something to do of an evening."

Cher arrives with the panettone bread pudding.

"Careful now, this is really hot," she says, lowering an enormous ceramic dish, with tea towels at either end, into the center of the table. Clive comes over with a steaming jug of brandy custard, which smells divine, all homey and Christmassy and comforting, with the kitchen boy behind him who's pushing a trolley with a big pile of bowls and spoons on it.

"You're in for a treat, ladies and gents," says Clive. "Kitty has excelled herself with this pudding." They exchange nods.

"And don't be worrying about the kids," Cher says,

looking at Molly. "We can set up a playroom in the games room at the back of the pub. There's a TV and DVD player in there." She beams, slinging the tea towels over her shoulders.

"And I'm sure my teaching assistant would be happy to help out," Beth jumps in. "She was just saying a few days ago that now her two grown-up sons are off gallivanting around Australia, she's at a bit of a loss over the holidays and really not looking forward to being home alone just twiddling her thumbs."

"Oh, is that Pearl? Lives in Rose Cottage down near the station?" Molly asks eagerly.

"Yes, that's her," Beth replies.

"Lovely woman. My four boys adore her. And I know lots of other mums that knit, and would most likely jump at the chance to join in the knit-off if their kids can play with my lot. They'll be climbing the walls by day two of the holidays in any case, that's for sure." She purses her lips and picks up a serving spoon to portion the pudding into bowls, which she then hands to Amber to start passing around the table.

"Well, that's settled then. I'll pop in and check with her on my way home," says Beth. "But I'm sure it'll be fine."

"Now, will you please all get stuck into your puddings?" Cher laughs. "You need to keep up your strength for the great Christmas knit-off!"

22

The following morning, and we've wasted no time in casting on. Cher's new beds arrived first thing, so after trying to help her put them together and failing miserably (she called Pete to help in the end, with promises of free beer until the end of the year), I managed to find the Ho Ho Ho pattern online, print off several copies on Lawrence's printer and brought them straight here to Hettie's House of Haberdashery so we could all get started.

It turns out that Mr. Tanaka, one of the Japanese tourists, has an uncle on the board of the English village theme park near Tokyo and they had a knitting factory lined up to produce sixty festive sweaters for the staff to wear over Christmas. But when the factory went into liquidation, and Mr. Tanaka was browsing all things Tindledale and getting excited for his annual trip, he spotted Hettie's new website, and my Ho Ho Ho sweater hanging in the window, and promptly told his uncle, who decided that a traditional hand-knitted Christmas sweater was exactly what was needed to replace the original order. Apparently, they had been trying to find another supplier and had almost given up hope because all the traditional British knitting companies they had contacted were already swamped with Christmas commissions. It seems wacky Christmas sweaters really are in great demand this year.

Half the payment was wired overnight, so Hettie immediately repaid the £500 she owed to Marigold, who was very reluctant to take it but finally caved in when Hettie threatened to expel her from the Tindledale Tappers if she refused, and seeing as this is the most fun that Marigold has had in years, she quickly accepted, and then called the bailiffs to clear some more of the arrears on the loan. The order has bought Hettie some much-needed time—we just have to knit the sweaters and get them to Tokyo so that Hettie has the rest of the money to have a chance of saving her home and the wonderful House of Haberdashery.

So it's all hands on needles here in Tindledale, and there must be at least thirty people crammed into Hettie's shop, every one of them knitting and nattering away, with every available chair, sofa and stool occupied. There are even a couple of guys sitting on the rug in front of the fire—fashion and textiles students home from university for the holidays, they saw Taylor's postcard in the village store and came right away to join in.

The most experienced knitters are working on sweater fronts with the Ho Ho Ho pattern on, while everyone else has been assigned to either backs, sleeves, sewing together, stitching on the *Handmade by Hettie's House of Haberdashery* labels or keeping the fire stoked and the biscuit barrel fully stocked—some of Taylor's friends turned up, which is wonderful and they'll get taught how to knit in time, but for now, it's definitely all about the great Christmas knit-off, as it's now known in and around the village after everyone heard Cher christen the project accordingly in the pub.

The click-clack of the needles is deafening at times, but brilliant too, a real feeling of community, of neighbors and friends, and strangers until today, all pulling together and having a laugh in the process—Leo has had us all in stitches with his outrageous tales from last summer in Marbella, followed by Edie telling us about her time in the fifties, when she worked as a waitress, or a Nippy as they were known, in a Lyons Corner House tea shop on the Strand in London. She still has a photo somewhere at home, of her in the iconic black-and-white uniform, which she's promised to bring along tomorrow to show us all. Truly fascinating. And one of the Women's Institute ladies brought along a big silver tea urn (currently installed on the draining board in Hettie's kitchen-cum-sitting-room) and her recently retired husband came too with instructions to "make himself useful and hand out hot drinks," which worked very nicely with the delicious big bacon sandwiches that Cooper sent down with Molly (minus the ferret) for our brunch break.

"Oh, Cher's here now," I say, on seeing her snow-covered car pull up outside the shop. She's scraped the windows clear, leaving about a six-inch chunk of snow balancing precariously on the roof, half of which slides down the front, caking the hood and windshield as she skids to a halt. I finish my row and place the knitting carefully into my bag, figuring I can easily get this section finished on the journey to Market Briar, and every moment of knitting time counts when you're working on such a big project as we are right now.

"Right you are, dear." It's Hettie, who looks up from her knitting. "Will you call me on the phone, the very minute you know?" she asks, anxiously. Ever since the order came in, Hettie has been panicking about getting the sweaters to Tokyo on time, especially as the last date for guaranteed delivery by Christmas with the Royal Mail is already long gone.

"Yes, of course, I promise." I jump up to pull on my parka and scarf. Basil doesn't even stir; he's far too busy being tickled by Taylor's friends.

"Leave him here; poor thing doesn't want to go out in this cold weather," Hettie says, seeing me looking his way. "He'll be fine here with us."

"Thanks," I grin. "And Hettie, please don't worry." It came to me in the early hours of this morning when I woke from a long, deep sleep, which is a welcome and regular occurrence now, regardless of my brandy consumption, and suddenly remembered Dolly's import and export business, so Cher and I are calling in on our way to Market Briar. "And if Dolly can't help then we'll find another way—there are lots of courier companies who I'm sure will leap at the chance to take sixty Christmas sweaters to Japan for us."

"But won't they be very expensive?" Molly asks, before taking a sip of her tea. "Dolly might give us a discount," she adds hopefully.

"Ah, we don't need to worry about that—Mr. Tanaka has already confirmed that he's covering the shipping costs. I just need to let him know in advance so he can transfer the payment; it'll all work out fine, you'll see." I smile again at Hettie, wishing she wouldn't worry, but it must be so hard for her—I saw the pile of ominous-looking post that arrived for her earlier and that hateful nephew of hers has been bothering her again; I overheard her on the phone saying, "I'm not ready to go into a home." And another time, Marigold heard her saying,

292

"My home is here in Tindledale. Your father would turn over in his grave if he heard you saying such things." It's such a shame, but at least, hopefully, now Hettie can hold on to her House of Haberdashery for a while longer.

"Oh, goody," Molly adds, helping herself to a chocolate cookie and a baby wipe to clean her hands with afterward. Hettie, quite rightly, has given everyone instructions to make sure the sweaters are perfectly pristine—"no sticky fingerprints on the wool please" is what she said at eight this morning when the knit-off commenced. *Or ferrets on leashes,* is what I had thought, which thankfully isn't the case today—the ferret is safely tucked up in its cage at home.

*

Forty minutes later, and Cher and I are traveling very slowly on account of all the snow piled up on either side of the Old Market Briar road when the GPS lady tells us to take the next left turn. I've managed to get quite a bit more knitting done and we've had a good gossip and catch up.

Cher manages to steer the car down a long, winding country lane, with even bigger banks of snow piled up high on either side, and up to the door of an enormous timber-clad barn. But there are no lights and a big "closed" sign is in the window. My heart sinks as we get out of the car.

"Oh no," I say, my breath making misty clouds puff into the freezing air.

"Come on, let's try there," Cher points, trudging through the snow to a detached house nearby with a big bushy Christmas tree twinkling merrily in the bay window. She rings the bell, but nothing happens, and we're just about to leave when an ancient old man bent over a Zimmer frame eventually pulls open the front door.

"Yeeeessss?" he rasps, lifting his watery eyes up to see us.

"Oh hello, um, I'm really sorry to bother you, is Dolly at home, please?" I ask, surreptitiously glancing over his bony shoulder to see down the hallway, the walls of which are adorned with a multitude of chintzy patterned china plates, hanging in little wire frames.

"Who?" he asks, pulling a hanky from his cardigan pocket to wipe the drip from the end of his nose.

"Dolly." I grin.

"Dolly? Who is Dolly?" He looks to Cher, as if for an explanation.

"Oh, um, she owns the business in the barn next door," I say, figuring this was a bad idea; he clearly has no idea who I'm talking about. "I'm so sorry, we must have the wrong house . . ." And just as we turn to leave,

Dolly appears on the path to the side of the house, wearing a black padded long coat and leather riding boots with an old wicker basket full of mud- and feather-daubed eggs looped over her left arm.

"Sybil. What a wonderful surprise. I was just seeing to the chickens." She pats the basket and then turns to the old man. "Dad, what are you doing at the door? It's freezing out here, come on, let's get you back inside in the warm." Dolly shakes her head and goes to gently lead him by the arm. "Let's have some tea," she calls over her shoulder to Cher and me.

Ten minutes later, and we're ensconced in Dolly's farmhouse kitchen, seated around a circular wooden table next to a buttercup-yellow Aga, and warming our hands on generous mugs of tea. The delicious cinnamony and orange aroma of festive baking permeates the air, and the old man is dozing in a patchwork armchair with a crocheted blanket tucked over his knees.

"Sorry, dear, his memory isn't what it used to be," Dolly mouths, after I've introduced her to Cher and they've exchanged pleasantries about the Duck & Puddle—Dolly's first husband, Basil, used to take her there for a stew and a pint of cider when they were courting.

"Ah, not to worry," I smile, eyeing up the plate of homemade mince pies in the center of the table.

"Go on, take one, or two if you like," Dolly chuckles, passing the plate to Cher and then to me. We both help ourselves and take big bites of the still warm, deliciously soft and crumbly sweet pies. "So, how is Hettie these days?" Dolly asks, ladling three spoonfuls of sugar into her tea and giving it a good stir. I've already explained all about the Tindledale Tappers and the Japanese Christmas sweater order and she's more than happy to organize the delivery, and there's absolutely no problem in getting them to Tokyo by Christmas Eve, which is a massive relief. Hettie will be thrilled when I tell her.

"Busy," I smile, figuring this to be the best answer; besides, it's not my place to talk about bailiffs or that horrible nephew of hers with his heart set on tearing down her house and ripping the soul out of the village with his big housing subdivision plans.

"Will you give her my regards, dear, and please explain that I'm not really one for knitting, otherwise I'd gladly help out with that too." She smiles apologetically. "Plus I've got my hands full with the business, and looking after Dad, now that he's living with us. I just couldn't leave him in that awful home up in London. Shocking, it was, and I have no idea what possessed him to move up there in the first place, all those years ago." She shakes her head. "I took one look at him last Thursday and was horrified—I'd been up to visit him when I met you on the train" (ah, so that's what she was doing in London and I wonder if I should inform Hettie and Marigold) "– and then I got home, and my husband, Colin, was horrified too, so we drove up yesterday and fetched him back, and here he is, being properly looked after and where I can keep an eye on him." She smiles fondly in his direction. "And Marigold? Is she still going strong, we were at school together, and I haven't seen her in years?"

"They certainly are. And Marigold has been a big help with the shop." I pause, and then quickly add, "and the knitting too," just in case she queries why Hettie might need help.

"Oh, God help you, she was never one for knitting." Dolly laughs, shaking her head, and the old man stirs.

"Is there one of those pies for me?" he says jovially, rubbing his hands together in anticipation. Dolly puts one on a plate and takes it to him with a paper napkin.

"You remember Hettie, don't you, Dad?" Dolly says, lifting her voice so he can hear.

"Who?"

"Hettie. You know, with the haberdashery shop in Tindledale," she prompts.

"Ah. Tindledale, yes, such a beautiful place—I was the postman there," he says to Cher and me.

"That's right, Dad," Dolly nods, then explains to us, "Bill isn't my father; he's the father of my late husband, Basil."

"Basil? Who's Basil?" Bill says, and Dolly stares at her tea momentarily, before giving us a sad smile.

"I'm so sorry," she says softly and I smile sympathetically at her, unsure really of what to say, but knowing that it must be so heartbreaking for her, with her father-in-law having no memory of his deceased son, which in turn means no fond reminiscing together over her first husband.

"Bill, tell us about Tindledale." It's Cher, who salvages the moment. She moves her chair so it's up close to Bill's and gives him a big smile of encouragement.

"It's such a lovely village. I was the postman there, you know," Bill says proudly, and Cher nods.

"How did you get around to deliver the letters, Bill? Did you have a van?" she adds patiently, and I'm surprised, I've never seen Cher like this before.

"Oh no, I had a bicycle. Glorious it was in the summer, cycling down the lanes with the wind in my hair and the sun on my back." He smiles and a light comes into his eyes. "Not so in the winter," he laughs, shaking his head and pulling a face now. "Harsh, it was. I remember one winter, 1959, at the beginning of December, when it was so cold the letterbox on the Honey family's oast had frozen tight shut!"

"Blimey, what did you do, Bill?" Cher asks, her face full of fascination and intrigue.

"I pushed open the front door, of course. Good job too, or heaven knows what would have happened to the lady." He pauses to take a bite of his mince pie. After dabbing his mouth with the napkin, he continues. "Lying crumpled at the bottom of the stairs she was, out like a light." Bill shakes his head, his face creasing with concern.

"Gosh, that must have been a shock for you, Bill," Cher continues. "So what happened next?"

"I ran to the phone box down the lane and called Dr. Donnelly up in the village; he came right away, but the ambulance took ages to arrive as it had to come all the way from Market Briar." And I spot a slight tremble in his hands; he's clearly still shaken by the event, even after all these years.

"Oh dear. And was she all right?" Cher places a gentle hand on his forearm.

"Who?"

"The lady," Cher prompts, softly.

"Oh, you mean Hettie?" Bill pauses, and then nods solemnly. "Yes, they patched her up good enough. But the baby not so; crushed underneath her body, you see!" And I let out an involuntary gasp as I bring a hand up to my mouth. Oh my God, poor, poor Hettie.

23

"Fifty-seven. Fifty-eight. Fifty-nine." And I lift the last, carefully folded, Ho Ho Ho sweater up high in the air, just like Rafiki held Simba up to the animals in *The Lion King*, and the whole shop bellows, "SIXTY!" as I bring it back down, wrap it in red tissue paper and place it in the box with the special *Hettie Wishes You a Wonderful Tindledale Christmas* card.

"Hurray!" A spontaneous whoop ricochets, followed by a massive sigh and a "thank God for that," from Molly as she slumps back in her armchair, clearly exhausted as she stretches her arms high above her head and wriggles her fingers around. But we did it! We knitted seventy-five sweaters between us, in total, and in little over two weeks. Surely that must be some kind of Guinness World Record?

Leo leaps forward to sprinkle in the festive red and green Christmas tree-shaped confetti, while I peel off a length of the special *Priority* printed packing tape that Dolly gave us to bind up the boxes securely. On Dolly's advice, we've put thirty sweaters in each box, just in case one goes astray, which she promised has never, ever happened before, so it's not likely to now, but better be safe than sorry and thirty is better than none and all that, although it hasn't stopped Hettie from worrying as always, even though Mr. Tanaka has already transferred the final part of the payment and she's cleared the arrears on the loan in full. Hettie is still concerned that her reputation could be on the line if the sweaters don't arrive, and that nobody will want to shop in her online store if word gets out, even though there are already lots of delighted customers. Only this morning, the woman who won the bone knitting needles auction sent a thank-you card, saying how delighted she was with them, commenting specifically on their prompt arrival and pretty packaging—Taylor had gift-wrapped them with a length of vintage William Morris wallpaper that we found behind one of the armchairs and a midnight-blue velvet ribbon tied up in a big bow. And the lemon lace-weight shawls have all sold too, as I knew they would, so Hettie's House of Haberdashery online shop has already got off to a very impressive start.

"What if they don't arrive and he wants the money back—I can't give it to him," Hettie said last night when the others had gone home to get some much-needed sleep. I tried to reassure her that everything will be fine, that Dolly knows what she's doing and that her company has an excellent reputation, with numerous glowing testimonials on the website extolling the super efficiency and promptness of service, but Hettie still doesn't seem very convinced. Or perhaps it was my mention of Bill, the postman, which has unsettled her—she just stared right through me before dashing out to the kitchen-cum-sitting-room. And just like the time before with the hanky in the suitcase, I let her be, sensing her desire to be alone with her thoughts. And I've not asked about the baby, figuring that was far too delicate a subject to broach. And besides, it really is none of my business, unless Hettie wants it to be.

Dolly arrives right on time, and I've just finished helping her to load the boxes into the back of her car when another car pulls up and Ruby jumps out. I wave goodbye to Dolly and walk toward Ruby.

"Hey, Sybs, do you have a minute?" she says, greeting me with a kiss on either cheek before blowing on her hands and stamping her feet on the ground to keep them warm.

"Sure, why don't you come on inside? We're about to have a party to celebrate the end of the great Christmas knit-off; you're welcome to join us for a mince pie and a mug of mulled wine, if you like—we filled up the tea urn," I laugh, remembering the look on the WI lady's face when she realized that Leo had swapped the stewed tea inside for several litres of Cher's deliciously festive concoction. And the urn is perfect for keeping the wine at an optimum temperature.

"Ah, thanks honey, but this is a flying visit. I'm due on the Picture House stage in two hours and I must brush out my rollers and get my timeless glam on," she says, doing her throaty laugh and gesturing to her hair which is piled up underneath a gold-patterned Hermès silk headscarf. She snaps open the clasp of her black crocodile leather, forties-style handbag. "I wanted to bring these back." She goes to hand me a bundle of letters tied up with a piece of pink satin ribbon.

"Oh, thanks, but what are they?" I ask, flicking through them—there must be at least twenty envelopes here, all in swirly black old-fashioned handwriting, written with a proper ink pen too, by the looks of it.

"Well, here's the thing . . ." Ruby pauses, and glances at the shop behind me and then back to look me straight in the eye. "I found them at the bottom of Hettie's old suitcase."

"Wow. I had better give them to her then, right away," I say, knowing that Hettie will be mortified to think of her personal correspondence going public. But Ruby carries on talking.

"I had to take a peek, of course, curiosity got the better

303

of me, so I read through them all last night," she says totally unashamedly, "and I am telling you, these are gold dust."

"Gold dust?" I repeat, and she taps her index finger on the top of the bundle before pushing them into the pocket of my parka.

"Yep, that's right. And they need to be kept clean and dry because I'm certain they're worth an absolute mint. I could find out exactly how much they're worth if she wanted me to?" Ruby steps in closer to me and lowers her voice. "And Hettie is some saucy minx. You would never think it to look at her—a little old lady—it's hard to imagine her as a twenty-year-old having the time of her life in Hollywood, dancing with icons and dating *legends*. Do you know who he was? Has she ever mentioned the love affair—you know, when you've been knitting and nattering away together? I'd love to hear all about it first-hand." Ruby eyes me eagerly, clearly keen to glean a smidgen of those halcyon days for real.

"Um, nope," I say, wondering what on earth she's going on about.

"Well, I'm telling you, those letters are history right there. The golden age of Hollywood captured on paper by someone who actually lived through it. *She kissed Cary Grant,* for crying out loud!" And Ruby looks as if she might actually faint with excitement. She takes a few seconds to compose herself. "Only on the lips, but still . . ." She flutters her eyelashes and shakes her head. "What I wouldn't give for a moment like that with a truly glamorous star. Do you think she'd talk to me about it?"

"I wouldn't have thought so, she's very private about her, well, private life."

"Hmm," Ruby pouts and ponders for a moment before adding, "I Googled her you know." And I can't believe I forgot to do that, or at least ask Lawrence about Hettie's seemingly amazing past, but then I have been kind of busy with the Christmas knit-off and everything. "Yep," Ruby continues, "did you know that she was a dancer in Hollywood?"

"Yes, she told me that," I say, enthusiastically.

"Ooh, and you didn't think to tell me? That's only, like, my dream job, if I had been born several decades earlier, of course." Ruby pulls a face, clearly devastated at having missed out on a whole other life entirely, and I feel deflated, having let my girl crush down so tragically. "So, what else did she say?" Ruby makes big eyes.

"Not very much," I start. "But she has a picture signed by Gene Kelly," I offer up like some kind of consolation prize.

"Oh. My. God." And Ruby grabs hold of me in a massive hug as if to thank me for bestowing such magical fairy dust from a glittering age on her, before quickly letting me go again and gushing, "Do you think he could be the man?" Her eyes are like dinner plates and I feel happy to be back in her good books—ridiculous, I know.

"What man?"

"The man in the letters. The man she writes about but only refers to as G? It has to be. Oh my God! You know, in the last letter, the one where she writes all about Cary Grant kissing her at a party, swoon, she even says that she thinks G is going to propose! Imagine that. I wonder why Hettie would turn down Gene Kelly?"

"Steady on. We don't know that any of this is true. It all sounds a bit far-fetched to me. Surely, if there was anything between them, it would have been documented? Wikipedia would have something, surely," I say, thinking it's highly unlikely that Hettie had a love affair with Gene Kelly. It's absurd.

"Hmm, I guess so, and he was married three times," she pauses, and her eyes flick to the side as if she's deep in thought. "But wait, he was divorced from his first wife in 1957 and didn't marry his second wife until 1960. And the letters were written over Christmas 1958, going into the beginning of 1959. Oh my God, Sybs, you must ask her. See what you can find out."

"I can't ask her! She's a very private person, and besides, she'll then know that you've been reading her letters," I say, momentarily wondering if I should mention Cher's

306

conversation with Bill, but immediately decide against it. It'll only tip Ruby over the edge if she knows that Hettie had a baby. A secret love child is how she'll dramatize it, for sure.

"Ah, yes, that's a very good point." There's a short silence and I can see that Ruby is mulling it all over. "Well, I guess it was a nice romantic notion while it lasted. I even had a dream about it all last night." She shrugs and I smile, thinking it must be a very bittersweet life to continuously hanker after a time you can never experience. She takes a big breath before carrying on. "But there is a bit about Hettie online, you know. She was the understudy for some really big names, like Debbie Reynolds, and she was in that famous film *Singin' in the Rain*. I wonder if Hettie was her understudy for the film? It makes sense if she has the signed picture of Gene. Oh, it's incredible." And she's clearly not completely letting go of her fantasy version of events if she's still hankering for Hettie having a famous Hollywood film star lover.

"Exactly, and wouldn't there be something about it, if Hettie *had* actually been Gene's girlfriend?"

"Yes, you're right. I mean, Gene's super famous, even now, after all these years, like Elvis, and there's a Wikipedia page all about Elvis's many girlfriends," she says, knowledgeably.

Ruby is revving up for more incredulity when Marigold calls my name from the shop door. I turn around.

"Cher's on the phone for you." And Marigold ducks back inside.

"Sorry, I had better go. Are you sure I can't tempt you in for a quick mince pie or a handful of Twiglets? There may even be a Terry's Chocolate Orange," I grin.

"I really can't, much as I'd love too—might give me a chance to chat to Hettie, but I can't be late, my fans will be waiting." She laughs, and then adds, "But please, see if she'd be willing to chat to me sometime. I can be very discreet."

"I'll try, but please don't get your hopes up," I say, knowing that it's highly unlikely that Hettie will agree.

"OK, honey. Fingers crossed—if only for posterity, living history, old times' sake," Ruby says hopefully, before turning and heading back to her car.

24

When I make it back to the Duck & Puddle pub, I take one look at Cher and Clive's concerned, but silently seething faces, before tearing upstairs to my bedroom. Just as I reach a hand out toward the door, it flings open and there she is, bursting from the en suite bathroom like crimson and cream streamers from a party popper.

"SASHA."

"There you are. Damn snow! No wonder I live abroad these days. And why haven't you got a mobile anymore? I've been calling you for months," she puffs, rolling her eyes and shaking her head, making snowflakes cascade from her glossy, poker-straight curtain of hair onto the carpet. "Hug for your big sister." Sasha flings her arms around me, practically crushing me in the process, and it completely throws me. She's acting as if nothing has happened. As if she didn't have a "thing" with my ex-fiancé, in secret, behind my back—Luke may be back in his storeroom, but still, it's *rude*, whichever way you slice it.

"Three and a half minutes," I mumble into her red riding jacket, the shock of her sudden appearance affecting my ability to think straight, let alone string a coherent sentence together.

Why is she here?

Why now?

And more importantly, what does she want?

And just when everything is going so well. OK, work is a bit of a mess, but being here in Tindledale for Christmas is amazing, and for the first time in a long time, I feel happy, and I don't want anything to spoil it, least of all my big betrayal by my twin sister.

"*What?*" Sasha pulls back to look at me and then realizes what I'm talking about, "Oh Sybs you're so funny; you've always had a thing about that. It's not my fault I was born first." She does her special operatic laugh before glancing around the room. "So this is where you've been hiding?"

"I'm not hiding. I'm staying with my friends for Christmas, Cher and Clive, you remember them, don't you?" I say, pulling a sarcastic smile onto my face as I try to bat away her implication that I must somehow have a reason to hide—why would I? I haven't done anything wrong. She has!

"Hmm," Sasha acknowledges rudely, before marching around like she's performing some kind of inspection. I close the door behind me and place Basil on the bed—even he's unnerved by her being here and won't settle like he usually does, preferring to sit up on his haunches and growl, his eyes hooked on to her, watching and following her every move.

"What are you doing here?" I eventually manage to get my mouth to cooperate with my brain.

"What are you doing, more like?" Ah, here we go, typical Sasha; always jumping in before engaging her brain—she's been like it ever since we were little—if there's a criticism to be had, then Sasha never fails to find it. "In this place," she says and pauses to lean down and sweep an expensively manicured hand over the coffee table while she conjures up a suitable description. "It's like a horrible little Hobbit hovel, for Christ's sake." I cringe all over, hoping and praying that Cher and Clive can't hear her insulting their quirky, and quite lovely, traditional old coaching inn.

"No, it isn't."

"Yes, it is . . . I very nearly twisted my ankle on this ridiculously sloping floor," and she does an exaggerated stagger in the space between the end of the bed and the window as if to demonstrate her point. "I bet Health and Safety would have a field day over this.

And there must be some kind of law against letting guests sleep in such unsuitable, and quite hazardous accommodations." She has her grand event planner attitude on now.

"Stop it," I hiss, in a low angry voice, horrified at how stuck-up she sounds. She definitely inherited Mum's Hyacinth Bucket gene, only a billion times worse.

"You know, come to think of it," and she places a little finger to the corner of her mouth, "have they considered letting film crews use this hovel? It would be perfect for one of those dreary Dickens dramas that always get scheduled on Sunday evenings just to depress everyone a tiny bit more before they go back to their dull jobs on Monday morning—talking of which, are you still working for the council?" I ignore her, but she just carries on regardless, barely drawing breath. "Hmm, I could put Cheryl, or Cher as she tries to glamorize her dowdy name," Sasha rolls her eyes, "and the dim-witted Clive in touch with one of my TV contacts."

"Right. That's enough. This place is perfect: far nicer than your sterile, chrome and Perspex box in Dubai, or wherever it is you live these days," I retaliate.

"Well, at least my box is clean!" I gawp at her momentarily, desperately resisting all the filthy comebacks that are currently flying around inside my head right now. "Unlike this dump."

"It's perfectly clean," I splutter, smarting from her sheer, bloody audacity and spitefulness.

"Oh yeah? What's this then, fairy dust!" And she points to a minuscule cobweb in the corner of the mullioned window.

"Why do you always have to exaggerate?" I say, thinking she has a flaming cheek to just turn up here out of the blue and start hurling insults around, after what she's done. She clearly has no shame, and why does she have to be so snarky and aggressive all the time?

"I don't."

"Yes, you do," I say firmly. "Look, I don't have time for this; just tell me why you're here. And why are you dressed up like something out of *Black Beauty*, or whatever those pony programs were that you used to love watching all the time." I want to get back to Hettie's and help her with the party. And I promised to put up the Christmas decorations too—we haven't had time until now, with knitting all the sweaters—and the Japanese tourists are arriving tomorrow. Mr. Tanaka has already said that they want to call in and see for themselves where their traditional English Christmas sweaters were made. Sasha plants her hands on her hips and cocks her head to one side. Mirroring her stance, I fix my eyes on hers.

"Well, I was in the area," she starts, jutting one jodhpur-clad leg out like she's channeling Angelina Jolie on the red carpet. "My charity event, the Christmas hunt ball, is in this part of the world this year, so I thought why not pop in and sort things out with you on my way through." She inspects a fingernail.

"Oh, I see. How very convenient for you." I can't resist. So she hasn't made a special trip to see me at all, to apologize, beg for my forgiveness, explain herself, say that she made a terrible mistake. All the sorts of things one might expect from someone in her position. No, I'm just a convenience! Well, she can bugger off with trying to make herself feel better because that's what this is about. It's about her being consumed with what other people might think. Yes, Mum does it, but Sasha has taken it to a whole new, horrible level. I know Sasha well enough to know that it's always about her. Always has been and always will be. And she's probably worried that word will get out and her so-called fabulous client list will dwindle away, because nobody will trust her—if she can steal her own twin sister's fiancé, then what's stopping her from coming on to a total stranger? That's what people will think, and that's all that Sasha is bothered about: other people, and putting on a show for them.

Take our thirtieth birthday for example. Sasha organized a hideous joint party at a flash private members' club in London, not my thing at all, and then after all the guests had whooped and wished us happy birthday,

Sasha had ripped off her dress, revealing a teeny-tiny tasseled silver bikini, and promptly leapt around a pole that swiveled down from the ceiling, glinting in the spotlight after the lights were dramatically dimmed and raunchy music pumped from speakers. She performed a full-on pole dance, like a pro, in front of the hundred or so guests, made up mainly of her business contacts (Sasha never misses an opportunity to network) while my small group of friends cringed over by the bar area. But that's not all; she then heckled me to join her, knowing I hate heights, until the whole crowd, apart from my friends of course, were chanting my name. Even Luke joined in. I was mortified; there was no way I could writhe around a pole without making an utter fool of myself, plus I didn't want to, it's just not my thing, so I ran away, finding out later that Sasha had been having pole dancing classes for months, and hadn't bothered to mention it to me, thereby ensuring the show was all about her.

"Well, what did you expect me to do when you don't *bother* to answer your phone?" And there it is again, the same accusatory tone that Luke used; it must be a thing for people who've messed up, a defense mechanism— blame the other person and hope they don't notice.

"And why on earth would you think I would want to talk to you? And how did you know I was here?"

"OK. Well, it's the bizarrest thing . . ." She purses her lips and makes big eyes. Sasha always did love a drama, especially someone else's. "Mum has left like a hundred messages," she starts, in a stagey voice, "practically hysterical she was, something about you losing your job—a massive cock-up she saw something on the local news—and then Luke called her saying your boss had rung him. So she begged me to find you and sort out the mess." Hmm, I definitely bet Mum didn't. "And then something about you and Luke working it out and that I should talk to you and say sorry so you can be happy with him, and then when I was schlepping through this toy town of a place, the village idiot approached me, twiddled her tacky loom band, did a crazy cow grin and then asked me how it was going with the doctor! Obviously thought I was you, God knows why, because we look nothing like each other anymore." And she actually gives me an up-and-down look as if I'm somehow inferior to her, when actually, we do still look identical, apart from the hair of course and the makeup and the way we dress. "Have you met a doctor? Is that why you've run away to this dump? To be with him?"

"Shut up! Just shut the fuck up. Tindledale isn't a dump!" I scream, flinging my hands over my ears and moving toward her. Sasha's mouth actually drops open. She takes a step backward and a dart of fear flits through her eyes. A short silence follows, interrupted by a knock on the door. It opens and Cher pops her head into the room.

"You OK, Sybs?" Cher gives me a look and I walk over to her, my legs still wobbling with rage.

"I'm fine. Honestly, I can handle her." I toss a disparaging glance in Sasha's direction and to my utter shock and disbelief Sasha is now crumpled on the floor, kneeling with her forehead on the carpet and her arms cradling her body. Sobbing!

Instinctively, I run over and reach a hand down to touch her back, but she shrinks away from me. Cher follows until she's standing beside me. We look at each other, both wondering what on earth we should do. I've never seen Sasha like this before; in fact, I don't think I've ever seen her cry, certainly not since we were little girls, and then it was probably because she couldn't get her own way. Tears of temper, never sadness or compassion, but this is different. She's seriously distressed. Is she having some kind of breakdown?

"Sasha!" Cher crouches down next to her. "Come on. Let's get you up." But Sasha pulls away from her too. "We're worried, love," Cher says gently, using the same voice she did when she chatted to Bill. Cher manages to loop her hand through Sasha's elbow and motions for me to get her other arm, which I do, and between us we lift Sasha up and onto the bed. Basil swiftly runs off to hide under the table by the window. "Do you think we should get Dr. Ben over here?" Cher looks at me. I open my mouth to reply, but Sasha mutters and pulls her arms free before yanking off the riding jacket and tossing it away. It lands in a sad heap by the bathroom door.

"Please, I'm not ill," she sniffs, wiping her nose on the cuff of her sleeve, which is so unlike her—usually she'd be the first to criticize that kind of behavior, and the silk shirt that she's wearing looks incredibly expensive, but it's as if she doesn't care, as if she's given up. How weird. Sasha may have her flaws, but she's never been a quitter. I grab a box of tissues from the nightstand and offer them to her. She takes a handful and blows her nose before crying some more.

"Sasha, if you're not ill, then what's going on? I've never seen you like this before." I can feel her body trembling against mine. Cher stands up.

"I'll get you a nice cup of tea, how about that?" she smiles, but Sasha doesn't respond. "Or perhaps something stronger?" Sasha manages a nod. "OK, be right back. I'll bring you one too." Cher nods at me as she leaves the room and I wait for Cher to close the door behind her, before trying again.

"Sasha, please tell me what the matter is," I start,

managing to keep my voice calm, even though I'm still fuming with her—I can't erase the mean stuff she said or the fact that she cheated with Luke, just because she's having a breakdown. But she is my sister, and I do still care about her, so I'm prepared to put it to one side for now, and find out what the hell is going on. "Are you sure you're not ill? I can get Ben, the doctor, to come over," I say, wondering how he'd react to seeing my identical twin sister here. Some people totally freak: I had a friend from Brownies home for tea one time who started crying and Mum had to call her parents to come and collect her. And then a horrible thought pops into my head, *what if Sasha tries to steal Ben away too?* Oh God. I will myself to get a grip. Ben isn't Luke. Besides, Ben isn't my boyfriend, plus it comes down to trust at the end of the day. I can't spend the rest of my life worrying that any man I meet is going to jump into bed with Sasha.

Sasha places her hand on my knee.

"Sybs, I don't need a doctor," she says quietly.

"OK. So what *do* you need?" I gingerly pat the top of her hand and it seems to calm her, as she takes a deep breath, stops trembling and tells me.

"About a billion pounds."

"What?" I say, wondering what she means. Is she joking? I can't tell, as her face is deadly serious.

"Oh, Sybs, I've messed everything up. I'm so sorry. I've ruined your life." *Hardly, I'm sure I'll survive.* But she's always been a drama queen. "And I've ruined my life. Mum and Dad hate me; my so-called mates have abandoned me. Most of my clients have deserted me; all I have left is the Christmas hunt ball. And it's all my fault—so you'll probably think it serves me right." *Hmm, maybe.* But what am I? Twelve. Yes, she betrayed me horribly, but if what she's saying is true, that she's properly ruined her own life, then I'm hardly going to sit here and gloat. I press on, keen to get to the bottom of it all.

"I don't understand."

"Sybs, I'm bankrupt! It's all gone. The lot. I've lost everything. It started shortly after . . ." she pauses to pick her words, but I save her the bother.

"You stole my fiancé." And she flinches.

"Please believe me when I say that it just happened," she says, crying again. "It was never intentional."

"Look, Sasha, I don't want to talk about it. What you did was unforgivable, but it's done, in the past. I can't change it, and to be honest, you might even have done me a favor; I'm starting to see that now. Let's just say that I would never do something like that to you, or any other woman for that matter." I turn away, determined not to make this about me. This is her doing, not mine.

"You say that now, but you have already done it," she snivels, picking at a hangnail on her left thumb.

"Whaaaat?" *Is she for real?*

"With Ian. He told me all about it, that you came on to him in the taxi that time, that he had to turn you down." Her voice is all quivery.

"Are you kidding me? That's a pack of lies. He came on to me!" I say, incredulously, remembering Sasha's barrister boyfriend who was named after Ian Botham.

"He said you'd say that, that's why I never asked you outright. I couldn't bear to, but I never forgot and it broke my heart, you know, everything changed from then on. I loved Ian, I thought we'd be together forever, I just didn't care after that, it's why I am the way I am. And why I—"

"Hang on," I interrupt. "So let me get this straight, are you saying that you got with Luke as some kind of sick revenge plan for something you thought happened years ago?"

"Nooooo!" And she actually looks genuinely horrified. "I truly didn't, Sybs, I was just saying, explaining that you're not perfect either."

"But I didn't betray your trust. I didn't come on to Ian. Like I said, I'd never do anything like that," I reiterate.

"I realize that now," she says in a very small voice. "And that's what makes me even more awful."

"You're not awful," I say quietly. I actually can't be bothered to argue with her anymore. I look sideways at my beautiful, glamorous twin sister and see instead, a wreck, a shell. On close inspection her hair is a mess, her red roots are in desperate need of a blond touch-up and her nails are chipped and bitten. Underneath her usually immaculate makeup her face is looking withered and weary because she's lost too much weight. Her fight has gone, the hard outer shell, and the snootiness has faded away, leaving a vulnerable and frightened woman. I feel sorry for her. Something's clearly very, very wrong.

Cher arrives back with two glasses and a bottle of Southern Comfort. She looks at me and I nod my head so she backs out of the room, pulling a face and mouthing, "good luck."

I pour us both a drink, hand a glass to Sasha, down mine and ask her to start from the beginning. And she does.

*

"Oh my God." I shake my head.

"So do you see now?" Sasha says, and I pour us another drink.

"I had no idea," I reply.

"I did try to tell you. I called and called and called to explain," she says, swallowing a mouthful of Southern Comfort. Sasha has told me that nothing happened with her and Luke before the wedding. He turned up at her hotel room the night before, confused, saying that he wasn't ready to settle down, and they started drinking and one thing just led to another and they ended up in bed together, and then when they woke up in the morning, an hour after the wedding was due to start, they both panicked—Sasha says she felt disgusted with herself. And the weirdest thing of all is that I believe her. I just know she's telling me the truth; so maybe we do have that twin thing, that sixth sense, that connection after all. But none of this changes anything between Luke and me. It wouldn't have worked, it wasn't right in any case. And he clearly thought so too, if he turned to my sister to pour out his heart to, the night before our wedding.

"I know you did. But you can't blame me for not wanting to talk to you," I say, "I thought it had been going on for a while."

She shakes her head vehemently.

"Yeah, I can also see that now. And I'm sorry I didn't come to you on the day of the wedding, explain everything, but I felt so ashamed, so revolted with myself, I couldn't have even looked you in the eye."

"But it doesn't explain why you thought it was OK to sleep with my fiancé. What do you have to say about that?" I ask, not ready to let her off the hook completely.

"There's no excuse. We had been drinking, and well . . ." She stops talking.

"Come on. You need to do better than that."

"I don't know."

"You must know. Had you wanted him for a while? Was that it, you fancied Luke and couldn't stop yourself?" I say, desperately trying to fathom it all out.

"No. It was never like that. I didn't want him."

"Why did you do it then?"

"To feel better, perhaps." She shakes her head. "Oh, I don't know, I've gone over and over and over it a million times."

"To feel better?" I say incredulously. "But you weren't unhappy, were you?"

"Ha! This is the thing," she sniffs, "everyone assumes that just because you have loads of money and a glamorous, high-flying life, it means you're happy. But I've never really been happy. Not properly. Lonely, more like. Not like you, with your cozy, secure life. Friends like Cher that you've known for years, people that really care about you. A future, getting married and then most likely having a family, and let's face it, I've always been the mean twin, the wicked one—and that's the thing about being a twin, there's always a comparison."

324

Silence follows. I had no idea she felt this way.

"So is that why you . . ." I pause, not wanting to kick her when she's down, I'm not that heartless, "um, are, *gregarious*?" I settle on.

"I guess so. When you're the black sheep of the family, it's sometimes easier to just carry on reverting to type, playing the pantomime villain."

"You're not the black sheep," I protest.

"Yes, I am. I know what you all think of me . . ." Her voice trails off.

"Well, you could always try being a bit more courteous, less judgmental in the future."

"I know. And I am trying. That's what coming here today was all about. A start. But I got scared. Scared of what you might do to me, scared you might not talk to me, let alone see me. I thought I had lost you for good and well, I suppose I did what I always do—"

"Lashed out," I finish, and she nods her head. "And what about the bankruptcy?" I ask, not wanting to talk about her, or Luke, or what they did to me anymore. "How did that happen?"

"Oh God, it's such a mess," she starts, and then takes a deep breath before exhaling hard and carrying on. "In Dubai, there are strict rules about kissing and drinking and that kind of thing in public. And it's ludicrous, but I, we, Luke and I—he begged to come back to Dubai with me after he missed the wedding, said he had to get away, and well, we got drunk on the beach. We both felt so wretched, and unhappy, and we had one of those horrible, sad, desperate, rebound kisses and got caught by the police. So as soon as word of my arrest spread faster than a bush fire, that was that, all my clients drifted away. Pouf! Just like that." She waves her arm in the air in a feeble attempt at a joke. "Nobody wants the drunk tramp organizing their daughter's sweet sixteen. People can be very particular about that kind of thing. And in my business, you're only as good as your last gig; hence I'm back here with only my charity event left. Plus a trillion bills to pay: my landlord in Dubai is suing me for nonpayment of rent on the penthouse and all the catering companies, celebrity singers—superstars like Kylie and Miley performing at your wedding reception don't come cheap—still have to be paid for because you can't just cancel them at the last minute, and I never bothered with insurance policies and all that; I ran my business on goodwill and charm. So now it's all an utter mess." And she starts sobbing some more.

Twenty-first of December, and Hettie's House of Haberdashery is adorned with colorful Christmas decorations and packed full with fifteen Japanese tourists all looking resplendent in their Ho Ho Ho Christmas sweaters, alongside various people from the Tindledale parish council and practically all the residents from the village too. We thought it would be nice to have Christmas drinks to welcome the Japanese guests to the village, and also give them the chance to meet Hettie and the rest of the traditional hand-knitters.

So, Hettie has a special Christmas songs tape in the cassette player and everyone is laughing and chatting and generally having a wonderful time. The tourists must have taken a trillion pictures, at least: individual ones of them standing outside the shop, individual ones of them with Hettie and the Tindledale Tappers and then the same thing all over again, but this time as a group. The whole process took over an hour, but was actually a very lovely, jovial experience helped along with copious cups of mulled wine and iced Baileys, followed by an exceedingly good selection of Kitty's cakes—mince pies, stollen slices and fruity, marzipan-topped Christmas cake. And Hettie is thrilled to be receiving such "international recognition for her little shop in Tindledale" is what she whispered to me when the others were busy chatting and laughing with our guests.

Even Cher has managed to duck out of the pub to come and celebrate with us, leaving Clive in charge with strict instructions not to flick on the karaoke machine or let the locals think there's going to be some after-hours drinking later.

"Do you reckon Sasha will be OK, then?" Cher asks, joining me by the fireplace.

"I hope so. I spoke to her last night and she said she's going to stay at Mum and Dad's in Staines while they're away on the Christmas cruise—she wants to give herself a chance to get her head straight and then see if she can sort out her finances somehow and salvage her career."

"Hmm, well that's good, and I'm pleased you and she are kind of OK now. You are twin sisters at the end of the day."

"Yes, me too. I'm glad she didn't hang around though— I can't handle all her dramatics, an afternoon seems to be my limit." I shake my head and sigh. I feel so much lighter now after having seen Sasha and confronted my demons. I think I had built up the scenario of what happened with her and Luke to such a monstrous thing in my head that I'd turned it into an insurmountable hurdle to get over, when the reality was actually quite sad and pretty desperate—two lonely, flawed and confused people who got it wrong, and they're both facing the consequences of their mistakes now. I guess that old adage of "*what goes around comes around*" really rings true sometimes.

"Ha! She sure can be a bit intense. I'd be lying if I said I wasn't relieved when she agreed that traveling on to the Christmas hunt ball venue was a good idea," Cher puffs, helping herself to another turkey and cranberry sandwich from a plate that Taylor is offering around the room.

"Me too, plus it was the right thing to do because it's all she has left and, putting everything aside, she is an excellent event manager, so if she has any sense, she'll make the most of the hunt ball and see if she can use it to jump-start her career here in the UK. Far less glamorous, but—"

"Oh well, I'm sure she'll cope somehow," Cher laughs. "She could always ask your mum to fix her back up with that awful Ian and his chamber!" And we both do childish sniggers as we finish the last of our champagne. "Look who just walked in," Cher says motioning with her head toward the door. I glance over and see Ben walking through the door, pushing the hood of his duffel coat down and smoothing his curls. He sees me, and waves, but before he has a chance to come over, a woman from the parish council grabs his arm and practically canters him toward the Japanese tourists, who, after being introduced to the village doctor, all do reverent little bows as Ben shakes their hands, each one in turn. And I know any chance to get near him is futile. "Awww, you have to feel sorry for Dr. Ben," Cher laughs as we see him surreptitiously glance in our direction with a "rescue me" grin stuck on his gorgeous face. I smile, wondering if we'll ever have a chance to be on our own together. I think I'd quite like that.

Lawrence arrives too, and after introducing Cher to Leo, I dash over to greet him. Then the bell above the door makes the now-familiar jingly sound, and an older man in a black overcoat and a very serious look on his face appears.

"Can I help you?" It's Marigold, who breaks free from the throng and turns toward this unexpected guest. I move closer, as there's something about his manner that's making me feel edgy, uncomfortable almost. His eyes are darting around the room, looking, searching for something or someone, and he seems taken aback by the crowd, as if surprised, annoyed even. He leans in to Marigold, says something, which I can't hear, and she shakes her head. I step forward to be right next to her, ready to help out if required. She says, "not here," in a stilted voice. Oh God, please, not another bailiff.

"Everything OK?" I smile breezily, inwardly praying this isn't what I think it is and that he's going to embarrass Hettie in front of all these people.

"No. This, er, gentleman . . ." Marigold pauses to give him an up-and-down look, "wants to see Hettie, but won't say why."

"Oh, I see." I glance at Marigold.

"In that case, you'll have to come back another time," I say, swiftly taking charge but keeping my voice low. I'm not having Hettie upset, not now, not when this party means so much to her. "Hettie's busy and we're in the middle of a private function," I tell him. And I can't even see Hettie. I scan the room, but it's no use, there are so many people squeezed into the small space that it's impossible, and probably a good thing as Hettie will only worry if she sees Marigold and I talking to this stranger.

"Is she here?" he asks, looking around too.

"Um," I start, and Marigold gives me a discreet nudge on the back of my leg with her knee. "Actually, she isn't, she er, had to pop out," I lie.

"So when will she be back?" The man creases his forehead and glances at his watch.

"We really couldn't say," Marigold answers airily, before crossing her arms.

"In that case I'll wait."

"But she could be ages. Why don't you come back another time?"

"Look, this is . . . er, a . . ." and he clears his throat as if weighing the right words to use before settling on, "family matter." And then I know.

I get it.

Marigold does too.

It's Hettie's vile nephew.

In one swift movement, Marigold places a hand on his forearm, the other on his elbow and practically frog-marches him out of the shop. I dart after them, just in time to see her propel Hettie's nephew into the snow-covered wooden bus shelter.

"Get off me, woman! Are you crazy?" the man huffs, shaking his arm free in an overly dramatic way. "You know, there are laws against physically assaulting people," he adds, brushing his coat sleeve with a look of disgust on his face.

"Oh, don't be ridiculous. I hardly touched you, and talking of laws—for your information, there are lots of laws to prevent people from pulling the wool over old ladies' eyes," Marigold hisses.

"What are you talking about? Just because I won't tell

you my private business. And as for *old lady*?" He pauses to give Marigold a disparaging glare. "I'd dispute both of those claims right now!" There's a short silence while Marigold opens her mouth and then closes it again, clearly trying to fathom what he means by this juxtaposed compliment, and then he clarifies, sort of. "Since when did *ladies* go around dragging complete strangers along the pavement and into bus stops?"

"Oh, well, if you put it like that . . ." Marigold pats her hair, the penny seemingly having dropped that he doesn't think she's old! And she's not, really; she's much younger than Hettie, which is who she was referring to having the wool pulled over her eyes. But still, mid sixties, which is what I'm guessing how old Marigold is, isn't really that old these days, not when people are living well into their nineties, or to over a hundred in some cases, so he has kind of got a point. "Then I apologize for dragging you out of the shop." And I swear there's a hint of a simper in Marigold's voice.

I jump in. We need to pull this back—we can't fraternize with the enemy, the man that thinks it's OK for Hettie to worry about being forced to go into a home, worry about having to drink stewed tea from a sippy cup. What kind of a way is that for her to live? It's not right. I take a deep breath.

"But you still haven't explained why you're here?" I

fold my arms and wait for an explanation, desperately trying not to shiver, but it's nearly impossible given how blooming cold it is out here. And then he throws me completely off-guard.

"Would you like my coat? Here." He goes to unbutton it. Hmm, trying to be a proper gentleman now, I see. Well, it won't work; he's not going to pull the wool over my eyes too. Not wanting to get distracted, I carry on.

"No." I shake my head. "Thank you."

"I will." Marigold leaps forward, but I quickly push out a hand to stop her.

"No, she's fine too." I give him a glare.

"Yes, of course. You're quite right, Sybs. Sorry," she mutters, checking herself.

"OK, seeing as it's so cold out here and we have a party to get back to, I suggest we get this over with quickly," I start, authoritatively, and fixing my eyes on to his Wedgwood-blue ones—just like Hettie's, so obviously a genetic Honey family thing then. "Tell me why are you here?"

"Like I said, it's a family matter."

"Then you must understand that we're Hettie's friends, so we're not going to stand by and—"

"That's right." Marigold jumps in. "I've known Hettie for years and to see her unhappy and struggle for so long because of you, is well, quite frankly, heartbreaking.

Have you no shame?" And to give him fair dues, the man flicks his eyes to the pavement as if Marigold's words have really unnerved him. Ha! So Hettie's nephew does have a soul then. Good. Perhaps we can persuade him to leave her alone and stop banging on about carting her off to an old people's home, away from everything she holds dear—her friends, her beloved oast and glorious House of Haberdashery—which is definitely on the up. Only this morning we had another batch of new knitting commissions. Baby sets, booties, bonnets and cardigans in mainly white, with a few pink and blues too, and a lovely Valentine's sweater which I thought might be popular—a gorgeous crimson mohair with a sparkly pink heart on the front. And the first order is from a guy who plans on presenting it to his girlfriend on Valentine's Day—he's asked, especially, if it can have a label sewn inside with "will you marry me?" on it, which we all thought was super-swoonsome. Taylor is all for delivering it in person just so she can yarn-bomb some hearts over the bonnet of his car or something, to really complete the whole hand-knitted romantic experience for them both.

"Look, I shouldn't have come here today," the man says, shoving his hands inside his pockets and hunching his shoulders against the swirling snowy air. I pull my scarf up over my chin, grateful for having the foresight to have

335

kept it on. Marigold huddles into me and I pass her a length of the scarf to wrap around her hands.

"Indeed," shivers Marigold. "Now, I think you should go and leave your aunt in peace to enjoy her twilight years." The man looks confused, but before I can work out why, a shiny black Range Rover screeches to a halt at the curb and a stubby, red-faced man jumps out and storms toward us. He's fuming—his eyes are flashing and an ugly vein is protruding down the left side of his forehead. And I'm sure I recognize him. Where have I seen him before? The car, the shiny black Range Rover! I've definitely seen it before.

"Yeah, you heard the lady. Now do one. Turning up here and throwing your weight around, who the fuck do you think you are?" the stubby man bellows, and then I remember. He's the man who barged into me when I first came to Hettie's House of Haberdashery and Hettie had to apologize on his behalf. The *stubby man* is her nephew—the nasty creep who is trying to steal her oast, her shop and pack her off to a home for old people to sip stewed tea from a sippy cup!

So who, then, is this other man?

Oh God. Please not another bailiff. But surely a bailiff wouldn't have let Marigold push him around or, indeed, have hung around inside a bus stop to take a tonguelashing from us either?

But what's happening now?

Mrs. Pocket appears. But she wasn't invited to the party, I'm sure of it. And now Hettie is standing close behind her. The nasty nephew wastes no time in laying into Hettie.

"Come on, Aunty, let's go. It's not safe for you to stay here any longer with all these strangers hanging around. Let's pack your things and get you settled in to the home; don't worry about all these people, I'll send them on their way." And he actually grabs the top of Hettie's arm. Marigold steps forward, but the man in the overcoat beats her to it, and pulls Hettie's nephew back.

With his face looking as if it's about to explode, Hettie's nephew lifts his left hand, which is now clumped into a fist, and goes to punch the man in the overcoat. And I've seen enough. Hettie is wringing her hands and shaking her head, clearly distressed. The man in the overcoat ducks just in time, and the nephew ends up punching the wooden frame of the bus shelter. I jump in front of him.

"How dare you," I yell, flinging my hands onto my hips and facing him square on.

"Get out of my way," the nephew spits, nursing his fist. "I'm warning you."

"Oh yes? And what exactly does that mean?" I say, holding my nerve and staring right into his eyes.

"Sybil, leave it, dear. Please, he has a ferocious temper," Hettie says, almost in tears now, and Marigold cottons on; she realizes that he's Hettie's nephew and walks over to stand next to me. She glares at him too, and out of the corner of my eye I see Mrs. Pocket put her arm around Hettie's shoulders. The man in the overcoat is standing behind Mrs. Pocket with his head bowed and his shoulders hunched as he goes to walk away.

"I know all about you. Trying to take over my aunt's shop." Hettie's nephew moves up close to me until he's practically touching my face with his nose. "Well, you've got another thing coming if you reckon you're going to steal it away from her—"

"No, that's more your style, isn't it?" I say. "Trying to push an old lady out of her home, con her out of money to finance your own business, take everything that she holds dear. You're disgusting." And I give him the dirtiest look I can muster, which is a massive mistake as, in one swift movement, he barges into me, forcing me to stagger backward into the corner of the bus shelter. I can hear my blood pumping in my ears and my heart banging inside my chest. I can see Marigold behind his back, trying to pull him away, and Hettie is crying now, tears pouring down her cheeks, and it breaks my heart. An old lady, an octogenarian, crying, is a harrowing sight, so I lift my leg and kick Hettie's nephew as hard as I can.

He lets out a yelp and instinctively backs off. Within seconds, the man in the overcoat is back in the bus shelter and has Hettie's nephew pinned to the wall, with his arm pressed firmly across his neck.

"See how you like it, you thug. Make you feel like a big man does it, pushing women around?" he says, sounding very old-school gentlemanly.

"Keep out of this pal," Hettie's nephew splutters, seemingly on the back foot now.

"I'm not your pal."

"Then who the fuck are you?"

Silence follows.

"I'm Hettie's son!"

And the minute the words come out of his mouth, Hettie gasps, clasps her hands up under her chin, stumbles forward and collapses into Marigold's open arms.

"Oh no he isn't!" the pantomime prince hollers.

"Oh yes he is!" the Tindledale villagers roar back in unison. It's Christmas Eve and the whole of Tindledale has turned out for the final pantomime performance, a matinée, including the Japanese tourists who've been given front-row VIP seats. I smile in admiration, thinking how fantastic they all look in their festive sweaters, and they're not afraid to have a good time, oh no, not at all, they're getting drawn in, laughing and cheering along to shockingly lame slapstick gags with the rest of us.

Basil is nestling on my knees, snoring away as always, and Lawrence is onstage in full regalia—extra-long, super-fluttery diamanté lashes, plum-colored nail varnish and the biggest hoop-skirted frilly fairy godmother dress I think I've ever seen. And the irony isn't lost on me; Lawrence really is a wonderful fairy godmother, and friend too—he certainly sprinkled some magic my way, helping to heal my broken heart. Coming here has been incredible and I'll always cherish my time in Tindledale. I inhale sharply and push thoughts of reporting to Mr. Banerjee on January 5 out of my mind. Cher, sitting beside me, senses my anxiety and gives my hand a quick squeeze. I turn to her and smile, and she leans into me. Lifting my hair, she whispers in my ear.

"Have you seen who's sitting over there? It's only the sexy doctor!" I look and see Ben at the end of the row in front of us. He's leaning forward with his elbows resting on his knees as if he's fully enthralled by the show. Lawrence cracks another cheesy joke onstage, and Ben leans back and roars with laughter, clapping and cheering along with the rest of the audience. Then, as if sensing my stare, he turns round and catches me looking. For some ridiculous reason, I quickly flick my eyes away and pretend to be enthralled by the show too. I even do a big wolf whistle, putting my fingers into my mouth and really getting involved when Ruby struts onto the stage in a puff of pink marabou feathers. She's halfway through a cheeky, but family-friendly, version of a burlesque sequence involving Pete, who is dressed up as the hapless scarecrow from *The Wizard of Oz*, when Ben ducks out of his seat and, keeping his body bent low so as not to obscure the view of the others behind, he bounds around to the end of my row and scoots into the empty seat beside me.

341

"Hello," he grins, his voice a whisper and gives Basil a stroke when he stirs, turns around and then settles back down again. There's another roar from the audience and Ben moves in closer until his shoulder is pressed next to mine. He yells, "Are you having a good time?" He seems far more confident than before; maybe it's the dimmed lights and the festive party atmosphere or because he's not in his office so not technically on duty, who knows, but whatever it is, it suits him, and I like it. A lot. And that feeling I had on first seeing the message on the newspaper floats right back, not to mention the furnace-like sensation radiating down my arm where his body is touching mine.

"I certainly am," I say, grinning right back and desperately trying to not let it become rictus as I attempt to ignore Cher's sharp elbow digging me in the ribs on the other side of my body. And I swear I can feel her bobbing up and down in excitement.

"Are you coming to the Christmas Fair after this?" he says, folding his arms. Ooh, his bicep is surprisingly hard, and for a second, I hold my breath, not even daring to move.

"Yes. I'm helping Cher with the drinks," I say, a little too loudly it seems, as a woman in the row in front of us, turns sharply to give me a filthy look, before treating Dr. Ben to a very flirty pout. Cher sniggers and when the

342

lights go down she gives my knee a firm squeeze, and I swear she's giggling now, just like that time in Guides—joint summer disco with the local Scout group and Matthew Start came over and asked me for a snog. Ha! And I had been so shy, covering it up by coming across all prim and proper and flouncing off in a huff. But not anymore! There's just something so appealing about Ben. I could quite easily move my face forward a few millimeters and press my lips to his.

"Great," breathes Ben, and he's so close now that I'm treated to a sudden and very welcome burst of his deliciously spicy scent. "Maybe we can catch up later. You never know, we might even get to grab a few minutes alone." And he actually winks.

Oh yes please.

I'm still fantasizing when the curtains swing together, signifying the end of the show and after three encores and a very cute rendition of "Ten Little Elves" by the children from Tindledale primary school, we all file out of the hall and make our way over to the village green.

*

"I can't believe you didn't just grab the doc's hand and bring him with you," says Cher, shaking her head and lifting the lid on an enormous vat of hot mulled wine with cherry brandy to give it a big stir. We're standing behind a trestle table on the edge of the village green with just a striped canvas awning for cover, which is OK as the wintery evening is surprisingly mild now the snow has stopped falling and the air is infused with the warmth and aroma from the various food stalls dotted around. Basil is spinning round in circles beside me and Cher is now lighting the grill so we can roast chestnuts too, so that will warm us all up nicely.

"And risk the wrath of the woman in the seat in front?" I laugh.

"Jealousy is a terrible thing, babe. And from what I've heard, our Dr. Ben isn't short of admirers; since he first turned up Tindledale, he's been causing quite a stir among the school mums in the playground." Cher does big eyes.

"He is rather lovely, in a very unassuming way," I say.

"Lovely? Bloody gorgeous, more like, and like I said before, he'd be perfect for you. Get stuck in, Sybs, before one of those mums grabs hold of him," she says, looking outraged now as we see him in the distance, walking across the snow-covered grass over by the trees, and surrounded by at least five women. Then Tommy Prendergast, the guy from the pub with the suspected hernia problem, lumbers across and embroils Ben in a lengthy and very animated tale of another ailment, by the looks of all the bending and the pointing to his knee that's going on.

"Mmm—chance would be a fine thing!" And we both laugh. At this rate, I'll never get a look-in where the lovely Ben is concerned.

The atmosphere on the village green is so buzzy and Christmassy and cozy and everyone is happy and full of festive cheer. The carol singers are getting into position over by the duck pond, each of them holding a flickering tea light lantern on a tall metal stake, which they push into the grass to create a magical, mesmerizing mirage across the water. Twinkling fairy lights sweep in and out of the many trees, and the cottages surrounding the green all have candles glowing in their windows. Beautiful. It really is like a magical winter wonderland. And it takes my breath away.

Clive is busy carving a giant turkey on the stall next to us for the villagers to help themselves to with a ball of stuffing to cram into a crusty roll with a generous dollop of cranberry sauce. Cooper is with Clive, but he's tending the hog roast, turning and basting it to perfection. Mr. Tanaka and his group are hovering eagerly nearby, finishing up their cups of mulled wine in anticipation of a hog roast feast. And Basil is sitting at Clive's feet now, sweeping the snowy-covered grass with his tail as two lines of drool slather from his jaw in anticipation of bagging himself a tasty turkey dinner.

"Will you look at the state of him," laughs Cher, pointing at Basil. "Honestly, woman, do you never feed him?"

"Apparently not," I grin, rolling my eyes at him and shaking my head.

"There you are." Molly arrives, with her ferret on the leash, looking flushed and harassed with her four boisterous boys in tow, who immediately dash over to snag some crackling from the hog roast. "Heyyyyy!" she bellows and each boy freezes on the spot. "Where are your manners?" She plants her woolly-gloved (hand-knitted of course) hands on her hips. "You know the rule—Mummy goes first," she beams and they all crack up as Cooper steps forward with a prime sliver of pork on a fork.

"Just for you, my big, beautiful, festive flower." And the boys all make barfing noises as Cooper gives Molly a generous kiss on the mouth.

"And enough of the 'big,' thank you!" Molly laughs before pulling the pork from the fork and popping it in between her plump lips.

Smiling, I help myself to a cup of mulled wine and just as I take a sip of the delicious fruity concoction, Hettie arrives, wrapped up warm in her good winter coat and matching felt hat with fur trim, the one she keeps for best. I place the cup on the trellis table and dash around to the other side to give her a huge hug. I've not seen her properly since that moment in the bus shelter.

Not alone, so we could talk properly—if she'd even open up to me; maybe she wants to keep the matter of her son turning up out of the blue to herself.

"I wanted to give you this," she says as we pull apart, and hands me a parcel wrapped up in red flock wallpaper with a length of navy yarn wound around and finished with a bow. "To say thank you," she adds, a little sheepishly.

"What for?" I smile and take the present, giving her hand a gentle squeeze in acknowledgment of her kindness.

"For holding the fort in the shop while I, um, tended to other matters," she says quietly, her eyes flicking about as Molly and her boys bound past on their way over to the pond to listen to the carol concert.

"Oh, don't be daft!" I grin to lighten the conversation, sensing her obvious discomfort at discussing such a personal matter in public. "I loved every minute of it." And it's true, I really did.

After the showdown in the bus stop, Hettie's nephew had leapt into his Range Rover and driven off, and as far as I know he hasn't been back since. Marigold then bustled Mrs. Pocket away, before taking Hettie and her long-lost son next door to the oast, where they could be guaranteed some privacy. I went back into the shop and acted like nothing out of the ordinary had happened, as I knew Hettie wouldn't want a fuss or for the party to be cut short. Later that evening, Marigold called me at the Duck & Puddle pub to ask if I'd mind looking after the shop for a few days, just until Christmas Day, when Hettie would be closing up anyway until the new year.

I open the gift. And gasp.

"Oh Hettie, I can't take this," I tell her, going to hand it back. Her picture, signed by Gene Kelly, is nestling inside the tissue paper.

"Please, dear . . ." She pushes it back toward me with an earnest look in her blue eyes. "You helped me so much, more than you'll ever know. It was like a miracle that day you walked into my shop."

Hettie looks down at her hands and I smile, thinking that yes, it was a miracle for me too. Everything changed from that moment on.

"But this is precious, Hettie. It's a part of your history, your past, and your passion for dancing," I say, desperate for her to keep hold of it.

"But that's just it. The past is gone, dear, and you know that as well as I do." A brief silence follows while we both ponder our respective histories. "I nursed a broken heart for so many years and this picture was a constant reminder of something that couldn't ever be fixed—or so I had thought."

"I don't understand," I say gently, tucking the picture frame into my pocket and looping my arm through hers. Her tiny frame is shivering. "Come on; let's make ourselves a bit warmer so we can have a natter. It's probably a bit too cold for us to knit as well," I say, just to lighten things a bit. I know this can't be easy for her—and it seems to work because Hettie is smiling as I steer her behind Cher's stall so we can toast ourselves next to the roasted chestnuts grill. And it's quiet over here now; everybody else is gathered by the pond listening to a sterling rendition of "Ding Dong Merrily on High"—even Cher and Clive have disappeared along with Cooper and the tourists. "Would you like a hot drink?" I ask, but before Hettie can answer, I ladle a generous serving of mulled wine into a mug and hand it to her, figuring she might appreciate a measure of fortitude. I know she's not very comfortable talking about herself. She takes a tentative sip.

"Mmm, I'm not really one for alcohol," she states almost as if to allay any suspicions I could possibly have of her being otherwise—it makes me smile, "but this is rather nice," she chuckles.

I pull two camping chairs across from Cooper's stall, I'm sure he won't mind us borrowing them for a bit, and as we sit down, Basil places a paw on Hettie's knee before tilting his head to one side and looking up at her as if he senses she may be in need of some comfort. She pats his head and he takes it as his cue to jump onto her lap. He snuggles into her coat to keep her warm and she strokes his little velvety ear.

I place the picture frame on the trestle table in front of us.

"Hettie, it's very generous of you, but I really can't take the picture."

"But I don't need it anymore. Not now that Gerry is back," she says.

"Your son?" I ask, tentatively.

"Yes, named after his father, Gerald Henry Mackintosh." Hettie takes another sip of her drink.

"Did you meet him in America?" I say carefully, in case I'm crossing the line, remembering the conversation with Ruby about the mysterious man with the initial G.

"Yes, that's right. In Hollywood. We courted for two years before he proposed."

"Oh, that's nice," I smile.

"That's why I came home, back to Tindledale. To make the arrangements for the wedding, you see . . ." Her voice goes quiet. "He had promised to follow me, but he never did . . ." Hettie turns away and my heart aches for her. Poor Hettie. She may not have got to the actual altar, but still . . .

"I'm so sorry," I say.

"And I never thought I'd see the day." She shakes her head solemnly. "This was all I had left of little Gerry." Hettie reaches a hand out to tap the picture and I crease my forehead. Basil hops off her lap and curls up next to her legs instead, resting his wiry chin on her booties.

"A photo of you? I don't understand," I say, feeling confused.

"Ah, yes, that's what they all thought. But behind the picture of me, was this. I kept it there, safe, but out of sight, and always close by." And she clips open her bag and fumbles around inside before pulling out a black-and-white image of two tiny babies lying on a blanket. "Gerry and his sister, Jean. Poor little mite, she died before she had a chance to take her first breath. Too tiny, you see, and they didn't have all the equipment that they do these days. I remember holding her—my hand was almost as big as her whole body—but there was nothing I could do apart from stroke her tiny face and tell her that I loved her," Hettie says numbly and quietly, and a long silence follows. I swallow hard, willing myself not to cry. "She's buried in the churchyard over there." And Hettie points toward the silvery glow of the cross high in the dark starry night above St. Mary's church on the other side of the High Street. More silence follows until I can bear it no longer.

"Oh, Hettie," I gasp, touching the tip of my finger to the corner of the photo; no wonder she always retreated to the kitchen-cum-sitting-room to be alone with her thoughts and memories. "I'm so sorry. Bill said . . ." I let my voice fade away in case I'm intruding, but then, as if sensing my apprehension, Hettie pops the picture back safely inside her handbag, and tells me what happened.

"Soon after I arrived back in Tindledale, happy and keen to show off my new wonderful husband-to-be, I realized that I was in the family way." Hettie hesitates, lowering her voice, and I notice that her hands are trembling slightly. "But then, when Gerald didn't arrive, well, I was on my own. My parents let me stay, of course, and my darling baby Gerry was just a few months old when I fell down the stairs with him in my arms—I was exhausted from sitting up all night, and I hadn't been coping too well, what with the whispers in the village and all." She lets her gaze drop down to her hands. "So it was thought prudent that he be adopted for his own safety. 'Best all round,' is what my parents had said."

Oh God, poor Hettie. And my heart feels as if it's cracking in two—I can't imagine how painful that must have been for her.

"Times were different then, dear," Hettie offers by way of an explanation, and I'm sure a segment of my heart actually crumbles away. "I wanted him to have a perfect life, to have everything I couldn't give him and be free from the whispers, the stigma of having an unmarried mother— sometimes love just isn't enough," she finishes softly.

Taking my scarf, I quickly brush it against my face, not wanting her to see the tears that are now pooling in the corners of my eyes. I swallow hard and will myself to be strong, but it's hard, seeing her pain laid bare like this. All I want to do is wrap her in my arms and comfort her, but I'm not sure how Hettie would feel about that. I pat her arm instead.

"So everyone just assumed the baby had died," she continues, "which, in a way, is exactly how it felt for me. Grief comes in many forms." Another silence follows. And then Hettie's voice lifts a little. "But I was always able to visit Jean, which was a comfort." Hettie pats her handbag and I feel utterly in awe of her strength and stoicism. Abandoned by her fiancé, losing her little baby Jean and then having to give up her son, how on earth does anyone deal with so much pain? But she did it. Against all the odds. Somehow, she survived. "You know, I named my baby Jean after Gene Kelly himself—he was such a lovely fella, so polite and such a tremendously talented dancer. He gave me some coaching and it took my tap-dancing to a whole new level!" Hettie goes quiet again. "I take the bus up to the village once a week to tend to Jean's flowers." *Poor, poor Hettie. No wonder she didn't want to go into a home. No wonder she didn't want to leave Tindledale and her lovely House of Haberdashery with all its memories. She needs to be here, to be close to Jean.* "And now her brother, Gerry, has come back to us too," Hettie adds.

"How does that make you feel?" I ask.

"I was apprehensive at first. Ashamed, even. You see, I knew he was coming, but didn't realize it would be so soon—he found me via Mrs. Pocket, you know. There's an ancestry place in the Internet," she explains with just a hint of marvel in her voice at this further phenomenon of modern technology. "And then when he turned up out of the blue, having stumbled upon the shop's new website, instead of writing to me first as she had suggested, Mrs. Pocket panicked and followed him straight down to the shop. That's when she pulled me out from the party and we found him embroiled in the showdown with my nephew and you and Marigold in the bus shelter."

"I'm so sorry," I say, trying not to snivel. "And I know Marigold is too."

"I know, dear, you thought he was another," she pauses, "bailiff," and lowers her voice again before casting a look over toward the pond. But there's nobody here, just the two of us, and to be honest, I'm not sure the rest of the villagers are judgmental in that way, certainly not the ones I've met. Everyone here seems so nice, warm, down-to-earth and kind. Just concerned and ready to help if they can, but Hettie comes from another era, a time when integrity and honor were all you really had. A time when you put on a brave face—didn't complain or tell everyone your business, and just got on with it in private.

354

"We really thought he was your nephew until he actually turned up."

"Hmm, I don't think he'll be rushing back in a hurry, not after that kick you gave him. Good for you." Hettie's face sets into a frown, but then softens again. "Gerry told me he was excited and just wanted to meet me right away." Her voice soars now. "He's so sorry for turning up unannounced like that."

"And that's a wonderful thing. But you've nothing to be ashamed of," I say, feeling sad that Hettie has carried this burden alone for so long. Nobody knew about the babies, not even Marigold. She told me during the phone call to see if I'd look after the shop that she had no idea Hettie had a son. She remembers as a child that there were rumors running around the village that Hettie was an unmarried mother, but when she had asked her own mother about it, Marigold was told that the baby's father was a soldier stationed far away in America who was then killed in an accident, which I suppose in a way had a grain of truth to it. And then over the years, the people died, or moved away like Bill did, and the ones that stayed—well, their memories faded.

"My dear, you're very kind, but you saw how bad things had got when you first arrived. I was heartbroken to think Gerry would turn up to see what a mess I had made of it all. I didn't want to be a disappointment to him." She pauses to take another sip of her wine. "It's all changed now though, thanks to you and your knitting and nattering, and wacky Christmas pullovers. I can stop worrying about the bills—and that dreadful nephew of mine," she adds, sounding lighter now as she finishes the last of her wine.

"Well, it's been my absolute pleasure to help you, Hettie." I smile brightly before cranking up the dial on the grill.

"Then please, Sybil, take the picture. Without you, I might very well have lost my home and my beloved House of Haberdashery, and that would never do. Not when my heart will always belong here with baby Jean, in Tindledale." She pats her handbag again. "The signature might be worth a few bob and you could sell it and pack in that job of yours that you hate. Wouldn't it be wonderful if you could come and live here too?" She lifts the frame from the table and hands it to me, her eyes all sparkly as they glance over toward the twinkling lanterns swaying around the pond. For a moment we sit together and just listen to the carolers singing,

Silent night, holy night
All is calm, all is bright

"Hettie, I couldn't think of anything I'd love more. This place is special. Magical. And you know . . ." I lean in close to her and whisper, "those wacky Christmas sweaters helped heal my broken heart too."

27

Christmas Day, and everyone is here in the Duck & Puddle pub. Slade are belting out that old favorite, "Merry Xmas Everybody"; Molly and Cooper have popped in for a pint while their turkey cooks at home, and their boys are busy toasting marshmallows on skewers in the blazing flames of the open inglenook fire; Basil is in his usual place, on the blanket by the hearth, with one eye closed and one eye on the marshmallows, presumably hoping one just happens to fall into his mouth.

Marigold and Lucan are here too, and I've just refilled Lucan's pewter tankard that he keeps behind the bar—I'm helping out, seeing as it's so busy in here. Hettie is with them, smiling and looking relaxed, but a little nervous too as Gerry is on his way to collect her—she's having her Christmas dinner at his house and he only lives twenty miles away, with his wife, their four grown-up children and numerous grandsons and granddaughters—twelve in total, I think she said. Leo and Beth are at the far end of

the bar with some of the other Tindledale Tappers—
Louise, Edie, Sarah and Vi—and they're all enjoying a
traditional Christmas drink with a goose-fat roasted potato
or three, from one of the many brimming bowls dotted
along the bar, courtesy of the landlady, Cher, and her
other half, Clive, aka Sonny. And this still tickles me. Pete
popped in earlier to pick up a barrel of beer on his tractor,
they're having a party at the farm, and he'd momentarily
thrown me when he asked if Sonny was up for joining
in the village football match tomorrow—it's a traditional
Boxing Day thing, apparently, when they all gather on
the green and attempt to kick a ball around in a desperate
attempt to start working off their festive food
indulgence.

Lawrence arrives, and after peeling off his coat, hat,
scarf and gloves (hand-knitted of course, courtesy of me,
as a little Christmas present) he goes to hang them on
the peg by the cloakrooms, before climbing on to a stool
at the bar.

"Happy Christmas, Sybs." He leans across to give me
a kiss on the cheek.

"Happy Christmas to you too," I say, giving his arm a
squeeze. "What happened to your Japanese guests?" I
glance over toward the door to see if they're following in
behind.

"Ah, yes," Lawrence smiles. "They're having a bit of a

lie-in. Seems they may have overindulged on the mulled wine last night and are now feeling a bit delicate. No requests for breakfast either, which I tried to explain wasn't a good idea and that you can't beat a good full English to soak up a hangover, but they weren't convinced." He shrugs. "I think they'll be joining us later," he finishes diplomatically.

"Ouch!" And we both laugh. "So, what can I get you to drink?" I grin.

"Ooh, I'll have a—"

"I'll get these!" It's Ruby, and she looks glorious as always, in a crimson faux fur swingy cape with a fluffy white collar and matching hand muff. She places the muff on the bar and sweeps the cape from her body, revealing a jaunty, and very kitsch, prancing reindeer print vintage blouse.

"Wow! You look sensational," I say impulsively.

"Thank you, honey. Wish I could say the same for you!" And she whips open her bag and pulls out her purse, as I try to reunite my jaw to the rest of my face.

"Oh, that was harsh, Rubes," Lawrence says, nudging her with his elbow. "Sybs looks lovely, she's a natural beauty." He nods.

"Thank you, Lawrence," I smile, having quickly recovered from her bluntness.

"Of course she does," Ruby continues, "but what I

meant was—she may want to get rid of that ratty tea towel she has slung over her shoulder." And she points a sparkly tipped finger at me.

"Why?" Lawrence asks, before I manage to.

"Because there's one very hot doctor waiting outside for her." Both Ruby and Lawrence look directly at me, and I swear my heart skips a beat.

"But—" I open my mouth.

"No buts." Cher is at my side now, having listened in on the conversation.

"He asked me to send you outside as he can't come in," Ruby says nonchalantly, smoothing her hair.

"Why not?"

"Why do you think? Because he'll get bombarded with medical questions if he comes in here, like he always does, that's why," Cher laughs. "Now, go on, shoo." And she grabs the tea towel from my shoulder and slings it in the sink underneath the bar.

"Are you sure?" I ask, checking it's OK—I did offer to help out, but right now, I really want to see him, even if the pub is heaving three-deep at the bar. Who knows when I'll have another chance?

"Yep. We'll manage," Cher says.

"And I know how to serve drinks." Ruby leaps down from her stool and sashays around to the serving side of the bar before bellowing, "OK, who's up for a tequila shot?" in her brilliantly throaty voice as she whips out four shot glasses from the shelf, places them on the bar and fills them up in one smooth movement, just like a pro. Grabbing a knife, she spears a lemon from the bowl, chops it into four wedges and dares Leo to have a go.

"Be quick," Cher groans, leaning into me and shaking her head in Ruby's direction, and I don't need telling twice so I dash out the back, grab my parka, scarf and mittens and after collecting Basil, figuring it'll do him good to galvanize himself into action and stretch his legs, I step outside into the silvery snow that's falling gently from the sky.

But Ben isn't here.

I look around while Basil bites the snow, before dropping onto his back and rolling around like a crazy dog, swishing his tail to make the snow flurry up and onto his tummy, and I swear if he were human, he'd be laughing and whooping like a lunatic. I'm just about to turn around to go back inside when the fifteen Japanese tourists come toddling along the lane, looking very delicate indeed.

"Ah, hello, Sybil," Mr. Tanaka says, doing his customary bow in greeting.

"Happy Christmas to you all," I say, hoping they hurry up and get inside the pub, because if Ben is out here hiding somewhere, there's no way he's going to show

361

himself with them all standing here taking more photos—the pub door, the pub sign, one of the wooden bench seats, one of Pear Tree Cottages, one of the merry woman from the other night who'd sworn to Ben she'd only had one drink with her blanket around her shoulders and her battered old Trilby hat (she'd turned up right on cue), and then finally the process is repeated all over again with me holding the camera while they all cram into view. And then they seem to muster up a modicum of fortitude as, for a grand finale, they stand in a line and whip off their coats, revealing their glorious Christmas sweaters for me to see while they all yell an obviously rehearsed, and very cheery "ho ho ho," patting the sides of their stomachs like they're Santa as they point to each other's sweaters as if it's the funniest thing ever. And I have to say, that it is pretty funny, to see them all guffawing; it's infectious, and I end up laughing with them. Eventually they stop, and after thanking me profusely, once again, for saving the day back home in the theme park in Tokyo, they toddle off inside the pub.

There's a rustling sound across the way by the village pond.

"Psst. Over here." And I stifle a laugh on seeing Ben crouched behind a bunch of snow-covered bushes with the hood of his duffel coat pulled up over his head so that it's practically covering his face. Basil bounds over to him right away, with me following on the end of his leash.

"What are you doing?" I breathe, covertly.

"Hiding," he says, as if it's the most obvious explanation ever. "It's the only way." And he has such a hunted look on his face that I end up laughing again.

"Oh God, please don't laugh," he says, trying to keep a straight face as he goes to move from his crouched position, but Basil darts in between his legs, making him lose balance and he plunges backward into the bushes. We both crack up.

"Ah, feck," Ben puffs, the first to recover. He sticks out his hand. "Jesus, will you pull me out of here, please?" His Irish accent gets stronger as he lunges forward in a vain attempt at propelling himself free.

And I do.

And he keeps hold of my hand.

With his body pressed against mine, his breath warm on the cold of my cheeks, neither of us speaks. He lifts off his glasses to wipe away the specks of snow and my pulse quickens as I look into his beautiful emerald eyes. A lock of dark hair falls onto his face. After pushing it away, he places his hand on my cheek, gently sweeping it inside my hood and under my curls at the nape of my neck before pressing his warm lips onto mine. And in this moment, I have absolutely no idea why on earth I ever thought he was nervous, awkward or inexperienced with women when my tummy flips and my heart soars as he kisses me hard and very, very passionately.

We eventually pull apart and I do an actual gasp, just like they do in the rom-com films.

"Merry Christmas, Sybs," he says gently. "I've wanted to do that since the first moment I clapped eyes on you on that train." Grinning, I touch my woolly-gloved hand to his face. "Sorry," he says gently, after pushing his glasses back on.

"What for?" I just about manage, wishing my breathing would slow, back to a normal-ish rhythm.

"I probably shouldn't have kissed you; I'm not sure it's an appropriate way for a doctor to carry on," he smiles, wrapping his arms around me and pulling me in close.

"Mmm . . ." I pause to ponder for a moment, and then look up into his beautiful face. "But you're not my doctor!"

"Well, technically I am—you came to see me in my office," he says, gently kissing the bridge of my nose.

"Ah, yes, but we first met on a train," I point out.

"Like *Brief Encounter*: wasn't he a doctor too?" And we both laugh again. "Come on, I'll walk you back into the pub," he says, slipping his hand in mine and giving Basil a quick stroke when he stretches up and lands both front paws on Ben's thighs, eager not to be left out.

"I'm on call this afternoon—I volunteered months ago, back when I had assumed I'd be on my own today, but maybe we could get together later this evening, someone said *Star Wars* is on if you fancy it?" he adds, in a very breezy voice.

And I freeze.

I'm rooted to the spot like a statue. Even Basil hunkers down and lets out a little yelp.

"Pardon?" I just about manage.

I hold my breath.

"It's not really my thing, but . . ." He shrugs.

And I let out an enormous sigh of relief before flinging my arms around his neck and squeezing him tight, thinking what a truly, wonderful, perfectly magical Christmas this is.

Epilogue

Five months later . . .

S pringtime. The gloriously warm sun streams through a perfect, cloud-puffed blue sky, while the gentle baa of the newborn lambs drifts over from the fields all around and the air is full with the heavenly scent of wildflowers.

"That's it. Oops, sorry, a little farther to the right. Whoa, stop. Perfect," I say to Pete, as he stands on the top of his tractor, making sure the new Hettie's House of Haberdashery shop sign is properly in place. And it looks magnificent—all art nouveau swirly gold lettering on a French-navy background—very shabby chic haberdashers. And exactly how I imagined it.

At last, the day I dreamt about, and fantasized over during those tedious long hours at my desk in the council offices, has finally arrived. I went back to work after Christmas and was reassured that I was in no way to blame for Jennifer Ford's unexpected windfall, and that they had been genuinely worried about me, hence the suggestion I take some time off. Seems I wasn't even in the office on the date and time when the transaction occurred—doctor's appointment is what it said on the online team calendar, so I wasn't the bungling employee after all. And they never did catch up with Jennifer Ford. The last that was heard of her—via a gossip magazine she had sold her story to—was of her swanking it up on a mystery man's yacht moored in the Cayman Islands, having got lucky on the roulette tables in Vegas.

Anyway, soon after, the council needed to make cost savings, so I was offered a buyout and jumped at the chance, gave notice on my flat right away, packed up all my stuff and paid a man with a van to drive it to Tindledale. That's right, I live here now. Marigold gave me first refusal on a tenancy for the Blackwood Estate lodge, set at the entrance to the farm, a tiny one-bedroom, turreted, Hogwarts-style house, and perfect for Basil and me.

I'm managing Hettie's shop now and today we're having a relaunch party, so she can take a bit of a backseat, and spend the rest of her years doing the things that she loves—knitting, dancing and getting to know Gerry. But the most wonderful thing of all is that he tracked down his birth father, Gerald, too, the mystery man, G, that Hettie had written about in those letters Ruby found in the suitcase. I did pass on the message from Ruby regarding their potential worth, but Hettie said she couldn't possibly part with them, not now she has them back. Hettie wrote the letters to her mother from America, and had no idea they'd been kept. But Hettie did agree to chat to Ruby, to share some of her glorious memories of the golden age of Hollywood and they've spent a number of evenings together, cozied up in Ruby's vintage shop, reminiscing while listening to Frank Sinatra and Gene Kelly on Ruby's Dansette record player.

And Gerald had never forgotten Hettie, or indeed stopped loving her, not deep down, but his parents were very conservative and had put pressure on him to stay in America, and not "chase after the English girl who lived so far away." Gerry never knew about the babies and said that if he had, then he'd have been there like a shot, even if it had meant never seeing his family in America again.

But the past is the past, and things are much brighter now, and Gerry senior and Hettie talk all the time on Skype—he's a widower with two grown-up daughters, and still lives in America, in Manhattan. So I persuaded Hettie to treat herself to her very own laptop to have in the snug of her oast, and she now spends hours chatting to Gerry senior and catching up on old times. She said they're planning an actual get-together very soon; Gerry's daughter is organizing it all for him to sail over on the

Queen Mary 2 from New York so he doesn't have to bother with airports and flying, and all that carry-on, at his age.

So now that everything is unpacked, the knitted contents of my old spare bedroom are artfully displayed on little hangers in the window, the tea cozies lined up on shelves and Hettie's mother's old Singer sewing table has replaced the flaky, chipped counter, the shop is finally ready for today's party. Even the bus shelter has had a makeover and is now adorned in a gorgeous sunshine-yellow yarn-bombed extravaganza, courtesy of Taylor and her mates last night, I assume, as it definitely wasn't here yesterday.

"Oh, it looks marvelous, Sybil," Hettie is standing next to me now, wearing her best floral frock and a lovely light expression on her face. Gone are the worry lines, replaced only with contentment, now that her heart has healed and she's finally found her peace. "You've done wonders with the old place, and I never thought I'd see the day—it would certainly wipe the smile off that nephew of mine's face." She loops her arms through mine.

"Have you heard anything more from him?" I ask, remembering when he turned up again shortly after Christmas, only to take one look at me and jump back into his shiny black Range Rover.

"Oh no, dear, he won't be bothering us anymore," Hettie says with a devious twinkle in her eye.

"Why? What have you done?" I smile cautiously.

"Told him of course. Well, not me personally, no, the solicitor that Gerry junior found for me, did—that you're in charge now, that the shop is yours and I'll be staying put in my home until the time comes for them to take me away in a box, thank you very much, and not to be thinking he stands to inherit a penny, oh no, not now that Gerry is back in my life." And she chuckles. I wrap my arms around her shoulders and give her a big hug.

"I'm so happy for you," I smile.

"And me for you. Now, come on, dear, it's nearly time for the speeches," says Hettie, breaking away and patting my arm.

Out of the corner of my eye, I see Mum whip a hanky out of her sleeve before nudging Dad and pressing the hanky into his hand with a "wipe the sweat off your bald head at once" stare. *What on earth will everyone think?* I chuckle inwardly. Mum looks amazing. They arrived yesterday and she went straight into Ruby's shop and bought a vintage Aquascutum dress with matching bag and cute lace gloves, said it was only right if she was coming to the relaunch of a "premier" establishment. Poor Glenda from next door has been getting a daily bulletin update on my move to Tindledale and plans for the shop for the last few months—anyone would think I'd single-handedly commissioned a shuttle to the moon, the way Mum's been carrying

370

on. You know, she even erected one of those electronic countdown clocks in the kitchen. Ticking away the days, hours and minutes. Won it on eBay, apparently, and none of us even knew she'd discovered online shopping.

*

"Sooo, I'll shut up now," Cher says, and after a smile and subtle nod of encouragement from Clive, she turns and cuts the ribbon. "I hereby declare Sybs's and Hettie's magnificent House of Haberdashery well and truly reopened!" Clasping my hands together up under my chin, I can bear it no longer and let out an enormous whoop of joy. It's been a long time coming, but I've finally achieved my dream, albeit in a different way to the one I'd imagined. There's an enormous cheer from the crowd—most of the villagers, people from the parish council, plus Dolly, with Bill in a wheelchair, Molly, Cooper, Marigold, Lord Lucan, Taylor, Louise, Edie, Beth, Leo and all of the Tindledale Tappers, and of course my dear friends Lawrence and Ruby, who between them well and truly helped me heal the broken heart that I had when I first arrived here in Tindledale.

Smoothing down my sundress—it has a fitted bodice with a swishy dirndl skirt, mint green and creamy white, and I made it myself from one of Hettie's old forties Butterick patterns so it's a walking advertisement for my new sewing classes that start next week. I leave my guests chatting and enjoying a scrumptious selection of Kitty's cakes, and head into the shop. Which reminds me. I grab the parcel from the low table just inside the door and call Kitty over.

"A gift for you," I say, handing her the present.

"For me?" Kitty smiles, but creases her forehead. "Honestly, there's no need—you've already paid for today's cakes."

"Please, this is different," I say, a wave of nerves sweeping right through me. *What if I got it wrong? What if it upsets her?* Spotting us together, Lawrence comes over and slips his arm around Kitty's shoulders in support, before giving me a wink of encouragement. I take a deep breath. Kitty peels off the paper and unfolds the gift. Silence follows as her eyes take it all in, and then she knows. She sees what it is—a memory quilt made from carefully cut pieces of Ed's clothes. That's what she had wanted Lawrence's help with that day in the pub, to clear out Ed's wardrobe, which Lawrence did, and then we came up with this idea. Kitty presses the quilt to her face and inhales hard, before handing it to Lawrence and flinging her arms around my neck.

"Sybs, it's amazing. I love it. Thank you so much, my friend," she says, softly in my ear.

"Phew. I'm so pleased you do," I say, clasping her hands and smiling as she lets me go. "I thought it might be a comfort, something for Teddie to treasure too."

"And she will. But Sybs, there's someone here who has a present for you," she says, looking a little nervous now.

"Oh." And Adam appears from the crowd. I've seen him a couple of times in the High Street, but he's always avoided making eye contact, and I didn't dare confront him to explain, for fear of getting another mouthful of abuse.

"Sybs, I wanted to give you this," he starts, before sweeping a hand nervously through his blond hair. I take the Tindledale Books carrier bag from him and peep inside. "It's a vintage knitting book, very rare. I, um," he coughs to clear his throat, "thought you might like it—a peace offering—to say sorry for yelling at you that day. It won't ever happen again. I was, am, well . . . going through a nasty divorce and I jumped to conclusions." He looks at the ground.

"Forget it. I have. And thanks so much for this," I say, waggling the carrier bag in the air, and he visibly relaxes. "Sorry to hear about your divorce though." And his shoulders stiffen again. "So, seeing as we're all exchanging presents today, I have one for you too, Lawrence," I add, to lighten the mood.

"Ah, you don't have to give me a gift," Lawrence smiles.

"Yes I do, after all that you did for me. It's the least I

can do." And after placing the carrier bag on the side, I point to a framed picture stored behind an armchair.

"What is it?" he asks.

"Take a look." I slide the frame out and he gasps.

"Studio 54! Oh Sybs, I adore it," he says, pulling me in for a big hug. I found it on the Internet, a black-and-white print of people queuing up to get in, and I'm sure there's a guy in the picture wearing peach cord flares. "I'll treasure this for ever," he adds, his eyes going misty.

Leaving Kitty, Adam and Lawrence together, I walk on into the shop, smiling as I pass the framed picture on the wall of the sixty Japanese staff at the English village theme park, all lined up doing *Wayne's World* thumbs-ups, and looking resplendent in their wacky Ho Ho Ho Christmas sweaters. I wander through to the kitchen-cum-sitting-room and stand quietly, taking it all in, remembering my very first day here, meeting Hettie, both of us heartbroken and sad. I smile, thinking how amazing it is, the way things happen in life, how they turn out, how sometimes they're just meant to be.

I turn to the mantelpiece and lift a finger to the framed picture—Hettie's picture signed by Gene Kelly. No way was I ever going to keep it for myself, or even sell it, no, it's far too precious for that. It was taken all those years go when she was young and carefree and full of dreams, before fate tore it all away and broke her heart. But she's come full circle and is happy now, with the chance to live out the rest of her life in her beloved oast house surrounded by a community that loves her and the memories she holds so dear.

And I got my dream too! My own broken heart has healed and I can knit and sew and quilt and crochet all day, and all night long if I want to, here in the picture-postcard village of Tindledale. It really doesn't get much better than this. I feel at home, happy and surrounded by friends too.

Footsteps break my reverie, and Ben appears.

"You made it," I smile, leaning in to him for a kiss.

"I wasn't missing this for the world, not even Tommy Prendergast's imagined hernia," he laughs, pulling a pretend face of despair, before looking around the shop. "Sybs, this is so amazing. And to think you've transformed it on your own."

"Well, not entirely on my own, I had a lot of help from my fellow knitting addicts, the Tindledale Tappers," I tell him, remembering the countless evenings, when, after lots of knitting and nattering and chocolate chip cookies and bars of Fry's Peppermint Cream, they got sucked in, rolling up the old threadbare rug, painting the stripped wooden floor a gorgeous shade of shabby chic gray, the walls too. Even the furniture has had a makeover, so now the comfy armchairs and sofa have a gloriously eclectic mix of floral, knitted and crocheted covers, with deliberately mismatched cushions and throws, creating a lovely, cozy, welcoming place for fellow crafters to come and relax. And they do. The last few months have been so busy, with villagers joining in the various knitting, sewing and quilting courses, residents from Stoneley and Market Briar too. We even had a bus load of knitters from Clapham who couldn't get enough of the wonderful new stock and they've been ordering online ever since.

"Well, I still think you're incredible," Ben says. "And I would have helped. I know I'm a clumsy doctor geek, but I can decorate and lug furniture around with the best of them," he grins, flexing his muscles like the strongman in a Vaudeville circus act, making me laugh.

Through the window, I can hear Mum chatting in her too-loud voice to the reporter from the *Tindledale Herald*.

"Oh yes, Sybil has always had an eye for the creative things in life, and she's a spectacular seamstress. You know she used to spend hours helping me sew and hem, um," Mum pauses and pats her hair, "things! You know, just watching to see how it was done. Takes after me. In fact, I've won awards for my embroidery. Third place at last year's summer fete and . . ."

Smiling and rolling my eyes, I glance at Ben. He smiles and steps closer to me, pushing a stray hair away from my cheek. Turning together, we peep through the side of the blind, eavesdropping like a pair of cheeky children, well, not children *exactly*, as Ben is standing behind me with his hands underneath my dress, his feather-soft fingers stroking the tops of my thighs. Mum waves a magnanimous hand around.

"And I'm not sure if you know already," Mum continues, "but she has a new boyfriend. All very discreet at this stage, with him being such a prominent pillar of the community, a doctor and all, saving lives every day." She taps the reporter's notepad. "Make sure you put that in," she instructs. "Yes, he's very eminent and has won awards for his pioneering work in, um, er . . ." She pauses, and her cheeks flush as she realizes she's caught herself out. "And he comes from a very good family in Ireland." Mum beams as she scans the crowd looking for me. I shake my head, and Ben and I both crack up laughing, but I guess Mum can relax now that I'm suitably paired up with a man, and a doctor, no less. *What will the neighbors think?*

After kissing the back of Ben's hand, I drop it gently and wander outside to be with my friends, and to find Basil too—last time I spotted him, he was sitting underneath the cake table, sweeping his tail and doing his usual feed-me-I'm-starving (hardly) face. A van pulls up and Lucy, from the florist in Tindledale High Street, leaps out and runs over to me.

"Flowers for you," she beams and hands me a beautiful

bouquet of pink and white roses, then adds, "Good luck, Sybs, I'll be down next week to sign up for your new crochet class. I've a new granddaughter on the way so the perfect pram blanket will be just the thing. Cheerio." And she's back in her van, waving with her arm sticking out from the open window as she drives off to do the rest of her deliveries.

"Mmm, they're beautiful." Hettie comes over with Basil under her arm. He leans around the flowers for a quick stroke, and I duly oblige by giving his black velvety head a good rub. "But who'd waste their money on such an extravagance, when we have a field full of flowers right here?" Hettie sniffs in disapproval, before sticking her nose into the bouquet. I shake my head and smile. Typical Hettie, she may have mellowed, but she's still as outspoken as ever. I pull out the card. Ah, it's from my old neighbor Poppy, in London. She couldn't be here today as she's on holiday with her new boyfriend, a senior partner from the law firm where she works—they're staying at his beach house in Nantucket.

To Sybs and Basil, and their bright new beginning in Tindledale.
Keep calm and carry yarn.
Love Pops xxx

Sybil's
Lovely Little
CHRISTMAS
Pudding
Pattern

You will need -

- 4mm knitting needles
- 10 meters of dark brown DK yarn
- White felt
- Stuffing
- Metallic thread
- Berry red beads
- Holly green bugle beads
- Sewing needle

Method -

- Using the 4mm needles, cast on 30 stitches

- Work 19 rows in knit stitch

- Row 20 — thread a darning needle with the remaining yarn and feed through the remaining stitches on the needle

- Gently pull to gather across the top and sew down the side of the pudding

- Leave the sewing needle and yarn at the side

- Place a little stuffing inside the pudding until firm and round

- Using the needle and yarn weave in and out across the opening and pull tightly to create a ball shape

- Secure by sewing over the opening
- Cut out the icing shape using some white felt
- Position and sew on the icing using some metallic thread
- Now sew on the pretty red and green beads
- To make a hanger, thread through a loop of yarn and secure from the bottom with a knot
- Sprinkle with glitter to really add some magical Christmas sparkle

And there, my friends, is your lovely little Christmas pudding.

Wishing you all
a very Merry
CHRISTMAS
and a wonderful
New Year.

Love

Sybs xxx

ABOUT THE AUTHOR

Alexandra Brown began her writing career as the City Girl columnist for the *London Paper*. She wrote the weekly column—a satirical diary account of her time working in the corporate world of London—for two years before giving it up to concentrate on writing novels and is now the author of the Cupcakes at Carrington's books. Set in a department store in the pretty seaside town of Mulberry-On-Sea, the series follows the life, loves and laughs of sales assistant Georgia Hart. *The Great Christmas Knit-Off* is Alexandra's fourth book and the first in a new series set in the fictional village of Tindledale, following the lives of all the characters there.

Alexandra lives in a real village near the south coast of England with her husband, daughter and a very shiny black Labrador retriever.

Website: www.alexandrabrown.co.uk
Facebook: www.facebook.com/alexandrabrownauthor
Twitter: @alexbrownbooks